So stood I, in Heaven's glorious sun,
And in the glare of Hell;
My spirit drank a mingled tone,
Of seraph's song, and demon's moan;
What my soul bore, my soul alone
Within itself may tell!

"My Comforter", Emily Brontë

Here and there on earth we may encounter a
kind of continuation of love in which this pos-
sessive craving of two people for each other gives
way to a new desire and lust for possession – a
shared higher thirst for an ideal above them. But
who knows such love? Who has experienced it?
Its right name is friendship.

The Gay Science, Friedrich Nietzsche

For in much wisdom is much grief: and he
that increaseth knowledge increaseth sorrow.

Ecclesiastes 1:18

I: HAMMEL

I

After the last long winter, I needed to get as far away from the city as I possibly could. My life there filled me with a weariness of disgust; I was tired of endless conversations in lamp-lit cafés with over-educated aesthetes like myself, tired of my apartment with its self-consciously tasteful artworks and its succession of witty visitors, of the endless jostling for status among the petty literati, the sniping envy and malicious gossip. There was also the question of a lady; there had been an unwise involvement, which on her part had flamed into an uncontrollable passion and which had caused me considerable discomfort. She was married to the General Secretary of the Writers' Guild, a man of considerable influence in the literary world and, if the affair had been pursued much further, it might have materially damaged my future prospects. This affair had caused me much nervous strain over the previous year, and my physician advised me that I ought to take a rest cure.

I thought idly of touring the glittering capitals of the wider world, but this seemed too much like my present life. More than anything, I hankered for solitude. Then I remembered my boyhood fascination with the wild men of the Black Mountains and the grim romantic landscapes of the north. Perhaps I could find what I needed in my own country… I made enquiries and at last, through a relative of a friend of mine, secured the lease of a house in Elbasa, a hamlet in the centre of the northern plains. It was, I was told, unusually luxurious for a hinterland dwelling, belonging to some scion of the northern royals, although it seemed he lived elsewhere. But its owner had not permitted it to fall into dereliction: an efficient couple kept it in order, and would act as my servants, should I take the lease.

Thus it was, in the early hours of a frosty spring morning, that I summoned a hansom-cab to convey me to the train station, and began the long journey to the Northern Plateau.

Naturally, despite my scientific and sceptical bent (I scorn womanly superstition), I had taken some precautions. There are too many stories about the naïf who travels into the wild with an arrogant faith in the superior qualities of civilization, only to find himself tragically undone, for me to be utterly inattentive to the protection of my person. I visited Aron Lamaga, the most famous of the city wizards, and availed myself of certain costly charms to protect me while I was on the road and in my remote residence. It seemed only sensible.

Aron Lamaga lives in the Wizards' Quarter, and although certain of my acquaintances frequent this area, for it has reputedly the liveliest taverns in the city, I confess that I do not generally join them. For the most part, the populace is a mass of quacks, charlatans, eccentrics, lunatics and criminals. The police watch of the city do not venture there, by tacit consent; it is not merely that the bewildering tangle of narrow alleyways, dark workshops and strangely dilapidated mansions holds perils for the unwary stranger, but that in this quarter – or so

I have heard – natural laws do not hold. It is said that maps are not reliable guides: streets which are bustling thoroughfares on one day are simply not there the next; buildings that are tall and substantial on Monday, on Tuesday might appear to be miserable hovels or a patch of wasteland punctuated by dock weeds; and those who venture there without guidance not infrequently disappear without trace.

There are some wizards of note whose workshops are in less disreputable quarters, but Aron Lamaga is generally agreed to be the most illustrious of all of his profession. The prime minister relies on his astrological advice, and, it is rumoured, consults him on certain tricky and secret affairs of state, such as when he wishes to rid himself discreetly of an inconvenient person. Lamaga is reportedly without parallel in the subtle business of disappearing citizens, and is capable, it is said, of erasing the memory of a man, even from those who have known and loved him all his life, so that it seems as if he never existed. He is said to be much in demand in the criminal underworld for the same reason. I cannot say whether this is merely dark gossip, but his reputation, whether true or no, certainly makes Lamaga a person whom it would be wise to fear.

Thus it was not without trepidation that I hired a guide and plunged into the crowded streets of the Wizards' Quarter, in search of Lamaga's mansion. But I was also, I confess, extremely curious. In the event, my meeting with the great wizard turned out to be a little anticlimactic. Instead of the exotic chamber I had anticipated, lined with an abundance of purple velvet curtains and smelling of exotic incense, its walls inscribed with sigils and crowded with grimoires and glass alembics and other suchlike magical apparatus, I was ushered into a room of surprising ordinariness, such as might have belonged to any one of my wealthier acquaintances. It was a conventional drawing room, comfortably furnished, albeit with some drawings and paintings on the wall which eschewed ostentation and showed him to be an art collector of considerable and informed taste.

The man himself was dressed like a rich merchant. He was slightly stout and had a curiously unexceptionable face, by which I mean that you would pass him in the street and think him like a hundred other reputable citizens. There was absolutely nothing about his appearance that gave any clue to his profession. He listened politely to my requests, nodded in a businesslike fashion, asked me to wait for a short time and returned with a small velvet bag. Inside were a silver ring, the inside of which was engraved with some arcane figures, which he instructed me I was to wear at all times, and a small glass phial with a dropper. It contained an emerald-green liquid.

"You must place one droplet on your pillow wherever you sleep," said Lamaga. "Also on the threshold of every outer door. This will protect you from most of the evil influences you are likely to encounter in the hinterlands."

"Most?" I queried, as I closely examined the phial. It was certainly of unusually exquisite workmanship.

A very slight spasm – perhaps of annoyance at my question – passed over his face, and for the briefest of instants I had an apprehension of danger, as if I had unknowingly brushed too close to a sleeping tiger. "I cannot protect you from imprudent behaviour on your own part," he said shortly. "If you act with common sense, you will avoid uncommon trouble."

He stood up, and my interview was clearly over. A little disappointed – I had, after all, expected somewhat more excitement from this visit – I handed over a considerable amount of silver and allowed myself to be bowed out of his house by his very respectable butler.

My journey to Elbasa was uneventful. I took the train to the end of the line, at the far edge of the lowlands, and from there

I hired a carriage to take me to the Northern Plateau. You can imagine with what eagerness I watched through the curtained windows as the green and fertile plains of my birth gave way to the stony beauty of the hinterlands. The well-cobbled thoroughfares of the city changed to rustic cart roads, and thence to roads which were sometimes little more than dirt tracks.

On the first day of travelling by carriage we began to climb. The lime trees and beeches and oaks of the lowlands thinned and then began to disappear altogether, giving way to conifers and low, wind-bitten thorn trees and scrub. The weather was clear and cold, the sky an icy blue. I felt my heart becoming lighter the further we drew from the city.

At noon on the second day we reached the Northern Plateau. We stopped at an inn for a hasty luncheon, and as I stepped out of the carriage I looked up and my breath was taken away: it was my first sight of the magnificent heights of the Black Mountains, which hitherto had been but a shadow on my horizon, cloaked in legend. The sheer brute fact of them was awe-inspiring: their crags heaved up into the distant sky, their crowns shrouded with grey cloud, their grim sides falling with an obdurate, oddly graceless beauty down to the Northern Plateau, the Land of Death, which now stretched before me, grey and flat under a thin sprinkling of snow.

Elbasa was in the centre of the Plateau, on the main road that ran through this region, and consequently one of the more notable settlements in this part of the country. When I had expressed my alarm at being near a town, speaking of my desire to leave all urban life behind, my friend Grosz, through whom I had secured my lodging, had laughed immoderately, and assured me that, in a region where most villages boasted at most a half-dozen houses, I was unlikely to encounter anything that *I* would recognize as a town.

"My dear Hammel," he said, when he had regained his

composure, "I know that you have not travelled, as I have, through the Land of Death. You may think the name fanciful; let me assure you, it is not. There are few grimmer visions than that desolate landscape of cemeteries! It is the home of vendetta, remember. Death has a different meaning in the north: its people live beneath its sigil, and death is the coin of their economy. The landscape has, I assure you, a most romantic beauty, but it is the harshest of beauties. Here you will see life in its most rugged state of nakedness! You will be longing for the crowded streets of the city ere long!" Here he even smirked.

A little offended, I reminded myself that Grosz was in his cups and thus not quite responsible for his expression; and I replied, somewhat tartly, that I desired, above all, the grace of solitude, and knew very well how to keep my own company. And that, moreover, having been brought up on a country estate myself, I was not unused to the rougher pleasures of country living.

Still smiling, my friend leant forward and poked me in the ribs. "Let me remind you, then, to avoid at least one of those rougher pleasures," he said. "The girls in the Land of Death are not for the taking, not like the country girls of the lowlands. They come at a heavy price."

"I am well aware of that," I said curtly.

"Well, don't you forget it," answered Grosz, more soberly. "I know your disposition, Hammel. And I swear, I have never seen such eyes as those of some of the upland women. But even to glance at them is perilous. And I'm not talking about the chance of being knifed. Cursing means something quite different in the Plateau…"

For a moment I caught his seriousness, and shuddered. I had a sudden vivid memory of having seen one of the upland wizards in town, a year or so before. He carried the staff of his vocation, but otherwise wore merely the coarse garb of a highland shepherd. He had with him a mute, a small boy whose tongue had been cut out, as all wizards did a few centuries ago. Like many barbaric archaisms, it was a custom still practised in the Land of Death. I shuddered to see the mutilated boy, and wondered why I had never heard what happened to these boys when they outgrew their use: were they killed, or abandoned? Or perhaps they received some reward for their services, and afterwards lived blameless but voiceless lives?

The wizard's bearing was arrogant to the point of insolence, and he walked with the long steps of one unused to narrow spaces; I noticed that even in that crowded street, people scrambled out of his way. He cast his flashing eyes around him, his mouth tight with contempt. As I walked past him, staring in my curiosity, I unwittingly met his eyes, and my heart went absolutely cold; for a moment I almost thought he had stabbed me. Filled with an inchoate terror, I managed to pass him by, and turned the nearest corner almost at a run. There I stopped, gasping for breath, at a loss to explain the panic that had so briefly possessed me.

Yes, everyone knew of the curses of the wizards of the hinterland, and of the Blood Laws and their vendettas. But, after all, it was the reason I wanted to go there, to see for myself the savage customs of those parts. There, my friend told me, life was stripped to its most essential: every action was inscribed with the sigil of death, and the hinterlanders, man and woman, obeyed its implacable laws unquestioningly. There, my friend said, waxing lyrical as he often did after a number of wines, life found its true, obsidian meaning.

"But stay away from the women," he said again, looking at me narrowly over his glass. "Unless you too wish to be drawn into its tragic mechanisms. For there is no escaping the northern laws, once you excite their attention."

I recalled this conversation as I gazed at the Black Mountains, whose sombre weight even from this distance oppressed my heart. For a moment I regretted my decision to come to the Plateau; I was on the verge of telling my coachman to turn and head south again, back to the orchards of my youth. But something in me – perhaps the thought of my friend's unspoken mockery should I return so swiftly – rebelled at my hesitation. And so I said nothing, but bowed my head to enter the low door of the mean inn, where I was to enjoy my mean luncheon.

I arrived at Elbasa two days later, on a day of cold, soaking rain. The Plateau, or what I could see of it through the veils of grey water, looked especially desolate and friendless. My spirits began to fail; I wondered what could possibly have possessed me to visit this cheerless part of the world, when perhaps I could have been lying in the pleasure barges of the Water City, or wandering through the incomparable artworks in the museums of the City of Light.

We passed several small villages, each of them, as my friend had said, no more than half a dozen houses. The houses were built of the black basalt of that region, and were humble dwellings for the most part, slant-roofed and tiled with grey slate. Few of them had more, I judged, than two or three basic rooms. Despite my friend's assurances of comfort, I began to feel rather less sanguine about the house that awaited me in Elbasa.

The only items of real interest along the road were the stone towers outside some of the villages. They stood like grim fingers pointing skywards, windowed only with glassless slits covered with shutters, sometimes reaching to four storeys high, but thin and narrow: they could not have been more than ten paces square at their base. These were, I knew, the *odu*, the houses of refuge where a man with the vendetta on his head could live unmolested but exiled from human society, emerging at night in the hours of amnesty to gather food. Fascinated, I wondered how many poor souls lived out their years cooped in darkness inside these comfortless places, and whether that life was really any better than a quick death by bullet on an empty road.

Spring was yet to visit the Northern Plateau: the fruit trees were stunted and innocent of blossom, and the flat grasses sere and yellow. The only green was the dark dress of some ragged-looking and solitary pine trees. Forlorn goats and damp chickens picked their way around the village middens in an apathetic fashion, and I saw the occasional dumpy woman, clothed in black from head to foot, going about the household tasks. Outside every village was a simple unfenced graveyard, with graves framed by squares of stone. Quite frequently, I saw single memorials by the road, nowhere near any visible habitation, grey cairns of rock dark with rain. After a few miles punctuated by these melancholy signs, I began to feel that I was travelling through a single vast cemetery.

On the road we passed very few people; there was the occasional darkly clothed traveller on foot, trudging stoically onwards, his head bowed against the rain, his rifle slung across his back, draped in sacking to protect it from the rain. I stared dully out of the carriage window, bored and cold, my spirits increasingly oppressed.

We were passing yet another solitary walker, when he glanced up incuriously at the carriage and briefly met my eyes. My breath stopped: although he was a young man, and of considerable beauty in the dark-browed fashion of those of the hinterland, he seemed a living corpse. His eyes were absolutely devoid of light, and his features pale and insensible as carven marble. The rain ran unchecked down his face, as if he really were a statue. My heart quickened as I noted the white band he wore around his right arm. This, then, was one of the Dead; my first sight of those who walked under the sigil of the vendetta. The band around his right arm indicated that he had killed a man, but was still in his month of grace; after the month passed, the band would be worn on his left arm, and he could meet his death at any time in the daylight hours. Unless, that is, he took refuge in the *odu*, fated never to see the sun again.

I looked back as his lone figure dwindled into the distance, struck to the heart by the man's tragic beauty. He seemed indeed like an angel of death, walking through a landscape of the dead. For the first time I began really to understand my friend's words about the Northern Plateau. But perversely the sight cheered me: perhaps, after all, I would find something to interest me in this godforsaken place.

My carriage clattered into Elbasa's tiny central square shortly before dusk that same day. A few vagrant sunbeams peeped through a low rent in the clouds and lent the square a little shabby warmth. While my coachman ventured off into the rain for directions to the house, I contemplated Elbasa gloomily out of my carriage window. On one side of the square was a tavern, on the other what I presumed to be the house of the mayor. In the middle was an ancient and stunted lime tree, still bare of leaf, a forlorn version of its gay southern cousins, and underneath that a worn stone seat by a rank pond of blackish water choked with rotting leaves. A grimy shop and rows of shuttered houses completed the melancholy impression.

After almost a week of constant travel I was anxious to leave my carriage and settle into a comfortable house. I longed for a hot bath and then a glass of Madeira by a roaring fire before I fell gratefully into a comfortable bed. That I managed to get these things at the end of my journey was, I confess, a source of considerable astonishment.

My friend's report had not erred: the house I had leased for the spring months was indeed luxurious by the standards of the Northern Plateau. It was but a little way out of the village, and set at a pleasing angle on a low rise, which was the closest they came to a hill in these parts. It could not escape the usual pines, which sheltered the house from the harsh winds that often swept down from the mountains. It was known as the Red House, because it did not have the ubiquitous slate roofing, but cheery clay tiles, which someone must have imported at great trouble and expense from the south. As I peered curiously out of my carriage I saw the last of the day's light touching its roof, making it appear almost luminous, and it seemed to me miraculous to see such a thing in this dour landscape of greys. I could also see a butter-yellow light streaming from the windows, and my heart lifted.

Once inside, I met the couple who kept the house, a taciturn and courteous man named Zef, and his wife, Anna. They were respectably dressed and mannered, locally bred but well trained, and although the house was not large – running perhaps to six or seven main rooms – it had about it an air of order and prosperity which was already a little alien to me, accustomed as I had become over the past few days to low-roofed inns with mattresses more notable for their livestock than their softness. Although it felt a little foolish in these polite surroundings, I carefully anointed the thresholds of the house and my pillow with a droplet from the phial Aron Lamaga had given me, as had become my habit since reaching the Plateau. To complete my satisfaction, I found that Anna was a superior cook: she made a dish of tripe and onions that evening that nourished the soul as much as the flesh. You can imagine how I congratulated myself on having found such an oasis of civilization in this rude country; with what relief I lay down that night between fresh linen sheets; and how, before I drifted off into well-earned slumber, I turned my mind with a fresh excitement to the prospects of my new situation.

I I

The morning of my arrival, after an excellent breakfast of blood sausage and chitterlings, I was sufficiently restored from the rigours of my journey to contemplate my surroundings with some degree of amicability. It helped that, after days of driving rain, the day dawned clear and bright. The pale sunshine of early spring struck blindingly silver off the puddles and made of the wet grass a wealth of trembling prisms. I stared out of my bedroom window as I dressed. It overlooked the back of the house, which boasted a wintry vegetable garden and the compulsory stunted orchard, and in the distance I could see the Black Mountains, clearly visible today, although their craggy heights were shrouded by mist. I found myself humming the mournful but beautiful ballads of my childhood about the shepherds of the Land of Death. The songs made me think of the youth I had seen the day before: he could scarcely have reached full manhood, but his face seemed ageless, as if death had already lifted him out of the stream of time.

I inspected my dwelling, which I had not had the energy to look over the night before, and confirmed my feeling of satisfaction at my situation. Indeed, it was perfect. The kitchen was large and well supplied, the amenities modern and well ordered. There was a pleasant dining room, furnished with surprising taste, a formal drawing room, a sitting room adjacent to my bedroom upstairs, and an attractive breakfast parlour downstairs at the front of the house, which captured all the morning light. In this room stood an elegant mahogany writing desk, surely the best piece of furniture in the house. I immediately requisitioned the parlour for my work room; I have brought with me several projects which I hope to complete in my time here, including the almost complete manuscript of poems which I have promised to S——. I thought of the lady who had inspired a good number of the poems; it is almost the anniversary of our first meeting. I confess to a moment's weakness, as I remembered a certain gesture, a certain turn of her head which displayed the graceful curve of her neck, and for a while I toyed with the idea of dedicating the book to her (I need only use initials, after all); but I discarded the notion almost immediately, since it would be taken as proof of an ardour which for me has now grown cold and which I have no wish to revisit.

After noon I found myself restless, and spent some time in the kitchen speaking to Anna, as I was more and more curious about the history of this house, which was so atypical of the dwellings I had seen in the Plateau. She told me that its owner, who was known only as Damek, lived not far away, less than two miles' walk.

"Well then!" I said. "I should, as a dutiful tenant, pay him my respects!"

"I fear, sir, that he might be from home," cried Anna, with what seemed to me a certain confusion.

"It would only be courteous," said I. "And if he is not home,

I have wasted no more than my time. I feel as if I should enjoy a walk."

"I think, sir, that the weather will turn later," Anna answered. "A storm can blow down from the mountains in a trice, and with a savageness as you lowlanders are not used to. And even if it is but a short distance, storms are no pleasure to walk in."

She looked as if she might say more, but instead turned to her cooking. My curiosity was piqued by this exchange; I felt that Anna was concealing something from me. I stepped outside to sniff the air and saw that the skies were clear and blue and showed no sign of unrest. So it was that a short time later, despite further attempts at dissuasion from Anna, I left the house, armed with meticulous directions (and checking that my silver ring was still on my finger, in case of unexpected meetings with Plateau wizards or the like). I found myself following a path that was little more than a goat track, which wound its way through scrubby fields of cabbages and barley in the direction of the Black Mountains.

I passed around a dozen sad memorials – the crumbling cairns of stones that signified where some luckless man had met his death – which seemed excessive for such a humble goat path. Then I remembered that my friend had told me that some two decades before, Elbasa had been under vendetta. "Vendetta can go on for generations," he said. "But in this case they found some way to stop it before it killed every man in the village."

It was, at first, as pleasant a stroll as I had anticipated, but as I neared my destination I began to realize that my housekeeper's warning had been well founded. The temperature fell abruptly, the wind began to gust in uneasy jumps and startles, and I saw to my alarm an ominous bank of purple cloud devouring the sky with an astonishing rapidity. I wrapped my coat closer around me and hurried on, keeping an anxious eye out for the house which, according to my directions, should soon appear to my left. It was with some relief that I spotted a gleam of light in the gathering darkness of the storm – it was only mid-afternoon, and yet the sun had all been eaten up, so that it almost seemed like night – and hurrying on, I found myself at the doorway of a large farmhouse just as the first drops of rain began to fall.

No one answered my initial knock. Puzzled, I tried again, growing concerned because the rain now began to pour down in earnest, liberally interspersed with hail. I thought that perhaps the deafening thunder drowned my knocking, and persisted, and after some minutes began to shout as well; but although there was a light in an upper window, indicating that the house was by no means empty, the door remained resolutely shut. At last I gave up and, shaking the water out of my eyes, started looking around for some rude shelter; perhaps the storm would pass quickly and I could make my luckless way home. There were, I saw, a couple of outbuildings, but more promisingly, I saw that at the back of the house there was a small courtyard. Perhaps this man Damek – if he was at home – was at that end of the house, and simply had not heard me through the din of the storm. The gate was locked, but when I clambered to the top of the wall I saw a window, and through the window, flickering against the wall, the reflected flames of a huge hearth.

By now I was soaked through and freezing – seduced by the pleasant morning, I had only worn a light coat – and forgetting how loud the storm was, I was possessed by an irrational rage, that anyone could have such lack of fellow feeling that they could leave a traveller unanswered by their door – and in such weather! And in the high country, where one's duty to a guest was sacred, a matter of honour, of life and death itself! Standing on an old water butt, I hefted myself over the courtyard wall and scrambled into the dark courtyard.

As soon as I dropped to the ground, I realized I had made a grave mistake: a very hound of hell, which had hitherto remained silent, rushed out of the shadows, barking fit to wake the dead. Had I not plunged forward in a blind panic for the door, it would have torn out my throat; even so, the brute attacked my leg, inflicting a most painful bite. I should have been done for, had the back door been locked; but to my great good fortune, it was not, and I and the snarling dog tumbled in a wet, graceless heap into the middle of a huge kitchen.

Somebody pulled the hound off me, but not before it had bitten me once more, and drove the animal out of the door with a stick. I sat on the floor gasping for breath, recovering from the shock of the attack, and it was a little while before I realized that I was crouched ignominiously on the floor, clutching my bleeding calf. A powerfully built, black-browed man in shirtsleeves, clearly a servant, was standing above me, regarding me with no great friendship in his face.

"Who the hell are you?" he demanded.

I attempted to draw together some poor shreds of what remained of my dignity.

"My name is Hammel," I said, trying to ignore the pain of my wounds and examining my trousers, which were sadly stained with blood. "I sought to pay my courtesies to my landlord, and find myself rewarded in this poor fashion. I knocked on the front door, but no one answered, and in desperation to escape the storm thought I would try the back..."

The man sneered and turned away without speaking, and my anger, fanned by my recent fright, reignited.

"Even if your master is away from home, it is no excuse to show such poor hospitality!" I said. "You disgrace his name. You can be sure that report will reach him, you cur. I'll see that he has you whipped."

The man turned back to face me, and to my astonishment

24

I saw that an infernal laughter flickered in his eyes. "And what of your manners, tumbling in here uninvited and messing up my floor?"

My breath was quite taken away by his insolence, and I sat there, gaping like a fish. But now he squatted down and, without further reference to me, examined my leg. He grunted.

"You're lucky," he said, standing up again. "Percha might have had your throat. But that's scarce a scratch; you'll live." He opened a cupboard and found a rag, poured some water from a jug into a basin and handed them to me. "Here, clean yourself up."

I took the items in a daze, still astounded by his rudeness. At last I found my tongue again. "Did you hear what I said, you dog? Your master will hear of this!"

"And whom, pray, are you calling 'dog'?" The amusement had vanished from his face altogether, and I began to feel afraid of him. He regarded me steadily for a few moments.

"I suppose," he said, "that it is not a mortal offence to be a fool, even if it ought to be. I expect you are my tenant; you look vapid enough. I had no desire or need to meet you, and I wish you would go home. Sadly, that is impossible at present, since this storm will not pass before the night is over. But since you have come to pay me your respects, I would suggest that it is inadvisable to call me names."

So this man, whom I had taken for a rough servant, was in fact Mr Damek, my landlord! Or was it some monstrous joke? What was the master of the house doing in the kitchen, dressed like a peasant? I thought better of arguing; a sudden uncomfortable image of the many cairns I had seen in my walk earlier that day passed before my inner eye.

I stuttered an apology, but the man merely gave me a look of contempt and told me to get off the floor. He returned to the table, where he had been cleaning a rifle before I had interrupted his task, and ignored me completely. Shakily, I stood and found a seat, as far away from my host as possible, but close enough to the fire to dry myself off. I cleaned my wounds, which smarted badly, bitterly regretting my hasty decision that morning. I resolved to listen to Anna in the future; it promised to be a long, uncomfortable and unamusing night.

III

Nor was I disappointed in my forebodings. I sat by the fire even after I became uncomfortably hot, not daring to move, listening to the storm outside and casting surreptitious glances at my sullen host and around the kitchen. It was a large room, and had once, clearly, been the heart of a prosperous and solid home: but everything, from the cracked plates stacked carelessly on a dresser, to the grimy windows and walls and cobwebbed eaves, spoke of neglect. The impression was reinforced by the smoky oil lamp, which cast most of the room into shadow: the only other illumination came from the hearth, which threw out a hellish red light.

Every now and then I made a nervous sally at conversation, which my host either ignored, or greeted with a grunt. He finished cleaning and oiling his rifle, reassembled it, placed it on a rack that hung on the wall, and took down another. While doing so, he glanced at me.

"You might as well make yourself useful, and put a log on the fire," he said.

Again, I was astounded by his discourtesy, but did not dare gainsay him, and did what he bade. At this point a door that I had not noticed at the far end of the kitchen opened, and a young woman entered the room. The last thing I expected to see in this house was a woman. I jumped to my feet in some confusion, and bowed.

The woman, I noticed at once, was very handsome; she had long black hair, no less thick for being dirty and uncombed, large, brown eyes set in a pale, delicate face, and a full, soft mouth. But her looks were marred by her slatternly dress and her sour, defiant expression. She started when she saw me, but my bow and stammered greeting merely elicited a sneer.

"Be polite to our guest, Lina," said my host. He sounded amused. "You need not betray your ill-breeding so grievously. This is Mr Hammel, from the city, who is currently staying at the Red House."

Lina turned and gave Damek a look of the purest hatred I have ever seen on a human face. She then sat herself down on a bench by the fire and, although I was scarce five feet from her, behaved as if I did not exist.

Now my situation was doubly uncomfortable; and to make things worse, I was getting very hungry. However, this last problem was resolved promptly, as after some sharp commands from Damek, Lina sulkily swung a black iron pot over the hearth and heated some soup, which she served out gracelessly in what had once been good porcelain bowls, but which were now, like everything in the kitchen, chipped and marred.

I thanked my hostess, and she favoured me with a contemptuous glare. Damek laughed.

"Don't waste your breath on her," he said.

Lina forestalled the objection that rose to my lips with a foul curse. But to my chagrin, she turned on me instead of Damek. "Don't think yourself so superior," she said to me. "I know your type. He might be a devil, but you're just a stinking louse."

Taken aback by her unprovoked attack, I found myself stammering like a fool. I concentrated on my meal, my vanity hurt by her open scorn, wondering whether she was mad, or if she was one of that breed of women that hate all men. For some time there was no sound except the scraping of spoons on crockery.

I tried, for the sake of ease, to strike up a conversation, since my mercurial host now seemed almost cordial; but everything I said was turned by Damek into an occasion for needling Lina. If she answered either him or me, it was in such a way as to lower her in my estimation. She was so surly and rude that I had a strong desire to slap her, and almost felt that she deserved the treatment meted out to her. I wondered if Damek had been soured by such unremittingly unpleasant company.

The soup was unexpectedly delicious, but my hostess received my compliments indifferently. Not that, by now, I expected anything else.

"As it happens," said Damek, with a malicious glance at Lina, "I made the soup. Lina is of no use at all. Except in one way, and even that has to be beaten out of her."

Lina didn't respond and I found myself, despite my better judgement, attempting to defend her.

"Sir, that is a churlish thing to say of a lady—" I began.

"A lady?" said Damek, and laughed. "I thought by now that even you would know better than that."

Lina started up, spilling her soup on the table, and flew at Damek, scratching at his eyes. He struck her full across the face, a sickening blow that flung her halfway across the room. She lay so still at first that I feared for a moment that she was dead; but then she stirred and scrambled up to her hands and knees, her hair swinging loose in rats' tails across her face. Her lip was bleeding.

"You son of a rotting whore," said she.

She spoke with such venom that I thought Damek would be momentarily silenced, but he merely glanced at me with what seemed to be complicity. I felt instantly revulsed.

"You see?" he said. "A certain superficial charm, I grant you, but such foulness within." Then he turned to Lina. "Get back to your room, lest I give you the beating you deserve."

She cringed away from him, so that I suddenly pitied her, and gathering herself together left the room. Damek followed her with his eyes until the door shut behind her.

"So," said he, turning back to me without the faintest trace of embarrassment. "Here you see the advantages of married life. I advise you to avoid it."

"She's your wife?" I said, with involuntary amazement. I was so stunned by the scene I had just witnessed that I scarcely knew what I was saying.

Damek didn't deign to answer, so I gave up my efforts to be companionable, and stared morosely into the fire. I had lost all sense of time, but it was now dark outside, and I estimated that it must be early evening. The storm, howling above the domestic popping of the fire, showed no sign of abating. My walk and the successive shocks of the day, combined with the heat in the kitchen, conspired to make me sleepy, and I found myself nodding off. I wondered, if I was to stay the night, as seemed inescapable, where I was to bed down.

I had passed around an hour in this fashion when the dog outside started to bark. I was wondering what other traveller could be so unfortunate as to be seeking succour from this cursed house when the door opened, letting in for a moment a gust of wind and mingled hail and rain which almost blew out the lamp. With it came a man so twisted by age and rheumatism that he was almost bent double. He was heavily cloaked, and water streamed from his cloak onto the flags as he cursed the dog.

He had one of the most unpleasant faces I have ever seen: all his features seemed to collapse into a lipless mouth, which was a thin line that expressed countless years of bitterness, spite and envy. His eyes were set close together, as if they conspired over his nose, pale blue irises floating in a web of blood vessels, and the nose itself was so red it was purple. This, I found later, spoke more of his drinking habits than the cold outside.

"One day I'll shoot that damned bitch," he said. "By the gods I swear I'll string her up…"

At this, he caught sight of me, and stopped short, turning to Damek with a wordless question.

"My tenant, Hammel," said Damek indifferently. "Hammel, this is my manservant, Kush."

Kush favoured me with a sour look, and returned to his grumbling as he removed his dripping outer garments and drew close to the fire. "I told you, Master Damek, there's a storm coming. But did you listen? Did you care? Not you. I could have been blown to the four quarters or frizzled up in a bolt of lightning. It's not a night fit for man nor beast out there. But no, nothing would suit you but—"

"Shut your whining, man," said Damek testily. "You're home now. Did you see the king?"

The old man reached inside his breast and threw a fat leather purse onto the table. "There, and much good may it do you," he said.

I was startled by the expression of lust that flickered over Damek's face. He swept the purse so swiftly into his pocket that I scarcely saw the movement, and then, suddenly aware of my observation, gave me a hostile stare. I averted my eyes; I had no wish to know what nefarious business concerned him. Our new companion gave me a sidelong suspicious look and helped himself to the remains of the soup, which he ate with disgusting slurps and sucking noises.

31

By now I was heartily sick of my situation. I have never wanted so passionately to leave a place in my life; if the rain had eased even a little, I might have risked getting lost in the darkness, just to escape. At last I told my host that I wished to sleep. He irritably ordered Kush to show me to a room and the old man took up a candle and, grumbling all the way, led me along an unlit passage and up some narrow stairs. On a landing he opened a door to a room furnished with a narrow bed, a washstand with a mildewed mirror and a wardrobe. The room had a fusty air, as if it hadn't been opened for years, and smelt strongly of damp. It was also freezing cold. Kush had every intention of leaving me in pitch-darkness, but I had a protracted argument with him, insisting that he leave the candle for my use, and in the end he acceded grudgingly to my wishes, and fumbled his way back downstairs.

I nervously checked that the silver ring the wizard had given me was securely on my finger and wished that I had not left the phial behind when I had departed in the morning. I set the candle on the washstand and found my matches and placed them beside it – I did not feel at all at ease in this house, and didn't want to be left without light should anything strange happen. I anxiously inspected the wounds on my calf, which were still very painful, for signs of infection, but in that poor light could tell nothing: I would have to wait until I could find a doctor on the morrow. Then I climbed into bed with all my clothes on, laying my coat on top of me for warmth, and blew out the candle, thinking regretfully of my cosy feather mattress in the Red House. But at least I was alone.

I V

Although it was so cold that my feet felt like blocks of ice, and the bed was hard and lumpy, I fell asleep quickly, exhausted by the events of the day. I passed into a night of dreams, the most vivid and horrible that I have ever experienced.

I was walking through a landscape very like the one I had walked earlier that day, still sere with winter, but something was wrong with the perspective: things that should have been close appeared to be very far away, but the mountains in the distance seemed to press up against me oppressively. The sky was a strange bruised purple. All around me, as far as I could see, stretched rows and rows of graves, some marked with crosses, some with mounds of stone.

I seemed to have been walking for hours without seeing a single soul, and the further I walked the more anxious I became. I was searching for something, although I didn't know what it was, something dear to me, the loss of which afflicted me grievously. The further I walked, the further I was from the possibility of finding it, and yet I knew I could not turn back. My heart grew more and more oppressed.

At last I saw a figure in the distance, walking towards me. Out of sheer relief, I started running; but then I saw it was Kush. He leered grotesquely when he saw me, in a parody of greeting, and held up his hands. From one dangled a leather bag, which I knew with a dreamer's clairvoyance was full of gold pieces; the other hand was empty. But in the centre of his palm was a wound, from which was falling a constant stream of blood. The blood fell to the ground and made a black puddle, in which was reflected my own face.

On seeing this, I was overwhelmed by loathing and horror. Kush began to cackle, and moved closer to me; I could smell his breath, an odour of decay. I wanted to run but, transfixed by terror, I could not move, and he reached out to touch my face with his bleeding hand. Just before his fingers touched me, I woke up.

I lit the candle with trembling hands and looked about the room. Although it was so cold I could see the breath hanging in front of my face, I was lathered with sweat. I took a few deep inhalations and admonished myself for foolishness: it was no wonder that I was suffering nightmares, after the day I had had, and probably I was feverish, from the dog's bites, maybe, or from catching a chill.

I told myself that the dream's dreadful realism stemmed from its echoes of my experiences earlier that night. I had sensed a dark tale behind that hastily hidden purse that my dreaming mind had transformed into deathly portents. So I comforted myself, noting that the storm wasn't so violent now; I must have been asleep for some time. Only a few more hours, and I would be out of here. I settled myself down and once again fell rapidly asleep.

I dreamt that I was in the room in which I now slept,

standing on the floor between the bed and the wardrobe. The grey light of dawn filtered through the grimy window, lending every object in the room a faint luminosity. I knew that the door was locked, and that I couldn't get out. For reasons I couldn't trace, I was filled with increasing apprehension, rising to panic: some dreadful event was to occur later that day, although I couldn't remember what it was.

Then, with the illogic of dream, I was in my own study at home in the city. With an intense sense of relief I sat down at my desk and picked up my pen, a new one I had purchased just before I left for the north, and began to write a poem which had suddenly occurred to me. But the ink was a strange colour, and kept clotting. I knocked the pen impatiently on the blotter, and tried again to write, but a haemorrhage of ink spilt over the page, and I realized then that it was not ink, but blood. As I stared at the spoilt paper, the blood began to pour impossibly from the nib of the pen, an increasing stream that collected into a red puddle and began to drip on the floor. The sound of its steady drip was, I remember, particularly dreadful. I lifted my hand to my eyes, and saw that it was covered with blood; then I realized that it was my blood, and that I was bleeding to death.

Again I woke in a sweat, all my limbs trembling. For a horrible moment I thought I was back in the nightmare: dawn-pale light was leaking through the shutters, giving the room the same ghastly luminosity that it had possessed in my dream. It was very quiet, a silence which seemed sinister until I understood that it was because the storm had blown itself out.

I swung my legs over the edge of the bed and sat with my face in my hands until I stopped shaking. I feel incapable of conveying the peculiar horror these dreams invoked in me: my entire body felt chilled through, the hair crept on my scalp and neck, and nausea crawled in the pit of my stomach. This house, thought I, is infected with more than the sheer unpleasantness of its inhabitants: some sick wizardry is at hand here. I checked that my protective ring was still on my finger; it was. I wondered, with a shudder, what might have happened, had I not protected myself in that way.

My only thought was to get out of that place as soon as possible. I had had more than enough of it. Perhaps I had had enough of the north, and should head back to the city ... though even then, the image of Grosz's mocking expression held me back from the thought of a humiliating return.

I stood up as slowly as an old man – all my body ached as if with ague, and my bitten calf felt more sore this morning than the night before. I put on my coat, and then leant towards the mirror on the washstand, to check the no doubt lamentable state of my person. And then I was plunged into nightmare again, because the reflection I saw was not my own.

It was the face of a woman who was perhaps in her twenties. She bore a strong resemblance to Lina, but was less conventionally beautiful. The same thick black locks tumbled over her face, and she had the same high, chiselled cheekbones, but her face was thinner, more asymmetrical, somehow more wild. In the mirror I could see that she was wearing a nightdress that fell immodestly off one shoulder and exposed almost the whole of one of her full breasts. Her mouth was luscious, preternaturally red, the colour of blood; but it expressed a wilfulness that lent its frank sensuality some other, thrilling, quality. Aside from her lips, her skin was deathly white. But it was her eyes that captured my fascinated attention. They were the violet eyes of a witch, and they blazed with unassuageable longing, a bottomless, reckless hunger, and they stared unseeingly straight into mine.

In those first moments I don't know whether I was more possessed by desire or terror. The imprint of that wild, beautiful face has never left my memory. I have seen – have even embraced – women more handsome, but never have I seen a face so passionate and yet, despite its utter abandon, so wholly itself.

Then it was as if something focused in that spellbinding gaze, and with a clutch of horror I comprehended that the apparition in the mirror was looking back at me. Her expression changed with astounding swiftness: now those extraordinary eyes blazed with anger. I was not what she had hoped and longed for; and even in my fright, I confess I felt a little shock of disappointment. Her gaze locked on mine, and I could see that she was speaking, although I could not hear what she said. I involuntarily flung up my hand in a gesture of helplessness. When I did that, she recoiled; I almost heard her hiss, as if she were in pain. I realized that she must have seen the ring on my finger. I tried then to turn and run away but found that I could not move my legs: my feet refused to obey me, whether because of sheer terror or because of some bewitchment I do not know.

In a moment she was close again to the surface of the mirror, as if it were a glass window that imprisoned her, and began to beat it frantically with her hands. When I saw this, complete panic took hold of me: I no longer knew what I was doing. I cried out, screaming at her to leave me alone, and hit out blindly at the mirror. The thing exploded in a shower of glass shards, some of which cut my face and hands. But I didn't care: now I could move. I ran out of the room, slammed shut the door and stood in the dark hallway leaning against the wall, panting, trying to regain my breath.

My host, perhaps awoken by my cries if he was not awake already – if indeed anyone could sleep at all in that infernal house – came running down the hallway in shirt and trousers. When he saw me standing by the door, his face darkened with fury; but I was at such a pitch I swear that even the Devil himself was beyond frightening me further.

"What were you doing in that room?"

The unexpectedness of his question pulled me up short.

"Why, you bastard," I answered furiously, "you put me there!"

"Not I," he said. "Not I. No one goes in that room."

"Then your filthy manservant did," I said, holding my bloody hand close to my chest. "Out of malice or mischief, I don't know. I wouldn't have chosen to sleep there for a million gold pieces. I'm going home, where that bitch of hell can't get at me. Even if I have to crawl there…"

I stumbled down the stairs, but I had not gone halfway before Damek caught me up and, grabbing my shoulder, swung me around to face him. "What bitch of hell?" he snarled at me. "What are you talking about?"

I attempted to tear myself free of his grasp. "A nice trick, putting me in a haunted room!" I shouted. "I swear, you're the Devil himself, and that woman…"

"Who?" he said to me with passionate urgency. "What woman?"

"That unholy witch in the mirror," said I. I looked up and met his eyes: they were blazing as intensely as the woman's in the mirror, though whether with longing or despair or rage or grief, or all of those at once, I couldn't tell. We gazed wordlessly at each other for a few seconds, both suddenly still.

"Tell me," he said, his chest heaving. "Tell me what you mean."

All of a sudden I pitied him, and I realized also that I was no longer afraid, although I hurt all over.

"I saw a woman in the mirror," I said. "A witch, sir! She tried to bewitch me, or come out of the mirror, or something – and so I smashed the mirror…"

Damek's face tightened as I spoke, and then he thrust me violently away from him, so I fell down the remaining steps.

He rushed upstairs, shouting his wife's name in a voice that sounded thick and hoarse with tears. I was momentarily baffled: what kind of husband was this, who reviled his wife with blows and scorn at one moment, and called for her with such passion the next? But all I knew was that I did not want to stay in that house with those people one minute longer. I ran down a wide passage to the front door, hastily unbolted it, and at last found myself outside, under a clear pale sky. Never has the dawn air smelt sweeter to me; and I swear that even with my wounded leg, I ran most of the way home.

V

My return, limping and bloodstained, to the village of Elbasa created in its own small way a sensation. The proprietor of the shop even came out of his dingy premises to witness open-mouthed my exhausted stumble over the cobbled laneways towards the Red House, and a couple of the mangy dogs crept up and sniffed me. I saw several faces peering out of dark windows, and in the narrow street a woman grabbed a small boy near by and whispered in his ear, whereupon he took off as fast as his fat legs could carry him, to bring the news of my reappearance – as I found when I arrived there – to Anna at the Red House.

My absence had, it seemed, created much consternation. Most of the village had known of my intention within an hour of my departure, and after much discussion had decided that I was doomed. Heads had been shaken and judgements pronounced on the foolish city dweller who so stubbornly had insisted on visiting the Devil himself. My survival must have been, therefore, a source of considerable disappointment: but

I have no doubt that the sorry spectacle I presented would have been some compensation.

I was past caring what anybody thought. When I shambled up the path to the Red House, Anna and her husband were already at the door. I have never been more grateful for simple kindness: they took me inside, and I found that Anna had prepared a hot bath and laid out fresh clothes, and there was a delicious-smelling breakfast already cooking. Anna inspected my leg, pursed her lips, and carefully cleaned it. I confess that I luxuriated in their fussing over me, although it was behaviour which would normally have made me irritable.

I bathed, ate and then, exhausted, fell asleep in the chair in front of a fire in the pleasant front room as I was reading a book. When I awoke, I was feverish, and Anna, despite my protestations (I had no great confidence in the skills of the northern doctors), became anxious and sent for the doctor, who lived not far away in the village. He arrived late in the afternoon and proved to be a lugubrious man of about sixty who took my pulse and looked under my eyelids, and then inspected the bites on my calf. My nervous enquiries elicited the fact that he was city-educated, and I relaxed a little. He pronounced that I was suffering from nervous shock and a chill, and that the wounds were slightly inflamed and likely to be infected, but with proper care should heal famously. He bled me and left a draught for me to take that evening, saying that I should be confined to bed for a week and that he would call the following day.

I found myself feeling bored and peevish, but mostly I was consumed by curiosity. Who were those people in that house? I had been educated to expect rustic manners and primitive behaviours among the peoples of the Land of Death – or the Black Country, as they call it themselves – but I had also been told that they were, by their own lights, people of strict propriety. They were bound by the Law of the Book, which governed their every interaction, from property rights to the Blood Laws. Damek, to the contrary, seemed utterly lawless, beholden to no rule but his own tyranny. Had I not been told he was a relation of the king? Did that mean that he held himself above the harsh laws of this place? What could explain his wild behaviour before I left that cursed house? And, most teasingly, who was the witch in the mirror? If indeed I had not hallucinated her in a fever, as I was half inclined now to believe…

Anna has at least solved the puzzle of Damek's mad cries for his wife that ghastly night: it turns out that the Lina whom I met at the farmhouse is in fact the daughter of the woman for whom he was calling with such passion, and who is now long dead. The confusion comes from the custom in the north of naming the oldest child after its mother or father, according to its sex. Moreover, Anna is convinced – a thought that chills me to the marrow – that the witch I saw in the mirror was no hallucination, as I have half convinced myself, but the spirit of the older Lina.

Now I am no longer in danger, the strongest sensation I feel is a powerful curiosity. I have determined to quiz Anna about Damek: she has lived all her life in this place, and must know its stories. I remember how she turned my queries about my landlord when I suggested that I visit him, and I fear that a natural reticence might prevent her revealing this country's secrets to an outsider like myself. On the other hand, she has been much more forthcoming since my return. I fancy she might believe that the wounds on my leg have earned me the right to satisfy my interest.

II: ANNA

VI

Many people say that Lina was born evil. They wrong her: Lina was as innocent as any baby is when it first opens its eyes on the world, and there was a spark within her that remained innocent until the last. If she was wicked, it was this pitiless world that made her so. All the same, there's no disputing that ill omen attended her birth. On the night she was born, the moon was in its dark phase, and a comet blazed its trail across the night sky. It was visible for a week, its brilliance weakening every night as the new mother sickened and died of the blood poison. She gave Lina her name and her first suckle, and after that she was too busy dying to take much interest in the infant, whose care fell to my mother, but lately lain in with me and with milk enough for the two of us. My mother, named Anna like me, was then newly married to my father, a stableman and farmhand in the household's employ; after Lina's birth she was quickly elevated to chief housekeeper, which was a post she filled for the rest of her life.

So it was that Lina and I were milk sisters. We played

together as children before the duties of the household took me away from that intimacy and it was made clear to me – although seldom by Lina, who for all her touchy pride never really took note of such things – that she was of high blood and I only of the servant class. Even so, our friendship continued until her death. And so there was a closeness between us that was often less of servant and mistress and more like a kind of cousinship, an intimacy that was, I confess, often as much trial as pleasure. I loved her dearly, not least because I had no sisters or brothers of my own; and I was one of the few people to whom she would attend. But with that love came much grief.

Lina's father, the Lord Georg of Kadar, was a distant cousin of the upland king and so a beneficiary of the royal tax, from which came much of the family's wealth. I should explain that royalty in the highlands is a different matter from nobility down south – older, for a start, tracing its lineage back to the dark years and, so legend says, before that to Judas Iscariot himself, arch-traitor to Jesus our Lord. One would think such lineage would shame a family of so much pride, and certainly – perhaps out of some sense of propriety – it is not marked in the genealogy of the royal family Bible (which I have seen with my own eyes, when I once had the duty of dusting it). On the other hand, in the ancient chapel in the family manse – not the chapel which is in use for regular worship, which is far grander – there is a fine stained window in the central place above the altar that certainly portrays Iscariot. He stands with his face downcast. In one hand he holds the bag that contains the thirty silver coins with which he betrayed Christ, and from the other dangles the rope with which he hanged himself. Inscribed on the stone plinth where he is stood are the words: "Error is the road to God".

Some heretics have argued that Iscariot was the true Christ, because it was through his abjection and treachery that man was redeemed by the Saviour, and without his action God would not have seen His will done. I see you look shocked? There was once a cult that believed it, and may still be, for all I know; most of its acolytes were burned by the Inquisition, but it may still thrive in the Plateau, away from the eye of the Orthodox Church. Such things are possible here. And whether that ancestry is real or no, the royal family of the north holds it as true; and perhaps this says as much about them and their wealth as anything I could tell you: most particularly, of their twisted pride and their obscure shame, which are twined together as inextricably as mating adders. Though as is never said but sometimes thought, there are many reasons why they might be considered cursed, and their ancestry the least of them.

Lina's mother, who was named Lina Usofertera, was a daughter of a powerful clan who count among them the most feared upland wizards. Her marriage to the master was a union of passion, and most impolitic. It was said afterwards that she cast a spell over the Lord Kadar; according to report, he certainly acted as a man bewitched, and ranted and raved until he had his way and his bride. After his wife died, my mother told me, the master was maddened with grief, and but for her intervention would have killed himself by his own hand. When he came to his senses he took himself and his new daughter away south, swearing he would never return to the highlands. My mother said he always blamed the wizards for his wife's death.

Of course, the wizards, who enforce the Lore, and the kings, who take the Blood Tax, are the two chief powers in the Black Country, and it might be said that they have many interests in common; however, in practice each keeps to its own, and the families never intermarry. The master married Lina's mother against the wishes of the king himself. The king forgave the master his transgression a few years after Lina's birth, when he called him back to the Plateau, although the king's later actions showed that his forgiveness held a modicum of poison. In marrying the master, Lina's mother defied her own family as well, as the clans don't hold with mixing their blood with the royal family. Some, including the master, believed that her death in childbed was the result of a curse from her father's cousin, the Wizard Ezra, who was the most implacably opposed to the marriage; others claimed further that this curse was a pact between the king and the Usoferteras. All these rumours are impossible to sort out one from the other, and the truth is anybody's guess. This is a country where secrecy is the chief rule, and so gossip blossoms here like nowhere else.

When Lina was born, she had the blue eyes of a new babe, and in any case the household was all at sixes and sevens because of her mother's death and her father's madness, so no one except my mother took much notice of the motherless scrap. It wasn't until her sixth month that her eyes attained their violet colour and showed her true nature. If she had been the daughter of any man but the Lord Kadar, she would have at once been abandoned naked on the hillside to die of exposure and her poor little corpse left to feed the crows, like every other baby girl born a witch in these parts. But by then, Lord Kadar had driven south with his household, and he said that he would be damned if he would kill his only daughter out of some black upland superstition. As some said later, recalling those words, if the Lord Kadar wasn't damned, his daughter was.

The southern estate is a small property by the sea which is famous in a minor way for making wine, and there the household repaired until Lina and I were ten years old. We had some of our happiest hours playing in that low, wide house, with its vine-twisted verandahs and red terracotta roofs, tumbling among the chickens and peahens scratching in the yard, or swimming in the tiny half-moon bay that lay beyond the garden. My mother cared for Lina as if she were her own daughter, treating her no differently from myself; and the master was kind, although he inspired me with the awe due to his authority. If he brought treats home from his travels, he never forgot me. I recall that as a blessed time, drenched with sunshine and laughter, although no doubt my memory tricks me: certainly, I was a contented child, and I think for Lina it was the only untroubled period of her life.

Lina's character was evident from early on. We all knew she was a witch – which was not such a bad thing down south, where they do not kill their witches – but she showed no early sign of magic. There was, however, no disguising her eyes, which were the vivid violet of the witchborn, and were large and luminous, surrounded by thick, long lashes. She was a startlingly lovely child, but oh! so wilful; she would lose her temper in a trice over anything that crossed her. Sometimes she would scream with rage until she vomited, setting the entire household in a fright; but then without warning the storm would pass, leaving her sunny and biddable, as if nothing had happened.

She could be cruel, but somehow it was never personal. She once sat on me to hold me down and broke my little finger by bending it back over my hand. I still remember the expression on her face as she did it: it was curious and intent, as if she simply wanted to see what would happen. Her dismay at the dramatic result was comical, as if my screams and the subsequent row – I didn't tell my mother how it happened, although she had her suspicions – were the last thing she expected.

The following day Lina told me that I should break her little finger, to make up for what she had done. She looked at me with unusual seriousness, and laid her hand down flat on the floor. "It's easy, you just pull it back like this. I won't stop you, I promise." To her surprise, I recoiled at her offer, and she pressed me until both of us began to get angry. When she realized that I really wouldn't do it, she looked hurt, but then she shrugged and laughed. "You are strange, Anna," she said. "It's only fair. But if you won't, I can't make you."

I suppose it's unsurprising that Lina's childish notions of justice should be shaped by vendetta: an eye for an eye, a tooth for a tooth, a finger for a finger. However, when she believed something was unfair, she could react in unexpected ways that had nothing to do with what she was taught. I remember vividly the day some of her friends, who were mostly children from land-owning families near by, began to tease me. They said I was only a servant and should not be allowed to play with them, and they mocked my clothes and held their noses to demonstrate how I stank. I was a shy child, and wholly unable to defend myself against their abuse.

As I stood in tears, Lina bristled with fury. "That's nice coming from you, Kinrek Tomas," she said, pointing scornfully at my chief persecutor. "Last week we had to take you home because you wet your pants! And Maya, I've never seen Anna with snot all down her front, like when you sneezed that time. Anna's cleaner than any of you. And she's six times more fun." (This last wasn't strictly accurate.) "I won't speak to any of you until you say you're sorry. You're all *pigs*." Then she took my hand and marched me home, where we played the games I liked best all afternoon, even though I knew they bored her rigid.

That day Lina won my undying loyalty. I did get my apologies, and I was never teased by those children again, though it took some time for me to forgive our playmates. Once they apologized Lina regarded the episode as finished, and she showed no resentment towards any of them. One of her virtues as a child – it changed later, although I never blamed her for that – was that she didn't bear grudges, and was mystified by those who did. It was another reason why I excused her excesses. That was the least northern thing about her: in the north hatreds are nurtured for generations of vendetta, as if they are precious family heirlooms.

We children treated Lina as if she were a perilous natural element, like the sea: we watched her with caution, and fled when she turned nasty. When she was in her sunny moods, no one was more fun: she led us into mischief, even the boys, because she invented the best games and was the most daring of all of us. We all admired her fearlessness, but her generosities inspired our deeper loyalty. Once, when we were caught raiding a neighbour's orchard for his plums, Lina stepped forward and took the blame for all of us, persuading the angry man to let the rest of us go. She was thrashed for her pains but, as she said to us with studied carelessness later, he wouldn't have dared to beat her nearly as hard as he would have beaten us, because she was the Lord Kadar's daughter.

Even then she was imperious and stubborn. It was, I suppose, the other side to her courage. My mother did her best to blunt Lina's edges and to instil in her some sense of womanly modesty, but this was undone by her father, who spoiled and indulged her, and whom she adored with a passion made all the sharper by his frequent absences.

One day the Lord Kadar returned home from a long journey. As was our custom, we all gathered solemnly in the dining room to welcome him home. After he had distributed gifts, he took Lina on his knee and kissed her cheek. She flushed with pleasure and buried her face in his neck, and he put his arm about her and announced, as if he were talking about tomorrow's breakfast, that we were going to move back north, to Elbasa. "As soon as the house is packed," he said. "I want to be home for the summer."

There was an immediate hubbub of astonishment. "But what about Lina?" asked my mother, her question cutting through the noise. It was typical of her that she thought of Lina first, although even then, young as I was, I knew that she was homesick for the north and for the family she had left behind when the master moved us south all those years before. "What will happen to Lina?"

The master looked my mother straight in the eye, but he hesitated before he answered her. "Lina too. The king has forgiven my family, and I think it's time we went home. And we are of royal blood, after all. The Lore doesn't apply to us."

Lina looked up at him, with a wicked laughter in her eyes. "I am a princess *and* a witch!" she said. "No one would *dare* to touch me!"

"Neither they would, my darling," said her father, and kissed her brow. "And a beautiful princess at that!"

My mother pressed her lips together, for she disapproved of such petting, which only encouraged Lina's excesses. She said nothing more: it wasn't her place to have an opinion about the master's decisions. The rest of the evening was a whirl of gossip in the kitchens as everyone talked about the news. My father, a taciturn man, went so far as to shrug his shoulders. None of us in the least expected it, not even the master's manservant, who was a little sulky at being taken by surprise: he felt it demeaned his status in the household. Later my mother was uncharacteristically impatient with me as she washed me and put me to bed, and I knew she was worried.

"Will they really try to kill Lina?" I asked, for like everyone else I had heard dark rumours of the savage ways of the north, although my mother never told those stories. I mostly picked them up from my southerner friends, when they wanted to tease me. And sometimes – always led by Lina – we had played hunt the witch, with Lina in the principal role. We dressed up as highland wizards, with sticks for our staffs, and dragged Lina from hiding, her hands tragically clasped; and we pretended to set her

52

on fire, while she cast her eyes to heaven and called down curses upon our heads. I have sometimes thought, although her father would never have countenanced such a vulgar occupation, that she should have stayed in the south and worked in the theatres of the city: she was a born actress.

My mother didn't answer me for a time, as if she were turning over things in her head. Then she said, "The master is right. She won't be killed, at least not by the common people, and maybe her royal blood will protect her from the wizards. I doubt she'll have an easy time of it on the Plateau, things are different there. But it is not for you or me, child, to question the will of the master."

And that was that.

VII

It was early spring, and the weather was still uncertain: everything that was to go north must be wrapped in sacking and oiled tarpaulins and packed on the drays in straw, and my mother, as chief housekeeper, had the responsibility of making sure that all the fine china and glassware didn't arrive in Elbasa shivered to smithereens. I had to leave behind my best friend, Clar, the red-headed daughter of the dairyman (Lina never counted as a friend so much as a condition of nature, to be borne with as best I could). Once I realized I would likely never see Clar again, the gloss fell off the excitement for me; I cried myself to sleep every night for a week, and we knotted bracelets of coloured wool for each other and swore never to forget our friendship. Lina, on the other hand, was radiant with excitement. She told everybody who would listen that she was going to claim her birthright as a princess of the blood, even after we were all heartily sick of hearing about it, and was determined to help with the packing. Although she was continually told off for being underfoot, not even the most severe scolding could darken her disposition.

I don't remember much of the journey, except that it was very slow and that it seemed to rain every day. I sat on the cart, numb with cold and misery, hating everything. Our arrival in Elbasa surprised me out of my glums, all the same: even though the master was to follow us later, the whole village turned out to welcome us back, crowding into the square in their best church clothes, which looked rude and strange to my southern eyes. In the north, a village without its lord is a village abandoned. No matter the scandal that attached to the master's wedding and his dead wife and, even more, to his witch-eyed daughter, blood is blood: and in this country, blood is everything.

I met my grandparents and uncles and aunts for the first time, and my cousins gave me dark looks and stuck out their tongues behind the backs of the adults, which made me act likewise and earned me a cuff from my father. Perversely, this had the effect of cheering me up: it seemed children up north were not so different from children down south, for all their crude clothes and muddy boots. I kept a wary eye out for the upland wizards, of whom I had heard much, and was disappointed when I saw no one who looked in the least wizardly; but there was some entertainment to be had from watching Lina, who took my breath away with her audacity. She ignored the children, and greeted the town dignitaries with the gravity of a highborn lady of the south. Such was her seriousness, nobody dared to smile: even at ten years old, Lina's sense of entitlement was a kind of enchantment in itself, persuading others to see her as she saw herself. There was much jostling among the peasants, because everyone wanted to get a sight of the witchborn daughter of the master, and she knew it too, and played up to it.

After the necessary speeches, which seemed to my mind quite unnecessarily long, we went up to the Red House. I think

I fell in love with it at once because, even though it was small, it reminded me of the home we had left behind. The master's grandfather had built it to please his southern wife, a delicate lady from the city who, so the story runs, quickly withered in the harsh plains and was carried away by the consumption in only a few short years. He bought the estate in the south when she was in her illness, and moved there hoping she would recover, but by then it was already too late. Some still whisper that it was back then that the rot set into the Kadar family. Black Country people do not trust southerners, begging your pardon; they consider them dishonest, weak and immoral, since they do not live by the Lore.

My master's father did much to rescue the family reputation, and lived an unexceptionable life. He married a hard northern woman who ruled the household with a hand of iron and had no truck with any southern fripperies. She moved the principal household to the manse, where Damek lives now, but she kept a canny eye on the accounts, and for all her disapproval of the south, didn't sell the profitable southern estate.

So my family were to live in the Red House, caring for Lina, and here too was the master's residence; the rest of the household was to move to the manse, and run the estate from there. There was much coming and going between the two households in those days.

One difference from our southern home I noticed right away, and it brought home to me more than anything else that we were in a place of unknown perils: every threshold was crowned with iron, and above every window was a sprig of rowan. It was, my mother told me, to keep out evil spirits; and because of the way she said it, I felt a run of goosebumps trickle down my spine.

I didn't have to wait long for my first sight of a wizard. The next morning there was a hammering on the front door, as if someone were beating it with a stick, which was in fact the case. I was in the kitchen with my mother and the cook, peeling turnips for luncheon, and I remember my mother started and dropped her knife. She must have known at once who it was, must in fact have been expecting it; and my father was out in the fields and the master not yet come. She stood up, gathering her skirts around her, and went to answer the door. She didn't forbid me to follow, which I am certain she would have done if she had not been so distracted, and I was alive with curiosity, so I dogged her heels through the hallway and peeked out from behind her as she opened the door. I'm sure my eyes were as round as saucers.

Outside stood a tall man who looked at first just like an ordinary highland shepherd: he wore a thick jerkin of unwashed wool and leggings of leather, and his rifle was slung across his back. The only signs of his vocation were the stout blackthorn staff that he carried, and the starveling boy who stood silently beside him, so pale and thin I thought he must be ill, and despite the cold weather dressed in rags through which his skin showed white. I stared at the strange pair and clutched my mother's hand, at which point she noticed I was there. She reached behind her to give me a slap, for my cheek.

"Greetings," she said. "The Wizard Ezra, is it?"

"Aye." The man lifted his head and met her eyes, and I felt my mother flinch. I couldn't stop looking at his face, which was as harsh and craggy as the mountains themselves: he had a nose like the beak of an eagle, and skin the colour of walnuts, weathered by wind and rain and sun, and a great scar ran across his face from one side to the other, across his nose, as if someone had slashed him with a knife. His eyes were like black obsidian: you could see nothing through them. "Aye, it is the Wizard Ezra," he said. There was a cold contempt in his voice, although his face was without expression. "Where is your master?"

"My master is not yet come, as you must know," said my mother. "And my husband is in the fields."

"Will you not ask me in to await their coming?"

"Nay," said my mother, and her voice was shaking. I had never seen my mother afraid, and it started a tremble in my own heart. "That I will not. You have no business in this house."

The wizard smiled, but there was no mirth in it, and somehow I knew my mother had won the first round. "I know you keep the witch child here," he said. "And that is an abomination, and of my business."

"She lives under the king's pardon!" said my mother shrilly. "You may not touch a hair of the child's head, and well you know it!"

"Maybe. Maybe not. Do not think yourself above the Lore, woman. Nor your brat there." Here he directed me a look of such venom that I felt myself go cold all the way through, as if the blood in my veins had turned to ice water. I was suddenly terrified, and could not move a muscle: I stared back like a rabbit before a fox, my heart pounding, until he turned his gaze away and released me. "I come to deliver a message, is all. On this matter there is truce between the king and the wizards, yes. Take care the truce is observed, else blood is the answer, as it should have been in the beginning."

"The truce will be observed, if it is in my power to observe it," said my mother. "And you may not curse me or mine."

"It's not for you to say what I may or may not do," said the wizard. "It is a matter for the Lore. It would be well to remember that." He turned on his heel and strode off without looking back, his boy stumbling after him.

My mother leant against the doorpost breathing hard, watching him all the way down the path and out of sight; and then she scolded me roundly for following her to the door. I said nothing at all, because I had just been frightened out of my wits, and I didn't know why. When we were in the south some of my friends had scoffed at the northern wizards, claiming they were charlatans who frightened the ignorant and superstitious peasants, but any scepticism I might have felt had vanished in the moment when the Wizard Ezra had looked at me. I remembered the stories of how wizards could turn a man's bones to water, or his marrow to hot lead, so he would die slowly in twisted agony; those stories no longer seemed far-fetched. When my mother had finished telling me off, I went back to the kitchen and finished peeling the turnips. I was burning with questions, but I knew even then that no one would answer them.

VIII

The master didn't travel with his household, preferring to avoid the bustle and inconvenience. It was some days before he arrived, and I remember that it rained almost constantly; great thick mists rolled down from the highlands so that sometimes you couldn't see six steps out of the windows all day, and a little boy herding goats was lost in the plains and frozen to death. Despite the weather, my father spent almost all his time with the livestock to avoid the chaos indoors. I think the rain relieved my mother's mind, because Lina could not go outside and get into trouble; at the same time it meant we were constantly under her feet. She had so much to do that she was sharp with us, so we tried to keep out of her way.

Lina was incandescent with impatience to see her father. She flew to the front window every time she heard footsteps or hoofbeats, and every morning she stated that he was *definitely* coming that day, and every evening she went to bed limp with disappointment, worried that he had become lost in the mist and died of cold, like the goat-boy. Her impatience infected me as well, and in my free time we made a game of it, running to the front room, even when we only imagined the sound, and driving my mother to distraction. She was setting up the household to her satisfaction, and in between was catching up with her own relations, whom she had not seen for ten years; there was a lot of news (most of which, when I was forced to listen as I sat in the kitchen peeling carrots, I found very boring) about who had died and who had been born and who had married and who had bought the short field down in the village south, or how Old Wanda had lost her mind finally and had been seen talking to the sheep on the high road, thinking they were her dead brothers, and so on.

Then, quite suddenly, the clouds lifted and a morning dawned fresh and sparkling, so the raindrops hanging from the buds on the bare hazels shone like jewels from a king's ransom. For the first time since we had arrived you could see the mountains in the distance, and I went outside and stared at them: they looked black and forbidding, jutting up into the sky out of the plains as sheer and dangerous as the steel knives in the kitchen; but I saw that they were beautiful too, and they sent a shiver through my soul. In that moment I remembered that I was born an uplander, and I felt the hard bones of this land beneath my feet and the high pale sky above me. I knew then that, for better or worse, this was my own country, and I belonged here.

At breakfast, Lina predicted confidently – as she had every day before – that her father would arrive that day. This time she was right: he arrived late that afternoon, when it had begun to rain again and shadows were gathering into nightfall. Lina was beginning to coil herself up into a tantrum of disappointment, and was picking a quarrel with me, poking me as I was trying to do my chores and generally being tiresome. She heard a horse coming up to the house, and then a rap on the door, and she started up, her face glowing with hope and excitement, and rushed to the door, with my poor mother wringing her hands behind her, telling her to mind her behaviour. She flung open the door violently and then teetered on the threshold, stunned with disappointment. Instead of her father, a boy stood on the step, wrapped in a cloak against the chilly rain.

"Who are you?" asked Lina rudely. "And where's my father?"

The boy stared at her sullenly and didn't answer. And then the master strode into view – he had been giving instructions to the groom – and she forgot her disappointment instantly and ran into his arms. He swung her up and kissed her and then set her down and said, "Lina, here is a companion for you. Damek, this is my daughter, Lina. Lina, this is Damek, who will be your foster-brother from now on."

I turned involuntarily to my mother, who was unable for a moment to hide her astonishment, and I knew she had been given no warning of this new charge. Lina stared at the boy, as amazed as the rest of us. "But I don't want a foster-brother!" she said at last.

"Nevertheless, you have one," said her father, and there was a grim edge to his voice that took the light out of her face. "And we have been riding all day, and are tired and hungry and wet, and I want to come into the house. If you will permit us to get past you, Lina."

My mother, flustered and perhaps a little angry, led the two travellers into the house, and took their sodden cloaks and sat them down at a table, which she laid with earthenware pots of soup and a casserole and fresh bread and tankards of beer; and for a while, there was no talk, just some serious eating. We had already had our supper in the kitchen, Lina with the rest of us, but I was allowed to wait on the master and pour his beer, and Lina sat at the table with both of them. There was a stormy expression on her face, and she darted hostile glances at the boy, who took absolutely no notice of her at all. She was jealous that he had spent all day with her father, and she blamed him for spoiling her joy at her father's return.

When he had eaten his fill, the master called the household to the dining room, and we welcomed him home. He had, as always, brought gifts for the children: for me it was a little deer carved out of wood, and for Lina it was a red scarf, beautifully embroidered in the way of the north with bright threads in curious patterns. She held it to her cheek, and her brow cleared; she loved pretty things.

"Now," said the master to the household. "I want you to meet Damek il Haran. He is fostered to me by the king, and will be a brother to Lina. He is of royal blood, and will be attended as a noble, and treated kindly by you all." Here he gave Lina a stern look: her black glances had not escaped him.

The boy stared unsmilingly back at the servants, and nodded distantly without saying a word. Lina scowled at him, but he ignored her, which lowered him further in her eyes. He certainly wasn't an immediately likeable boy, and he looked none too pleased to be in our house; his expression was clouded with what looked very like resentment. His proud manner obscured his good features: he was in fact handsome and strongly built, with thick black eyebrows, dark eyes and a sensuous mouth. He lacked the white skin of a noble, possessing instead the swarthy hue of a shepherd, which made me think he must be of mixed blood.

"I shall have to find a room for him," said my mother, which was as close as she came to expressing her annoyance at having to house another soul in a house that was already too small. "Perhaps Lina and Anna can share again."

"They are too old to share a room," said the master. "Lina is of an age when she must begin to mind her position."

My mother forbore to answer that it would be even more

improper to put Damek in Lina's room, whatever the propriety in rank, but I knew she was thinking it. Instead she sighed, saying that for the moment he would have to sleep in the room usually occupied by the master's manservant, and said nothing more. The next day she cleaned out a small room she had just filled with odds and ends from the southern estate, sending them on to be stored instead at the manse, and turned it into a bedroom for Damek. That was only the first of the inconveniences he represented for our household.

That first night he didn't endear himself to anyone. I noticed the shadows underneath his eyes, and excused his manner as exhaustion, but even so, he displayed little inclination to be pleasing company, and answered any question with a monosyllable or a grunt, if he bothered to answer at all. His stubborn indifference confirmed Lina in her dislike, and she too became sulky, as if each were competing to be the most ill-mannered. This angered her father, although he wouldn't rebuke her in front of us and instead gave her stern looks, which only had the effect of making Lina sulk more.

This threw a pall of gloom over the company, and we retired rather earlier than was usual. As Lina and I washed ourselves before bedtime, she made a face at me. "What do you think, Anna? Isn't he the most horrible boy? And he is to be my *brother*! The shame!"

I answered that perhaps he was just very tired, and might be more friendly on the morrow, when he had had some rest. Lina tossed her head.

"I think he has a soul as black as pitch," she said. "And even if he was nice as nice and sorry as sorry, I won't be friends with him. I don't believe he has royal blood at all. I don't know why Papa has to bring him here. He'll just spoil everything."

That was hard to argue with, after the evening we had just enjoyed; but it wasn't my place to comment, so I said nothing.

I went to bed and before sleep overtook me spent some time wondering who Damek was, and why my master had chosen to foster such an ill-favoured boy.

Such wondering became a common hobby about the village, but we never did find out his provenance: he was heir to no house that anyone could discover, even though the king claimed him as kin, and that meant that he had no part of the royal tax as his birthright, and no fortune of his own. He appeared to have no mother, and indeed said later that she had died when he was a little boy and that he didn't remember her, although it is hard to say whether that was the truth, or whether he simply didn't want to acknowledge that he was of low birth. It is most commonly supposed that he is one of the king's bastard children, perhaps of a favoured mistress, since the king acknowledged him, but he may have been a by-blow of any of the near relations of the royal house.

I should explain that fostering used to be a means of making an alliance among the various factions of the northern nobility; male children would be exchanged between houses as guarantees of peace. But it was a custom that was dropped long ago, and fostering is all but unheard of in these present times. It must have been a condition of the king's pardon that the master fostered this child, although he never explained one way or the other. If Damek was indeed a bastard child, which seems most likely, then it was as close as may be to an insult, and certainly no child was sent in return. Perhaps it was just a fancy of the king's, that he could at once solve an inconvenience of his own and saddle the master with a responsibility that was in fact a royal rebuke. All agreed that it was at best an odd arrangement, and the old women shook their heads and said no good would come of it.

IX

I remember the first days of Damek's residence as a kind of dark tunnel, a memory reinforced by the continual rain which kept us indoors. It seemed endless, although it must have lasted little more than a week or so. The master left the day after delivering Damek into our care and Lina blamed Damek, for no reason at all, for her father's absence. It simply confirmed the boy's evil in Lina's eyes; she resented him bitterly, and did her best to make him run away.

She confessed as much to me the first morning. "We don't want him here, do we, Anna?" she said as I brushed her hair. "He's nothing but a dirty peasant. Look at his skin! Why has Papa done this to me?"

"I'm sure he has his reasons," I said. "The king—"

"Oh, the king!" Lina swept that aside impatiently. "What could the king care for a lowborn bastard?"

I was shocked, and told her that she ought to show some respect. At the back of my mind, I saw the Wizard Ezra and his talk of some mysterious truce; although I didn't understand the complex dealings of adults, which took place in a universe over the top of my head, I couldn't but believe that somehow Damek's presence and the wizard's obscure warning were connected.

"I'm going to make him run away," she said. "I hate him. I don't want a brother. And if he runs away, Papa can't do anything about it. It's not his fault, is it? How could the king blame him then?"

I began to tell her that if Damek ran away it would shame our house, but Lina tossed her head and said she didn't care. And nothing I said in the following days could persuade her to care for the honour of the king or her father.

Her strategy was simple: she made herself as unpleasant as possible to everyone in her vicinity. This was sufficient to turn the household into a purgatory. There was Lina at breakfast, brows like thunder, throwing her plate at Damek and scalding him with hot porridge; Lina in the passageway, screaming and kicking my mother, who was attempting to stop her pulling Damek's hair; Lina brooding in the front room, sending black clouds of dolour through the entire house, so that everyone was cross and impatient and out of sorts.

The part of me – a very small part – that wasn't irritated with Lina beyond endurance couldn't help but admire her stubborn persistence in the face of every rebuke and punishment; there was not one moment where she wavered from her obdurate hostility. I have sometimes wondered whether that week showed the first sign of her powers, because when she walked into a room, everyone flinched against the turbid energy she brought with her. Even when my mother, her patience tried to breaking point by Lina's perversity, whipped her with a belt and locked her in her room without meals for a whole day, she shouted and screamed for hours until her voice was hoarse, hammering on the door so her knuckles bled. My mother only let her out because she was afraid that she would make herself ill, and I vividly remember the flash of triumph in Lina's eyes as she stalked out. And then the first thing she did was to find Damek and slap his face for causing her to be locked up.

I confess that although in those first days I could not like Damek, I admired how he bore with Lina's persecution. Even when she threw porridge at him, he didn't react; he merely stared at her expressionlessly and wiped it out of his eyes. He never once attempted to hit her back, and never answered any of the horrible names she called him, nor complained to anyone. Once or twice I saw a flash in his eyes that hinted at a danger-ous and implacable anger, but he suppressed it at once. I have since wondered where he learned such stoicism; I suppose he must have come from a place where he suffered much cruelty. This lack of response, as I think he knew, only irritated Lina to further extremes: she pinched him until his arms were mottled black and green, and kicked him in the shins, and pulled out chunks of his hair. Nothing my mother could say or do abated Lina's behaviour. Used as I was to her, I was shocked: this was different in kind from her tantrums. It was unforgiving and bitter, with no swift following laughter to clear the sky.

Without warning, when all of us were limp with exhaus-tion and despair, the oppression lifted. Lina came down late to breakfast, her face set in her now habitual scowl, and as she sat down a beam of sunshine broke through the clouds and shafted across the table. It scattered a spectrum of colours over the white cloth as the beam broke through the glass decanter and struck fiery sparkles from the silver cutlery. As it glanced on Lina's face, she looked up with a sudden luminous delight, her dark mood ambushed and destroyed by this stray sunbeam; by chance her eyes met Damek's, and she stopped, arrested. I don't know what passed between them in that moment; I remember her sitting in the room, as still as if she had been caught out of time, the smile lingering on her lips, her eyes serious and dark, but quite without hostility. She looked most of all as if she were remembering something important that she had forgotten.

I've often wondered what happened when Lina was ambushed by that stray sunbeam. It was such a tiny thing, but it changed all our lives. She would never tell me, even when I asked her directly; she would simply laugh and say that someone like me would never understand. I'm not sure that even she could explain it. I surmise that in her unguarded joy, her soul flung open its doors, permitting her to see Damek for the first time. But what did she see? A brother, perhaps, moved by the same passions as she was, a wild kindred soul who chafed as she did against the mean laws in which we lived, a will as stubborn and obdurate as her own? I never realized until much later how lonely Lina was. Even I, who was closer to her than anybody else, often failed to comprehend her. It may be that her sense of isolation sparked her childish rages: while every human being desires to be loved, perhaps we crave understanding more.

For the first time for days, breakfast passed peaceably. Lina was atypically demure and polite; she was playing the southern-born lady again, and said please and thank you, instead of haughtily demanding my service and trying to slap me if I was too slow. (Not that I accepted such behaviour without giving her a sharp telling-off. She ignored me, but it relieved my own anger.) She didn't speak to Damek, but at the end of the meal, when she pushed her chair back to leave the table, she met his eyes again and nodded slightly before she left. Damek seemed much struck, and it was a few moments before he too laid his napkin on the table and left.

As I tidied up after them, I drew a deep breath. Perhaps this was the end of the storm, and our little household would be an easier place. I had chores to attend to and didn't see either of them all morning; I was therefore wholly taken aback when

Damek and Lina walked in together to the luncheon table, and sat down as if they were intimate friends.

"What?" I said to her. "Are you talking now to your brother, Miss Lina?"

"Oh, Anna, he's not my brother!" said Lina. "That's the mistake. He's my *friend*." And she smiled radiantly and leant forward, in a pretty manner she then affected, to brush a lock of hair out of his eyes. "Aren't we the best of friends, Damek?"

He muttered something I couldn't hear in response, and she laughed and turned to me.

"He'll be less surly soon, I'm sure," she said. "It's only that he's shy." At this I saw the back of Damek's neck redden. "But he has forgiven me my lack of manners."

"Well, Mr Damek is a better human being than you are, Miss Lina," I said. "Look at those bruises on his arm! For shame!"

Lina tossed her head, quite unembarrassed. "If he don't mind, I don't see why you should, Anna. And you're just a servant anyway. It's not your place to make remarks."

Lina had never before asserted her rank – it was of the nature of an unspoken agreement – and that stung me. I had opened my mouth to protest when my mother came into the room with a roasted peahen and put an end to our conversation. After that I was coming and going from the room, waiting upon the two of them. I was still hurt by Lina's remark and was, I fear, excessively formal, though I'm sure Lina never noticed. I studied her change in manner towards Damek with amazement, unable to believe that she was sincere. She pulled her chair closer to his and murmured to him as they ate, her eyes flashing mischievously. He said very little, mostly nodding now and again in response, and I mistrustfully wondered what devilry she was hatching now.

I confess a little pain of jealousy started in my heart, watching the two of them huddled together so intimately; Lina and I had always been close, for all our differences in rank and sensibility, and now it seemed that she was replacing me in her heart with this sullen, mysterious boy.

X

It's difficult to remember things precisely. All this happened so long ago, and when I reflect it seems to me that I have forgotten many important things, while others which perhaps seem trivial stand out vividly from the shadows. I was, you know, a most ordinary child, with no precocious abilities; I had all the usual childish griefs and joys and my life has been, for the most part, remarkably without incident or tragedy. Lina used to laugh at my equable nature, claiming I had all the sensibility of a stick, and as a little girl I did feel that I was a dim and shadowed lamp next to her brilliant flame. Yet for all that, I never envied her; I would always have far rather been as I am. Which is a happy chance, really, since I have no choice in the matter.

In my education I was fortunate above most of my peers, because when the master employed a tutor from the south for Lina and Damek, he instructed him to teach me as well. This was not really an enlightened decision on the master's part, although I certainly benefited; his kindnesses were almost always self-interested. Lina was at best an erratic student, and predictably she regarded the classes (as I think her tutor did) as a means of torture, which she thought was especially devised to frustrate her deepest desires. Even her father's disapproval, which could cast her into a pit of despair for days, did little to make the necessity of staying indoors to study verbs and history palatable, even with Damek for company. However, when I joined the morning lessons, her natural competitiveness was fired, since she couldn't bear to be outshone by a mere servant. I enjoyed the classes, and even earned the tutor's praise on occasion, and this made her turn furiously to her work.

Thus it was that I learned my letters, and was given one of the great consolations and pleasures of my life. It is no boast to say that I am probably as well read as any on the Plateau, since Master had collected an excellent library and permitted me to read freely in my spare time. Like many things in my life, it altered me, and made me different from my kin. My mother disapproved of my education: she would never dare to gainsay the master, and did his will as always, but I think no decision of his angered her more. She said it would give me ideas above my station, and would take me away from my roots. In this, her instincts were correct: although I can't say I have suffered from it, I have always been a little outside things. I was fated, it seems, to be between: neither northern nor southern, neither an illiterate servant nor a noble. Once, when I was young and foolish, I did wish that I was the same as everyone else and could fit in more easily; but I was lucky enough to marry a good man who saw my virtues with a straight eye, and I have led a decent and hardworking life, which is more than can be said for some of my kin.

But forgive me; I am wandering from the story.

After that day, Damek was Lina's slave. I watched them

suspiciously, unable to believe that it was more than a passing fad on her part, but all I saw was sweetness and light. Certainly, their friendship made a great deal of difference to Damek. I think it likely that he had never had a friend before. As in everything she did, Lina approached the friendship with all the force of her fierce passion, and any resistance he may have felt quickly melted. At the time I was surprised by his instant capitulation – given those bruises, I would have coddled my resentment for much longer. But now I suspect that they might not have become so close if Lina hadn't behaved so cruelly to begin with, and that part of his respect for her stemmed from his initial experience of her demonic temper.

Patiently, with her rare gentleness, she coaxed him out of his sullen silence, and he began to seem more like any boy of ten; she drew him into her games and pranks and, although he never quite lost his wariness, for the first time we saw his face animated with laughter. I know you will not believe me, but I began to like Damek myself then; he was a handsome boy, and could be an amiable playmate. I am sorry for what he became. Perhaps he would have become what he is in any case, but I think he could have been a different man, had things turned out otherwise.

Lina and Damek would disappear for hours on end, returning with their clothes torn and filthy with mud and their eyes shining with secret mischief. Their antics were the despair of my mother, who felt both their impropriety and their inconvenience, since they doubled her laundry and darning. I was moved by less pragmatic considerations: to put it baldly, I was jealous. The pair stole away on their excursions without telling anybody, and after they returned home would whisper together like conspirators. I was locked out of Lina's private world, and I felt my exile keenly.

I caught them leaving the house one day when I knew they

had been expressly forbidden to do so, and demanded that I should come too, or I would tell my mother. Lina stared at me impatiently, biting her lip.

"Why would you want to come with us, Anna? You know you wouldn't enjoy it."

"I would so," I said.

"You wouldn't," she said. "We don't do anything special, do we, Damek? We just go racing in the wind by the river. You know you don't like running much. You'd just get puffed and spoil it all and we'd have to come home."

"I won't spoil anything!" I said heatedly.

Lina exchanged a glance with Damek that I couldn't read, but its intimacy fanned my jealousy. Damek shrugged. "Come, if you want," he said. "But you'll only get into trouble."

I was already regretting my importunity, but it was too late now to withdraw. Lina cast me a dark look, but she tolerated my tagging behind. As we reached the meadows that led to the river, she broke into a run. Damek cast a swift glance over his shoulder, which was not without sympathy, and then raced to follow her.

I plodded stubbornly behind them in the distance, sweaty and uncomfortable. I finally caught them up by the river. Lina was swinging from a willow branch with her back to me, as Damek sat on the ground looking up at her. With a pang of envy, I saw that for once his face was unguarded. He was staring at Lina with the same intense expression of worship I had sometimes seen on old women praying before the Madonna in church. Even as this incongruous thought crossed my mind, he sensed my gaze and turned his face away, and I saw a flush spread across the back of his neck. I already knew that I was pushing myself where I was not wanted, but suddenly I felt a new discomfort; it was as if I had glimpsed something that shouldn't be witnessed. I hadn't seen them doing wrong, don't misunderstand me; what

I saw was completely innocent. I felt clumsy and embarrassed, as if I had stumbled without permission into a hushed church in the middle of an important ceremony.

Lina dropped down from the tree and turned towards me.

"See," she said. "I *said* you wouldn't enjoy it!"

"But I am!" I said stoutly, and sat down to catch my breath. "Maybe we could make a house now. You could be the mistress." Even in my confusion, I wasn't going to admit that Lina was right and I wanted to return to the world of our ordinary relationships, undisturbed by the strange depths that had briefly opened before me.

"Sometimes you're so dreary, Anna," said Lina. "What do we want with houses here? Look at the mountains!" She pointed into the distance, where the Black Mountains stood clear of haze on the horizon, their flanks shading to deep purple. "Aren't they beautiful? They're just like Damek."

"You mean he's purple?" I said, bewildered by her fancy, as Damek cast her an angry look. I think she must have broken a confidence between them, because she coloured a little.

"No, stupid. If you can't see it, I'm not going to explain."

Before long, Lina announced that she was bored and we went home. We were gone so briefly that nobody had missed us, and the next time Lina and Damek disappeared, they took good care to avoid me. I was cured of wanting to join them, and I told myself that I didn't care, but of course that wasn't true.

Shortly after Lina's rapprochement with Damek, the master came home again. Had he returned while Lina was still torment- ing Damek, the consequences would have been unthinkable, and all of us – with the exception of Lina herself – felt the relief of disaster averted. In all my life, I have never met anyone with such a talent for ensuring her own unhappiness as Lina; despite his partiality, her father could not have countenanced her cruelty, and even his mildest disapprovals had the power to cast her into the depths of despair. And Lina in despair, in the midst of the extremity she had already so gratuitously created, was a vision none of us wished to contemplate. I knew even then that my mother feared for Lina's health, perhaps even for her sanity; for all the trouble she caused her, she cared for Lina as if she were her own child.

Thus we all covered for her. On his first day home, the master noticed the fading bruises on Damek's arm and frowningly asked whence they had come, and whether Damek had suffered mistreatment. We all started, unable to know how to answer without delivering an outright lie, but Damek steadfastly denied any abuse and claimed they had come about from a fall during play. The master studied Damek sceptically, and I was sure that he didn't believe him, but since it seemed that all was well, he forbore to say anything further.

This time, to Lina's delight, the master stayed at home for the entire summer. He spent much time in his study going over the accounts, and when he emerged he was often grey-faced with exhaustion. I still have the ledgers, and once went through those for that year out of, I confess, a vulgar curiosity. The southern estate had suffered an early frost followed by unusually severe tempests, which had devastated the vineyards, and there had been besides an outbreak of foot-and-mouth disease in the cattle. The bulk of the annual income came from that estate, and those disasters I think accounted for his presence, as the accounts also showed that when he was away from the Plateau, he led a life of considerable extravagance – indulgences to which his finances would not stretch that year. We believed that his constant absences were due to what we all vaguely referred to as "business", but the plain truth was that the master had no great love for the Black Country. Ties of blood, honour and money kept him here, and those bonds, which he could not break, were twisted tightly with threads of resentment or even hatred. Of course I only understood this much later. I don't think even my mother, his most faithful servant and perhaps one of the few people besides Lina who really loved him, knew this.

As the spring turned towards summer the rains abated, and it was as if a heavy lid had lifted off our heads and we could stand tall and breathe freely. The Plateau was then at its most beautiful. I know you think it a grim and ugly place, but to my partial eye even its winter dress has a rugged grandeur. When the many-hued grasses are strewn with wildflowers dozing in the sun, and the mountains rise in the distance like benign gods, their grey shoulders thrusting into white plumes of cloud, I think even you would think that the Black Country is a misnomer. Then this place is all colour and light. The air has a special clarity which picks out the edge of every blade of grass and gives all colours a muted radiance, so that each object seems to glow from within. There is no place like it in the world.

For all the relief of the sunshine and the general harmony in the house, there was a troubledness to this time that, looking back, seems like a foreshadowing. The Wizard Ezra again came to our house, and although he was not permitted over the threshold, the master spoke with him for some time. I was polishing the table in the front room, and could not help but watch them with fascination, ready to duck if either turned my way. I couldn't hear what they said, but both were stiff and angry. I thought the master won that encounter: finally the wizard turned and stalked back down the path, dragging his poor little mute in his wake.

I assumed the argument was about Lina, who was oblivious to the scandal her presence caused. Her behaviour was outrageous even if she had not been a witch; when she was free of lessons or the other tasks like needlepoint that my mother considered essential to the qualities of a lady, she ran wild about the estate with Damek, and would come home with her dress torn and her hair in tangles. She was now reaching an age where these actions in a girl are seen as the signs of a wanton, and are a dishonour to her household. Even the master, who in the softer regions of the south had looked on Lina's behaviour with a lenient eye, began to be alarmed: in the north, such behaviour is not merely ill-advised, but dangerous.

The chief peril was, of course, the Wizard Ezra. Like most northern wizards, he used his powers seldom, but when he chose to exercise them it made a lasting impression. Not long after I witnessed the argument with the wizard, one of the labourers on a neighbouring farm, a man called Oti, made some slanderous comments about the Usofertera clan. He was known as a simpleton, and at the time was much the worse for drink, or even he would never have said such things in a public place. A man less prideful than Ezra might have thought the incident beneath his notice, but, unfortunately for Oti, word reached the wizard's ears, and retribution was swift.

The entire village was summoned to the square to witness this poor man's fate. The master, to Lina's deep chagrin, forbade her to go, and my mother likewise refused his summons, out of loyalty to our house. As for me, like all the rest of the village children, I was beside myself with curiosity (not unmixed with fear) and made sure I turned up at the appointed time, safely hidden behind my uncle.

Oti was dragged out into the middle of the square, his arms tied behind his back, and was made to stand on a makeshift platform, so we could all witness his punishment. There followed a long and dull speech, in which the Wizard Ezra expatiated on Oti's crime, which, he said, betrayed not only the Usoferteras, but the entire vocation of wizarding, and which deserved the most summary retribution.

My eyes were fixed on Oti; I could see his limbs trembling

from where I stood. His face was absolutely white, and it seemed all his features – aside from his eyes, which were stretched wide open so that the whites around his irises were visible – had sunk back to his skull. His terror was so pitiful that I started to cry, trying to be as quiet as I could, as I was fearful I might attract the wizard's attention. I began to feel very sorry that I had come, and yet I didn't dare to steal away.

At last the Wizard Ezra stopped talking, and a dreadful silence filled the square, as if everyone there was holding his breath. The silence was broken by a thin, tearing shriek. I knew it was coming from Oti, but I could not see why: neither he nor the wizard had moved a muscle. He kept on screaming, the same high, horrible note, for what seemed like an eternity, writhing against his bonds as if he were in the most unspeakable agony. I was as baffled as I was appalled, for I could see no reason for his distress.

Then, just as suddenly, Oti was struck silent, although he still twisted as violently, and a spark shot out of his throat. Within moments a torrent of flames was pouring from his open mouth, and almost at the same instant I smelt burning meat. I realized with a clutch of nausea that I was watching this man being consumed from within by fire. Even as I watched, his skin blackened and split open, so that briefly it appeared as if flames were shooting out of every part of him, surrounding him in an infernal aureole; but almost at once he ceased to have a human shape, and the house of his body twisted and collapsed, until the whole was consumed to ash.

The fire burned with such ferocity that the whole process, from the moment that Oti began to scream to the dying out of the flames, took less than five minutes. The platform where he had been standing was barely touched: it was marked, my friends told me later, only with scorch marks where his corpse had fallen. Myself, I had no desire at all to examine the site:

I ran off from the crowd and was violently ill, and for months afterwards could not pass the spot where Oti had burned without feeling sick with horror.

After that, I needed no persuasion that there was good reason to fear the Wizard Ezra. I suspect now that this demonstration might well have been for the benefit of the Lord Kadar, to impress upon him the perils of crossing a wizard's will. I think the master took note: certainly, he employed the tutor shortly after this incident, telling us that he was ashamed of the ignorance and rough manners of his charges.

The tutor, Mr Herodias, was well chosen. A tall, thin-lipped man who affected a pince-nez, he was in truth a bit of a dandy: he was an exotic sight indeed in our village when he ventured out for his regular Sunday stroll, with his polished boots, embroidered waistcoat and carefully folded neckcloth. But his effete appearance belied a steely will that even Lina found difficult to bend. He was impervious to her sulks and threats and indifferent to her charms, and she was never able to deceive him. She was the most difficult of his charges: Damek was a stolid pupil, neither enthusiastic nor rebellious, and I was frankly studious, which exposed me to Lina's mockery.

Calmly and coldly, with a switch on his desk, which he didn't hesitate to use, Mr Herodias set about instilling an education into even the most recalcitrant of subjects. He rented a small but comfortable cottage in the village, and walked up to the Red House every morning, swinging his switch around his legs, and calmly returned home each night to eat his supper. We spied on him sometimes, peeping through his window in the evenings: he always sat in his front room, sometimes reading, but mostly writing in a book. We never dared to ask him what he was writing about; the rumour was that he was a naturalist and was writing a treatise on butterflies, but I never heard the truth of it.

His presence gave our lives a routine that summer that I, for one, found at once stimulating and comforting. Although all of us had been taught our letters, our ignorance was profound; as I've already said, the two years Mr Herodias spent at Elbasa I count as among the more precious gifts of my life. He opened for me the universe of books, and through books I have been able to address the gaps in my knowledge. I have continued his education all my life. I have wondered whether that odd, cold man knew what he gave me; sometimes, thinking back, I am sure he did. For this reason, I remember that summer as a happy time. But that is an entirely selfish memory; if you mention the same year in the village, you will see people shudder and cross themselves. That was the year the vendetta came.

XI

Because I am a woman, what I say counts for little in the world. But all the same, I watch and I think my own thoughts, and if I say little, it's not because I have nothing to say. A wise woman, as they say here, keeps her face in a shell. If I were to speak some of my thoughts freely, it would be cause enough for a curse to be set in my flesh, or for a knife to open my throat. People here think the vendetta the central mystery of the Plateau: none dare speak against it, out of pride and terror. It would be like denying our own souls. Vendetta is at the heart of our honour. Here in the bitter north, where scratching a living from the soil is for most people the height of aspiration, a man who has no honour has nothing.

When the vendetta comes to a village, it is a calamity. It is worse than flood or fire, worse than the tempest that sweeps down from the mountainside and tosses about trees and walls and houses as if they were the playthings of a child. It is more like a plague which, instead of flaring for a brief deadly moment, leaving the survivors in peace to mourn and bury their dead, stays virulent for years, for decades, even for centuries. It's a fatal malady of the blood that slowly, inevitably, destroys whole families, whole clans, whole villages. I'm sure you've passed through some of the hamlets where vendetta has burned until there is no one left: the fields are returned to the wild, with weeds waist-high where once there were crops and vegetables, their stone walls tumbled and broken through lack of anyone to mend them year after year; the houses are empty, their roofs fallen in, the paving stones cracked where saplings have split them open, the wind and the rain their only guests. All that is left is perhaps a mad old woman with her chickens and scrawny goat, stubbornly clinging on because she has nowhere else to go.

Vendetta is a black vine, a parasite that fruits only graves. But it is a crafty predator: if all the Plateau were in vendetta, there would be no one left for it to devour, and vendetta itself would die out. And so it sets one seed here, another there: never too much, never too little. Over the centuries, there is no village that vendetta has not harvested, taking its tithe of death; yet at any time, it will be only a few families who suffer.

The death of vendetta is a special death. Vendetta is not the accident in which a man slips and falls from the side of a mountain, or is bitten by an adder, or where a child is lost in the snow of winter and is found days later clutching his staff, his face blue and icy. It is a death of honour, and a man's household is judged by how he faces his fate. It is at the heart of the Lore and its ritual, and is behind the authority of wizardry. And this is why, although it is a calamity we dread and fear, northerners never complain against vendetta: it is as much part of us as the ground beneath us, as the cycle of the seasons. To speak against the vendetta is a blasphemy, like pitting your face against the will of God.

Vendetta has, like everything here, its stern courtesies, and its laws are intricate and ancient. As it is about honour, it is the concern of men: women might suffer its cruelties, but they are not permitted into its workings. At root, for all the complicated rulings around it, vendetta is brutally simple. It begins with the murder of a man (the murder of a woman is considered a crime against property, not against honour). After a murder there is forty days' truce; then the man deemed responsible for the crime may be killed at any time. The murderer must pay in two ways: with the Blood Tax, and with his life. His death must be at the hands of the victim's nearest male relation. Once the killer is slain, however, the avenger must in turn pay for his crime, the second murder sparking the third, and so on.

During the forty-day truce, the killer must travel to the king and hand to him one hundred silver pieces. To fail to pay the Blood Tax brings undying shame upon his name and upon his family. The royal treasuries depend on vendetta. It will not surprise you that those of royal blood are exempt from vendetta: the laws that apply to peasants do not apply to them. As farmers tend their crops, so the king tends his populace, growing fat on the shedding of blood.

The penalties for those who do not pay are severe indeed: after he is killed by hanging, a dishonourable death, the defaulter's hands and feet are cut off so that he will never find his way to heaven, and he is buried at a crossroads as if he were a suicide. If his family or nearest relations still fail to pay the tax, any property they own may be confiscated and their homes burned to the ground, and they are banished. Their shame is absolute and may never be gainsaid. So you can imagine the ruinous lengths to which people will go to pay the tax. I know of no one who has not done so; but I have heard many stories of those who have bankrupted themselves, or have even sold their daughters and sons into slavery, in order to raise the money.

The wizards do not partake in the Blood Tax, but as they

administer the legalities of the vendetta, they stand to gain as much as those who do. It is the root of their absolute spiritual authority over the people of the Black Country. You know, I am sure, that each village has its wizard, and that the wizard's word is law. Their judgement is final; each wizard carries the Book of Truth, which has more authority here than the Bible, and the wizards' rulings are known among the people as the Law of the Book. The wizards live humbly, eschewing worldly wealth, and for the most part spend their time dealing with petty disagreements: whether one man has stolen another's goats, for example, or whether a boundary is three feet nearer a river than another man claims. Such punishments as were visited on the unlucky Oti are rarely administered, but the dread of them underlies the obedience paid to the wizards. I am sure they have other duties, but they are unknown to anyone outside their order: they keep their ranks closed, and to reveal the secrets of their magic is punishable by death.

There is much I don't know: what the bond is, for instance, between the wizards and the royal family. Then there is the constant war between the church and the wizards, both of which have strong claims on the royal house and fight jealously for its notice. The priests think the wizards are godless, and the wizards believe the priests are frauds imposed on the north by some fiat of the south. The latter assertion has enough truth to ensure that church attendance in the north is regarded as a matter of social appearances, while true God-fearing is reserved for the wizards. In the Plateau, Christian piety is, begging your pardon, secretly regarded as a sign of disloyalty, even though there wouldn't be one soul in the Black Country who doesn't believe in the wrath of God and the torments of hell, and who doesn't cross himself for fear of the Devil or call for the Last Rites when he is dying.

I will leave you to contemplate these contradictions yourself: some mock the northerners as heathens and pagans, but that seems as inaccurate to me as claiming that they are pious Christians. There are those who say that the king placates the wizards because there would be an insurrection if he did not, and I think there is a truth in that; but it doesn't account for the whole. If nothing else, it demonstrates that human beings are complicated creatures, and that even we stern northerners demonstrate an elasticity of being which might surprise the dogmas of city folk like yourself.

I don't mean to say that wizards are evil, even if they are feared: to be stern is not to be unjust. But some wizards are dark in their power. The Wizard Ezra was one of those: a bitter rage seemed knitted in his very bones, and what in some was a harsh justice, was in him cruel and vicious. He was not above using his powers for private ends, although wizards are supposed only to deal in public law. It is well known that he cursed a girl of the village when he was a young man because she would not have him: he set a cold spell in her bones, so she was twisted and distorted with agony, and her beauty was destroyed. It is a byword here, when speaking of impossible things, that it is like asking mercy of a wizard, yet there is still a difference between those who are pitiless and those who revel in the pain they cause.

To my mind, the northerners are like cattle that run willingly into the pen where they will be slaughtered for the table of their lord. Worse, we will fight to the death for the right to fill the coffers of the king with our own blood and to kiss the feet of the wizards who spit on us. I know you southerners think the vendetta a strange and romantic thing, and that your poets speak of it as part of the harsh and tragic beauty of the north, but I see no romance in it. I see a savage transaction which keeps the poor in their place, the wizards in their power and the kings in their comfort.

I should not say these things, even to a stranger. But I have watched and suffered, and this is what I believe.

XII

The vendetta at Elbasa began undramatically enough.
You might have seen the tinkers and the men who travel
from one end of the Plateau to another, offering their
wares and labour in return for a few coins or their keep. There
are many such in the Black Country, men without a household or a village who have nothing to call their own except the
skill of their hands or the strength of their shoulders. I know
that in the south, these travellers are considered to be beneath
contempt and treated as outcasts. It is not so here: they have
the dignity of their names and their strong bodies, and even
when a village cannot offer them work, honour demands that
they are given a roof and a meal before they move on to the
next village.

That year the autumn was long and warm. On a clear, moon-
less evening when the stars were so bright they threw shadows,
a man known only as Surinam came to Elbasa, seeking work.
He was a stranger to us: many itinerants like Surinam arrived
through the harvest season, staying for a night or a week or a

month before moving on elsewhere, but he wasn't one of our regulars. We already had our full complement of workers and he was directed to my uncle's house, where he was given a meal and the hayloft for the night. He left early the next day, as dawn was lightening the Plateau. Later that morning his body was found slumped on the road by a shepherd boy. He had been shot twice, first in the stomach and then through his right eye.

He was lying next to the border stone of the village, but we children, alerted before anyone else, didn't think about what that meant. Most of us had seen corpses in our short lives, but few had seen a shot man, and this was an event. We stared with a fearful fascination at his deathly pale skin, at the dark, congealed pool of blood that seeped from beneath his body, at the pink mess that had erupted from his skull. Lina was pale with excitement: she bent down to peer at the body, her eyes bright, high spots of colour on her cheekbones, holding Damek's hand so tightly that her knuckles were white.

"He looks like a dead pig," said one of the children.

"No, he don't," said another scornfully. "You cut a pig's throat. You don't make its head explode." He mimed the man's brains gushing out of his skull.

"He just looks dead," said Damek. He alone seemed unimpressed, even disgusted. "That's all. I don't know why you're all so beside yourselves. There's nothing special about being dead. I wonder who shot him?"

Lina glanced at Damek reproachfully, as if he were spoiling one of her games, and he glared back at her with something like contempt. Then he pulled back his hand from her grasp and stalked off by himself. Taken aback, Lina watched him leave, and turned to me and shrugged her shoulders. She picked up a stick and, despite my best attempts to stop her, poked the body, so it rolled stiffly. Its arm flopped back and we all flinched, afraid for a moment that it was still alive.

It was probably fortunate that at this point some adults arrived, including my father, who boxed my ears and sent me home.

XIII

It was far from the end of it, of course. All the village children were agog: it was the most exciting thing that had happened that year, aside from Fatima's two-headed chicken (which was later taken to be an omen of doom) and Kintur the Younger drowning when he fell off the bridge on his way home after a late drinking session. We were still considered too childish to be included in conversation; we were expected to be silent when adults spoke, and to obey their orders without question. But we knew everything the adults said to each other: children were invisible and everywhere, like mice, and we all had sharp ears. We heard the talk as we polished dishes in the kitchen or worked in the fields and orchards, and that evening as we gathered after our household tasks were finished, we told each other what we heard.

At first it seemed to have nothing to do with us. Surinam was a stranger, after all. All that day, as the man's body was brought to the town and washed and laid out for burial, the village hummed with disquiet. Who was Surinam? Where were his people? Was he in vendetta? Why else would anyone murder such a harmless-seeming, unimportant man? Or perhaps he was not as he seemed: some suggested he came from Skip, a nearby village towards which we harboured an ancient enmity, in which case evil goings-on were to be expected; others whispered that he was part of a gang of bandits, and that he was the victim of one of their feuds. At this, everyone checked their houses and sheds, but nothing seemed to be stolen. It was, everyone agreed, a deep mystery, and the old women declared that we would all be murdered in our beds and locked their doors.

That evening, as the long summer twilight deepened over the plains, the Wizard Ezra was seen at the border stone, and the village's curiosity was suddenly edged with fear. Old Yuri, who had seen him from a distance as he brought his goats in for the night, reported that the Wizard Ezra bent to the ground and sniffed the bloodstains, and then smeared a little of the blood – or was it the earth of the death-site? – on his forehead. Others saw the wizard striding through the village towards his house, where he shut himself in. When Fatima knocked on his door on some pretext, only the mute opened it, and he made clear that his master was not to be disturbed. Ezra wasn't seen for two days, although his mute was sent out to bring him raki and food; and for those two days the villagers went silent, as if they didn't dare even to whisper their fears in case the Devil heard them and came running.

We discussed the murder in the schoolroom the next day. Lina had heard of the Wizard Ezra's visit to the site of Surinam's murder. "What's it got to do with him?" she said scornfully. "Wizards are always poking their noses in where they're not wanted."

"You shouldn't speak about the wizards like that!" I said, scandalized and a little admiring.

"They don't frighten me!" said Lina. "Just because you're a

quaking goose doesn't mean that everyone else is."

There was a short silence, and then Damek, who had been scowling at his book, looked up. "If it's vendetta, it is wizard's business," he said.

"Well, I still don't see what it has to do with Wizard Ezra," said Lina. "It's not *our* vendetta. Though wouldn't it be exciting if it was?" She looked up, her eyes sparkling. "Nothing interesting ever happens here."

Nobody had mentioned that possibility out loud, but I suddenly understood why I had been hushed that morning when I had asked my mother about the murder, and why people were looking sideways at each other, as if they were communicating in a secret code. Everyone was afraid that it might, after all, be our vendetta. I felt a clutch of foreboding in my middle, and for a moment almost felt as if I might be sick.

"No, Miss Lina, a vendetta here would not be at all interesting," said Mr Herodias, who had been listening to the conversation with his mouth drawn into a thin, disapproving line. "And I would thank you to pay some attention to the irregular verbs on the page before you, if you would be so kind."

After that it was all Latin and Greek, and my oppression dissolved in the steady concentration the lesson demanded. Later, when the village children gathered after dinner to play in the long evening, we chatted in a desultory fashion about the dead man, but nobody had anything new to report. After Lina declared that it would be much better if the murder was part of a bandit war than a boring old vendetta, we decided to play a game of bandits instead. We were young and heedless, after all; although events made deep impressions on our minds, they were rapidly effaced, just as finger holes in a lump of rising dough will plump out and disappear.

The Wizard Ezra emerged from his house the following day, but such was the expression on his face that no one dared to ask him any questions. He demanded a bag of provisions from the inn, then took his staff and his mute and strode off down the road that leads towards the mountains. He wasn't seen for two weeks, and by then the anxiety of our elders had faded into the background of our little concerns, and we had mostly forgotten about the whole affair.

XIV

Achild's perceptions are partial and often mistaken, and there was much that happened in the following weeks that I didn't fully understand until later. As I told you, I was very happy that summer: my lessons were opening a new world, and I was making friends in the village and no longer missed my old home so fiercely. Damek and Lina remained close (which made a great deal of difference to the atmosphere of the household) and were the king and queen of our small domain. In the long, luminous twilights we ran free like young goats, kicking up our heels and pursuing our petty squabbles.

As in the south, Lina was the most daring of us all. The only person who could check her impulses was Damek; if he made a rare objection to one of her suggestions, she would wrinkle her nose, but would accede. Most of our games were harmless, but sometimes we did things that now make my hair stand on end.

A couple of miles from the village there was an ancient tin mine, long played out, which was one of our favourite destinations, in part because we were all warned to stay away. We played games among its crumbling walls and lit fires in the stone chimney, but what fascinated us most of all was the shaft, a black square hole that plunged straight down into the earth. Once there had been a ladder, but all that remained were a few rusted iron spikes stuck into the shaft walls, with red streaks staining the rock below.

Sometimes we all lay around its rim, trying to see how deep the hole was. The light petered out fast, leading to a bottomless blackness. It gave me a windy feeling in my tummy to look down, so I never dared to go too close to the lip, but others were braver and hung their heads over the edge, peering in.

"If you got to the bottom," said Damek, "you could look up and see stars in the sky, even in the daytime."

"You wouldn't be able to see anything, because your head would be broken and you'd be dead," said another boy.

"I bet there's bones down there," said Lina. "Human skulls and animal bones. Or maybe it just goes on for ever, and everybody who's fallen in is still falling."

That thought made me crawl back a little further.

"I bet I could see something if I could get closer," said Lina. "Why don't you hold my feet, and I'll have a proper look?"

I shrieked with dismay, but my playmates thought this was a grand idea. Neither Lina nor Damek nor anyone else took any notice of my objections. After some discussion, it was decided that Damek should hold Lina's ankles and lower her down into the shaft. Their only concession to safety was that someone else should hold Damek's waist, in case he slipped.

I stood up and watched this operation with my knuckles in my mouth, fearing at any moment there would be a dreadful accident.

Lina's voice floated up, echoing in the shaft. "Can't you get me any deeper?"

The boys shifted slightly, their feet slipping on the turf.

Damek's shoulders were straining with effort.

"You're very heavy," he said, panting. "Can't you see anything?"

"No," she said. "It's just the same, really, only darker and colder. I don't think there's any bottom at all."

Damek announced that if she didn't come up now, he would drop her, and the boys pulled back, landing Lina on the edge of the mine like a big fish. It was only then that I realized I had been holding my breath the entire time.

Lina stood up, all her clothes smeared with mud, her eyes sparkling. "That was fun!" she said. "Imagine if you had let me go! I might still be falling."

Despite Lina's report, nobody else was keen to repeat the experiment, and soon our attention was diverted to safer pursuits. That night I had horrible nightmares about falling down a hole, but that was the worst effect of our adventure. All the same, the memory of Lina's recklessness still gives me goosebumps.

We were all busy with chores. The summer had been unusually golden, and there was a fat gathering in for the winter. We laid out quartered apples and peaches to dry, and pickled mountains of cherries and walnuts and beans, and fattened pigs were brought in and slaughtered and turned into sausages and great sides of bacon, and hard cheeses laid in the cool cellars, and fields of barley and spelt harvested and threshed and ground to the rough flour that makes the good, sour bread of the northern plains.

The Wizard Ezra returned just as the last of the harvest was gathered, and called a council with the village elders. He told them that on the day of Surinam's murder, he had called up his powers and had seen the murder in a vision. Surinam had been shot, he told them, by Lovro, the second son of Kutsak Eran, a landholder in Skip. At this, there was a sigh of relief:

it was generally believed that the people of Skip were capable of every sort of iniquity. But Ezra held up his hand to silence the murmuring. No, he said: it was not as simple as it appeared. For Surinam was a man with no one to avenge his death: extensive enquiries had been made, and no one had found his family. And therefore the question hinged upon where he had been killed. Until he passed the borders of this village, he remained our guest: and as he was our guest, the man who had killed him had also insulted the honour of the men of our village.

A dead silence fell over the gathering, and then Petar Oseku, in whose barn the unfortunate man had slept, stood up and angrily disputed that Surinam had been killed while under his protection. He had died at the border stone, and had therefore passed out of the village. No, said Ezra: the border stone marked the outer boundary of the village, but it was inclusive. Here he raised the Book, the root of all Lore, as his witness, and who was to dispute his word, since no other man in the village save my father and Mr Herodias could read it? The Book, the Wizard Ezra thundered, was unambiguous upon this point: and further, he had himself travelled far to consult with his brethren, and also with the wise counsellors of the royal family, to clarify this very point. It was on the honour of the House of Oseku, he said, to avenge this most shameful death. Now fifteen days had passed, and Petar Oseku, as the head of his family, had only twenty-five days of truce left. Once it was over, his duty was clear, if this village was to clear the filth of insult from its honour: he must travel to Skip and kill the second son of Kutsak Eran, may the Devil take his soul.

Petar Oseku was my uncle, my father's brother. He was, by the standards of the north, a good and gentle man. My aunt told me many years later that when he came home from that meeting he seemed to have aged a decade in a day. He wordlessly placed his rifle in the corner of the kitchen, and turned his face to the wall. My aunt, a true daughter of the north, wasn't a woman whose tears came easily, but she threw her skirt over her face to muffle her weeping.

What they both most feared had come to pass. Their children would now be fatherless, and within a year their two oldest sons – the first just now preparing for marriage – would be dead, and their youngest son – now growing his first straggling beard – would attain his manhood only to kill and then, in turn, be killed. In less than five years all the men of their family would be devoured by the vendetta. Perhaps some might escape to the living death of the *odu*, never to walk in the daylight again. Such a choice would have never occurred to a man like Petar Oseku, since it would only hasten the doom of his sons, who would have to make the revenge themselves. And how would they pay the Blood Tax? They were not poor, but they were not a rich family either: it was likely that by the time all my aunt's sons were dead, she and her daughters would no longer have a house to mourn in, and would be reduced to begging for the charity of others.

Once her family was destroyed, the duty would pass to the next male blood relative, until the curse had killed the men of the next family, and then the next. There was no peasant in the village who was not related to the Oseku household, even if it was some distant cousinship. The vendetta would burn through all the bloodlines of our village, leaving in its wake a desolation of graves. Beside them would stand a line of empty-eyed women, their faces hardened by sorrow, shivering against the cold wind in their ash-coloured rags. So my aunt wept silently for herself and for everyone she loved, and her husband sat beside her with his face turned to the wall; and they said nothing to each other, because there was nothing to say.

XV

The forty-day truce passed, and Petar Oseku was clearly in no hurry to kill his man. As custom demanded, his wife hung the sheet on which Surinam's blood-weltered body had been laid from the top window of their house. It was a constant reminder of duty, and it flapped and snapped in the wind as the year turned towards winter. I crossed myself every time I passed: the sheet was like a shroud, and its rattling voice in the bitter air had a deathly sound.

My uncle had until the stain faded to take his revenge. The blackened clots washed off and the marks faded to brown and then to an ever paler rust, but still Petar Oseku didn't make his move. All the same, he wasn't idle. He was gathering together money for the Blood Tax: being a man of forethought and thrift, he made arrangements to cover not only his own payment, but that of his sons. He sold an orchard of almond trees, his most valuable property, as well as a couple of family treasures, including a small clock designed like a temple with tiny golden cherubs flourishing trumpets at each corner, and he put the money aside. Even if his household were stripped of its modest wealth, his wife and daughters would not now wander homeless.

By then winter had its bite on the plains, and soon the roads would be snowed out. Winter was considered as good as a truce, since travel was impossible. Strictly speaking, Petar Oseku should have pursued the vendetta with all possible speed; but since it was not his own blood that he was avenging, no one, not even the Wizard Ezra, would look askance if he took his time.

The snows came early that year, harbingers of a season of vicious blizzards punctuated by long, ice-bound nights. It was more than two months before the roads opened again, and in that time Petar Oseku made his peace with God. As soon as the spring melt came, he hefted his rifle and went, as a dutiful northern man, to preserve the honour of his family and his village. After he had shot Lovro, he immediately travelled to the King's Palace to pay the Blood Tax. When he came home, we held the honouring feast for him. It was the first I ever attended, if not the last, and was one of the few times that Lina envied me. As she was of royal blood, and therefore exempt from the laws of vendetta, she was also forbidden from its celebrations.

The honouring feast is a strange affair: proud and grieving and darkly joyous, all at the same time. We sang the mournful, keening songs of vendetta, and garlanded Petar Oseku's neck with spring flowers, and he was in that moment a king, because he had kept faith with his honour, and so honoured all of us. The least admirable man blossoms into his manhood at these events; I have seen mean and vicious spirits attain a grace that was otherwise unimaginable. A good man could seem like a demigod.

Petar Oseku sat at the head of the table, his back as straight as a poker, and lifted his cup with what seemed to me a mysterious elation. He had then thirty days of truce, his last as a free man: after that, he was the living dead. He could be killed at any time, as he took his goats to pasture, or tended his crops, or simply walked along the village street to meet a friend to play cards. I don't think it even occurred to him to take refuge in the *odu*, in that way escaping his fate; in any case, doing so would only hasten the doom for his sons, since the vendetta would then pass to his closest kin.

I have often wondered what that must be like, constantly to feel death stalking you, its charnel breath brushing your cheek, its skeletal footsteps dogging your own. Does such a man spend his entire waking life in a chill of sweat, and each night in restless dreams? The waiting must be anguish in itself; perhaps the murderous click of a rifle in the clear air would arrive as unutterable relief. As the vendetta burned through the village, I watched each sentenced man with, I confess, an almost indecent curiosity, and it seemed to me that my uncle was of all of them the most dignified, in death as he was in life.

Petar Oseku died a week and two days after the truce lifted, the first death of that black spring. He was shot on a goat path outside the village: the killer was Lovro's brother. The rapid revenge was, no doubt, driven by Lovro's brother's own grief and anger as much as the impatience of youth, and perhaps its swiftness was merciful. I think this boy was no more than nineteen years old when he was killed in his turn by Petar's oldest son.

The mechanisms of vendetta are slow. Rather than the quick fever and agony of plague, its effect on a village is like the wasting disease which gradually strips the flesh from the skeleton over months and years. The outcome is ultimately the same, but as it runs its course the village adjusts and continues with the routines of living. Perhaps this is also how people survive: after all, you cannot think about death all day, however heavily its presence weighs upon your mind, or you would go mad.

So it was that, after the initial excitement of fear and anger (this latter mainly directed towards the village of Skip), those of us not directly affected returned to our ordinary lives, and the presence of vendetta faded to the background. For me, this meant lessons and household duties, and in the thoughtlessness of childhood these immediate concerns overlaid any anxieties I might have felt about the vendetta. Lina began to adopt some of the manners of a lady; her father had managed to impress upon her the signal importance of behaving with at least some propriety. Both Lina and I were approaching the threshold of womanhood, and we no longer played as the small children did, boys and girls all together, but gathered with our own sex. I began to look upon boys with a bashful but not indifferent eye.

The exceptions to this separation were Damek and Lina, whose intimate friendship seemed, if anything, more strong. They broke all our childish rules of association, but they were an exception that we simply accepted: girls didn't play with boys, but Lina and Damek were different. The adults cast a less tolerant eye. On occasion the pair still disappeared together for a whole day, leaving before dawn with food stolen from the kitchen to make their lunch. Not even the Lord Kadar's displeasure could stop them, and he was more and more displeased.

Once, after a particularly stern scolding, I found myself comforting Lina, who had thrown herself in despair on her bed. When she stopped sobbing, I asked her why she kept opposing her father's will, when his anger made her so unhappy.

"It's so unfair!" she said, lifting her tear-stained face from her pillow. "If Damek and I were both boys, nobody would take the slightest piece of notice."

"But you're not a boy," I said.

"No, I'm not. It's the unluckiest thing in the world." She sat up, wiping her hands over her eyes. "God must hate me so, to make me a girl."

"It's not as if you and Damek can't talk together at home," I said reasonably. "Nobody would say anything then."

Lina sat up, her eyes blazing. "I hate being stuck in this house like a – like a broody hen or a sow in a sty. Don't you feel it, Anna? Sometimes I can't bear it. I just have to get out or I'll burst."

Usually I had little patience with Lina's overdramatic statements, but this struck a pang of empathy. I too felt the walls closing in around me as womanhood approached. I hesitated, unsure what to say, and Lina clutched my hand.

"Sometimes I want to feel the wind in my face and the rain in my hair and earth on my feet. I want it so badly that I could die with wanting… And when Damek and I are out in the plains without a single house in sight, with the sky above in all its changes and the rock beneath us, going down further than you could ever imagine, and us between them as light as blossom, I feel so alive! Then I'm free, Anna… It's the only time that I'm free…"

Not only what she said, but the passion with which Lina spoke, went beyond my understanding. I felt the same disquiet that had ambushed me years earlier, when I had glimpsed Damek's adoration of Lina; perhaps it was a dim presentiment of what would follow. Unconsciously I pulled my hand away and sat back, and Lina stared at me, the light ebbing from her face.

"Oh, go away," she said at last. "You don't understand. You'll never understand. Damek's the only person who knows what it's like. The rest of you are all sheep."

I was used to Lina calling me names, but this hurt me. She refused to say anything more, and since her distress seemed to have abated, I left her there.

For all its intimacy, Lina and Damek's relationship was not more than cousinly; but her father began at this stage to feel some concern about its future implications. He had accepted this cuckoo into his house more generously than he might have, and treated him fondly. Damek was interested from the beginning in the mechanics of money – the legacy, I'm sure, of a childhood blighted by poverty – and he badgered the Lord Kadar to teach him about the running of the estate. Lina's father wasn't nearly as interested in accounts as Damek was, but the boy's hunger to learn amused him. They sometimes spent hours closeted in the master's study; I suspect that he thought that Damek could make himself useful when he grew up, as steward of the estate. He certainly wouldn't have welcomed the notion of Damek as his son-in-law. It was then that he began to speak about sending Lina south, to pursue an education appropriate to her social standing.

This proposal created a major squall. Sending Lina to the southern estate was a sensible idea from many points of view, not least because it seemed that her witch powers were beginning to be manifest. Lina had no idea how to work spells or charms – in fact, her father had forbidden her even to think about exploring her abilities, and had told her that if she felt anything witch-like, she was to suppress it at once. Unusually for Lina, she made no signs of defying her father; I think that in this case she understood that his prohibition was in her best interest.

Even so, she couldn't hide her nature. Sometimes in moments of extreme emotion a faint shimmer seemed to inhabit her skin, and once, when she teased me to distraction and I slapped her face, I was thrown against the kitchen wall without her laying a finger on my body. Our squabble stopped immediately: Lina was as astonished as I was, and helped me up with unaccustomed meekness. We pretended nothing had happened and never mentioned it again; I think we were both equally shaken.

In the south witches were not persecuted, even if they were considered, with a couple of notable exceptions in the city, to be of lower status than their male counterparts. If Lina were living on the southern estate, the master could have hired a wise woman to teach her the witchlore, and perhaps she might have found a useful way to spend her time and her powers.

Lina's response to this suggestion was violent and absolute. She refused point-blank to leave the Plateau, if it meant leaving Damek behind. Even the mildest hint of moving would summon one of her fits, which as she grew older were at once less frequent and more frightening. She would scream at her father as if she were possessed by a demon, and then run off and lock herself in her bedchamber. We would stand anxiously outside her door, listening to her violent sobbing, but she would answer no one. Not even Damek could persuade her to open her door; until her father promised that he would not, for the moment, consider such a move, she would speak to no one. After two or three such incidents, the idea was quietly dropped.

And there things stood. Lina's life – and the lives of others – might have turned out a lot better had she been sent to the south. But if wishes were horses, I would be a great general. It's no use sighing for what might have been.

Despite such occasional explosions, life in our household continued uneventfully. The master seemed to have reached an accommodation with the Wizard Ezra, and there were no more disturbing interviews between them; we thought at the time it was because Ezra was busy with the vendetta, and was no longer concerned with the trivial business of a young witch in the village. My mother in particular was greatly relieved; for all the trouble Lina caused her, she was fond of the child, and would have been grieved by her suffering.

The year after the vendetta started, our finances improved considerably. Having spent almost a year in the Red House kicking his heels, the master embarked on one of his extended trips as soon as the roads cleared in the springtime. His departure left Lina desolate, and our household to manage the estate without him, which, to tell the truth, was somewhat easier in his absence. The master was never more than dutiful in his management, if you understand me. My father became steward of the estate, and between him and my sharp-eyed mother, there was more care given to detail than the master could ever be bothered to deal with. So it seemed that we prospered, like a man with an illness deep in his body that nevertheless leaves him looking hale, even if the flush in his cheeks betrays a deadly fever.

XVI

N ow I come to a time which remains among the most painful of my life so far; I still cannot think of my fourteenth year without suppressing a sharp anguish. It is well said that troubles are never lonely.

As Petar Oseku was a close blood relation, I should have known that it was only a matter of time before vendetta touched my own family. Perhaps, underneath, I did know, and kept the knowledge from myself; perhaps it was simply that I was young, and so consumed by the minor joys and sorrows of my life that I never thought of looking beyond my own concerns. The world of my girlhood is so far away, and there is much I have forgotten, but I find it difficult now to believe that I was then so blind.

Whatever the reason, it was a shock when my father was named to avenge the death of Johannik, Petar Oseku's middle son. His youngest, Orlu, was still to cross the threshold of manhood, and my father was Johannik's oldest male relation. My parents had known since the vendetta was first declared that it would be that way, unless the wizards of the two villages negotiated a blood settlement. For complex legal reasons that no one except the wizards understood, the Wizard Ezra had declared at the beginning that this would be impossible; and so the relentless logic of the vendetta reached into my own house. It was again the beginning of winter, two and a half years after Petar Oseku died.

My mother and father had not thought to warn me of this danger, out of a feeling of mercy perhaps, or because they assumed I would already know; although I think it most likely that it was because they considered me too young to be included in the conversation. And so, when the bloodied sheet was hung from the Red House (the back window, because the house belonged to the master, and not my father), it came like a bolt of lightning out of a blue sky. I had been on an errand, to buy some eggs from Fatima, and I was walking slowly, taking care not to swing my basket, and watching my step in case I tripped. I arrived at the back courtyard, unlatched the gate and looked up: and there was the sheet, hanging like a blasphemy from our own window.

I knew at once what it meant. I don't know how I didn't drop the basket then and there, but I did not: instead, I carried it into the kitchen and placed it with special care on the table. My mother was preparing a lamb casserole with lemon and egg sauce, and she thanked me and took the eggs as if that day were the most ordinary in the world. I remember the light that shafted through the door fell coldly on her face, and her skin looked waxy and slightly blue, as if she were a corpse herself. She said not a word about the sheet, not a word about my father. Her face was closed and stern, as expressionless as a rock.

That night, when I went to bed and cried until there were no more tears to cry, she came in when she thought I was asleep and stroked my hair; but that was the only time through those endless months when she thought to treat me with gentleness. My father acted much as his brother had, and refused to hurry his task; shortly after the sheet was hung, the winter snows blocked the roads, and earned him a respite. Every day when I walked out of the door, I saw the sheet, frozen stiff and hung with icicles, and every time I shuddered. All that long, dark winter death hung over our household, bruising the very air with dread.

My mother was never the most demonstrative of women, but that winter it was as if her soul withered inside her. She became a different person: harder and less forgiving. It was a lonely time for me. I felt as if she had abandoned me and had wandered off into some rocky, barren place where I was unable to follow her. Sometimes I hated her. Other women were softer with their daughters, and I would watch them from the corner of my eye with burning envy, as they held their girls in their arms and kissed their faces. Oh, I have long forgiven her; it was sorrow that froze the loving woman inside her. But it made a hard time harder for me.

I wasn't close to my father; although he was fond of me, I knew that he had always wanted a son, and to have only a single child, a daughter at that, was a trying disappointment in his life. Sometimes after a night of drinking he would beat my mother, but in that he was no worse than many of the men in the village, and better than some, since he never hurt her beyond a few bruises. I was, if anything, afraid of him. I'm not sure that I ever really loved him. But for all that, he was my father, and I didn't want him to die.

Lina was not so insensitive as to crow with excitement when the vendetta came to the Red House, but she couldn't conceal her interest. Vendetta was something that excluded her, and she hated that: she always wanted to be at the centre of everything. I turned to her in my loneliness, and our friendship, which had become a little distant in the previous couple of years, blossomed again under her quick sympathy. I think she really did feel sorry for me, and did her best to console my grief; she could be a charming and thoughtful companion when she chose.

Curiously, perhaps, I found most solace in Damek's company at that time; he said very little, but there was something in him that responded with profound empathy to another's suffering. One day he found me weeping behind the woodstack, where I had hidden after some hard words from my mother. I was insensible to his presence until he laid his hand upon my shoulder, which made me jump. I looked up through my tears, embarrassed to be discovered, and he squatted down and offered me a kerchief to mop my face.

"It won't hurt so much in a while," he said gruffly, when my sobs had subsided.

My awkwardness vanished, because I knew that Damek wouldn't tell anybody that he had found me crying like a baby. "It doesn't feel like it," I said at last.

"It always feels bad to begin with," he said. "But then you get used to it, and it's not so bad." I wanted to ask him how he knew, but stopped myself; we all knew Damek never talked about his past before the Red House. He stared at his feet, as if he were looking there for more words, and we sat in silence for a while as I gathered myself together.

He helped me up and studied my face. "Nobody would know you've been crying," he said. "Better that way, eh?" He smiled, and I gave him a wobbly smile back. He had a very sweet smile, I remember. After that I sometimes sought his company when my spirits oppressed me. He never asked questions: we would merely talk idly of this or that, until I felt better. It was simple kindness, and I have never forgotten it.

Perhaps you will find this difficult to understand, as Damek has since become so cruel: but maybe the cruellest people, those who are most crafty in the ministration of hurt, are those who fully understand what it means to feel pain. I sometimes wonder if that boy lives somewhere inside Damek still, or if Damek murdered him in his manhood. If he did, that might have been his worst crime.

When the thaw came, my father went to kill his man, and duly travelled to the palace to pay the Blood Tax, and on his return we held the honouring feast. You will no doubt find it strange of me, given what I think and believe about the vendetta, but when I looked at him sitting at the head of the long table with the soft flush of rushlight on his face, I was proud of him. It was the only time in my life I felt such a surge of affection towards my father; he was gentle with me that evening, and called me his dear as he stroked my cheek. I treasure that memory still, since it is one of the few times in my life when I felt some sense of redemption in our relationship. It is one of the paradoxes of the north, that the vendetta, the evil thing at our heart, is what brings out our most noble character.

The day after the truce elapsed, my father was shot dead on the road just outside the village. As with most of these killings, it occurred at dawn. The news was brought to us by Johka of the Low Pastures, who found his body. I remember it vividly: Fatima had just arrived with eggs and gossip for my mother, and I was making a tea, when there was a knock on the kitchen door. Johka was standing on the threshold, clutching his hat in his hands, and before he said a word, all the blood drained from my mother's face. Fatima nodded to Johka, indicating that this was women's business, and he mumbled his sympathies and went away. My mother stood, unseeing and unhearing, as Fatima took her elbow and made her sit down. It was only then that she began to weep.

For all the unhappiness it caused, the death of my father did not seriously affect our circumstances: my mother and I were protected because we worked at the Red House, and the master's family was immune from vendetta. We were not in danger, as others were, of losing our home and our livelihood. But my father was scarcely cold in his grave when disaster struck, and our lives changed for ever.

XVII

As is so often the case, it was a small chance that exerted the greatest leverage upon our existences. One evening in the late spring, the master saddled up Ruby, the impetuous chestnut mare, since he intended to ride to the manse to conduct some business. Normally my father would have performed this task, and since he was no longer with us we were a little short-handed in the stables. Had my father been there, he would have advised the master to choose another mount: Ruby had in the past few days developed a tiny sore on her ribs, which chafed against the saddle-girth. She was fiery at the best of times – one of the reasons the master liked to ride her – but the abrasion made her irritable. The master had ridden less than half a mile before Ruby threw him. His head hit a stone when he fell, and he lay unconscious on the path for hours before the alarm was raised. The men set out from the Red House with lamps when he failed to return, and found him at midnight. Ruby was grazing peacefully near by with her leg through one of the reins.

He was laid across his horse and brought home, as if he were already a corpse. In truth he was barely alive. He was near dead from exposure alone – he was drenched through with the dewfall – and although the head injury had not broken the skin, it showed an ugly bruise across his temple.

Lina was waiting up for him, curiously calm in the midst of the hubbub, and when she saw her father coming home through the rising mist she didn't move or make a cry. She watched, her eyes dark and luminous in the lamplight, as he was brought in and made comfortable in his bed while the doctor was sent for. Only her paleness – she had turned absolutely white when she saw the horse – and the small drop of blood on her lip where she had bitten it, betrayed her bitter anxiety. I confess that I was mightily relieved: had she behaved in her usual manner and had hysterics, I don't know how we would have coped. Instead she pulled a chair close to the bed and sat next to the master, holding his hand and stroking his brow. Damek stood uncertainly by the doorway, impeding everyone who wanted to enter or leave the chamber. He reminded me of a swan I saw once, whose mate had been fatally injured by a gunshot: it stayed day and night beside the wounded one, uselessly starving itself, unable to help and equally unable to leave.

The doctor arrived within the hour, and we were all banished from the chamber. It was the same doctor who tended your dog bite, sir, although he is much older now; a city-educated man, as you know, who possesses a store of something that cannot be taught: ordinary human compassion. Lina waited wordlessly with the rest of us outside the room, her head bowed, her hands twisting nervously together; and when the doctor at last emerged, her eyes sought out his with a silent plea of such ferocity and passion I saw him sway with the force of it.

For a moment it seemed he would pass by without making any comment, but then he changed his mind. He sighed, and taking Lina's hand in both of his, he met her gaze. "I'm sorry," he said quietly. "My condolences."

Lina drew in her breath sharply, but said nothing.

"He is dead, then?" said Damek quickly, from behind Lina.

"Nay," the good man answered. "I fear he will die before the dawn. I should be very surprised if he should wake before then."

Lina threw aside the doctor's hands, flung open the bed-chamber door and scrambled to her father's side. Snatching up his hand, she cried, with a piteous desolation, "Papa! Papa! Wake up!" When she saw no answering change on her father's face, a violent storm of grief possessed her; she let go of his hand and threw herself to the floor in an attitude of the deepest despair.

My mother, who looked as if she wanted to slap Lina, began to push past us into the room, but the doctor stopped her. "Let her weep," he said. "It will make no difference to him, and may help her."

"You don't know her, sir," said my mother. "She will make herself ill with it. I never saw one for such wailings over the smallest things."

"The death of her father is no small thing," he answered, and he looked sternly at my mother, who quailed before his expression. "I'll give her a draught to bring sleep later; I'll not leave the house until the lord's life is over. For the moment, leave her to mourn."

"But the master—"

"There is nothing further I can do for him. He is not in pain, and if he does not regain consciousness, as I believe he will not, he will not suffer. He is comfortable and warm in his bed; but it is his deathbed, I fear."

When the first violence of Lina's grief passed, she sat unspeaking by her father, her eyes fixed on his pallid face, where the darkening bruise slowly spread down from his temple along his jawline. She clutched his hand with such force that her knuckles were white.

Soon afterwards, against my protestations, my mother sent me to my bed, but neither she nor the doctor had any success in moving Lina. The doctor was correct: the master died in the small watches of the night without emerging from his coma. Lying sleepless and restless in my narrow cot, I knew the exact moment of his death. Lina's shriek of lamentation echoed through the silent house; and I felt as if a knife had entered my own heart.

XVIII

In his will, the master left his estate to Lina, who was then but thirteen years old. A will in these parts is a serious matter, which involves much affixing of seals and at least seven signatures by men of importance. The Lord Kadar was, as I have said, a man ever careless of detail, and he had failed to find two of the seven witnesses the law requires. No doubt he thought he had time, since he was a man of robust health and could have reasonably expected to live for many years; but it was not to be. His oversight proved disastrous. As the master partook of the royal revenue, his will needed to be approved by the king, and to our horror, the king ruled it invalid and claimed that the properties of the Lord Kadar reverted to his own estates, to apportion as he saw fit.

There was a long correspondence which took the best part of a year. The master's notary made a compassionate appeal, invoking the master's professed intentions, for the rights of Lina to inherit the estate; but he may as well have held his breath. The king, in his wisdom and malice, awarded the estate in trust to a royal dependant, one Emerek Masko. Masko was one of the palace hangers-on, a sycophant of sufficient distance from the royal bloodlines to partake minimally of its rewards; indeed, at the palace it was said his rights to claim royal blood were so minimal as to be non-existent. For all that, after the months of negotiation were settled, he lost no time in taking up his good fortune.

His entrance into the village square was, as he clearly intended, spectacular. Masko had instantly availed himself of his new-found wealth by buying a second-hand carriage, a *britzka* which he had painted with the royal coat of arms and which was drawn by two showy but impractical hacks. He reclined in the back in an ostentatious frock coat of green velvet, with turquoise frogging and a froth of lace at the throat, and the coat of arms embroidered upon its breast and lapels. It was a badly cut copy of city fashion hastily turned by some back-street northern tailor, and its cheap gilt buttons strained across his ample stomach. The effect was not as kingly as he imagined: more than anything he looked like an absurd bullfrog.

Behind the *britzka* came a wagon that bore his possessions. This was driven by a surly farmhand dressed, as his groom was, in an improbable livery of emerald and turquoise, which unhappily failed exactly to match Masko's own costume. As the procession wound its way to the Red House, Masko attracted all the notice he desired, but behind his back there was a lot of sly sniggering.

At the Red House, we were lined up in the entrance hall to greet him. When we had learned the hour of his arrival through a letter sent post-haste, Lina had initially refused to greet him, but somehow we had prevailed upon her to be present; to snub thus the king's chosen heir would have been perilous indeed. As the daughter of the late master, she stood first in line to greet the new lord. She was dressed in deep mourning, but out of courtesy she had her veil drawn back from her face. Grief had if anything heightened her dramatic beauty: she was yet young, and rather than darkening her face in shadow, sorrow set her cheekbones and eyes in relief, and enhanced the superb pallor of her skin. Damek, as the next of royal blood, stood behind her, and behind Damek were my mother, myself and the other servants of the household.

Masko was preceded by his groom, who threw open the door, bowed clumsily and announced his lordship. We were taken aback by this unexpected formality, and when Masko himself entered, stepping like a peacock, he was greeted with a dead silence. In our innocence, we had never seen such a sartorial exhibition as he then presented: for a fatal moment, out of surprise and embarrassment, not one of us could think of anything to say.

I felt my mother stir, feeling it was her duty, if Lina remained silent, to welcome the new lord to his home. But she was forestalled by Lina. Lina, whom all of us had thought would never laugh again, couldn't contain herself: her snort of amusement spilt over into helpless giggles and then became a long peal of laughter. We all stared at her, horrified, as she doubled over, her eyes streaming; it was soon clear that she couldn't control herself, and that there was indeed something hysterical in it. Damek had the sense to usher her hurriedly out of sight, and at last my mother stepped forward and said the polite words.

Masko flushed, pretending to ignore what had just occurred, although Lina's awful mirth, now beginning to dissolve into wrenching sobs, was still audible from the back of the house. He bowed icily in response to my mother's greeting, but didn't grant the rest of us even a nod. He snatched the inventory from my mother's hand and demanded to be shown the drawing room, where he would be served a glass of wine. We hurried to see to his orders, and in doing so I accidentally caught his eye.

In that moment, I saw that this man was more than a graceless fool: in a flash of intuition I perceived the depths of his capacity for cruelty and petty resentment. I turned cold: almost as cold as when I had caught the attention of the Wizard Ezra. Although this man had not the powers of a wizard, he was now lord over all of us, and our lives lay in his palm, to do with as he would. It boded very ill that Lina's first act in his presence had been so gravely to wound his vanity.

The first order he gave in our household, after he had consumed his refreshment, was that Lina must be thrashed for her impertinence. When my mother pointed out – with an unusual temerity – the unseemliness of thus punishing the former master's daughter, he answered that her blood made it all the more imperative that she learn some manners. Since his household servants were unwilling to carry out his order, he said, in a voice that rose to a scream, his groom would do the job.

This groom, a man called Kush, remains one of the most ill-favoured men I have ever met. You might remember him; he serves yet in our household, and is now Damek's chief manservant at the manse. Then age had not twisted him, and he still had the strength of his hale manhood. He took Lina's arm roughly, but she tore herself away and ran to her chamber, where she locked herself in. It was to no avail: Kush shouldered down the door and dragged her out, kicking and screaming, by her hair. He flung her over his shoulder and carried her outside, and flogged her with a switch until the blood seeped through her dress onto the ground and she fainted from the pain.

Masko watched the while, a smile on his lips, standing a little apart from the rest of the horrified, silent witnesses. When Lina fainted, I think he was afraid for a moment that she had been killed: for all the dislike the king showed to the master's family, it would not have been politic for him to have killed the heir whom he had supplanted on the day of his arrival.

He hurriedly bade his servant to cease the beating, and had her brought inside. Nor did he gainsay my mother when later that day she requested that the doctor be brought to salve Lina's wounds, although it would make his savage treatment of Lina widely known.

Lina was abed for two weeks after the thrashing, with Damek her constant nurse, and I attendant every moment that other tasks did not demand me. She didn't speak for three days. On the fourth she sat up in bed, despite the anguish it caused her to do so, and she cursed Masko with every fibre of her being. She summoned boils for his skin and cankers for his mouth and eyes and anus; she swore that he would eat ash and drink dust; she said he would bear neither sons nor daughters and would never find satisfaction in bed or out of it; she called the Devil to haunt his nights and days with such anguish and sorrow as she now suffered, but multiplied a thousandfold, as salt in his wounds and acid in his soul; and she swore his death would be early, and slow, and agonizing, and ugly, but that none alive would pity him. It was a terrible curse that echoed through the house so it could be heard even in the drawing room where Masko sat downstairs, drinking his porter.

My soul chilled as I listened, but I didn't dare to interrupt her. When she had finished, she turned to me, panting with exertion and pain. I don't know how to describe her in that moment. Her hair was tumbled wildly all down her back and breast, her face was as white as a corpse, and her eyes blazed with a hatred the like I had then never seen in another human being. But that wasn't what made my heart stop. I knew then that she was really a witch, and that the curse she had uttered was no empty threat. I almost felt sorry for the man.

"He'll have you beaten again for that," I said at last, my mouth dry.

"He wouldn't dare," said Lina.

I watched Masko closely over the next few days, but to my disappointment the curse seemed to have no immediate effect. He ate as much as he ever did, and slept as soundly. However, it was true that he did not beat her – perhaps the doctor had made his displeasure known – and when Lina rose at last from her sickbed, he chose to ignore her, although I sometimes caught him covertly studying her through narrowed eyes.

He did take other steps, however. The day after the beating, he let Mr Herodias know that his services were no longer required. Mr Herodias received this news with his usual ironic coolness; he read us a short lecture on the continual improvement of our minds by constant reading, gave us a parting gift of a book each, packed his bags and rode off to the city, presumably to find himself another position. I think in truth he was relieved to go: he wasn't a man of the north, and the unvarying society here had wearied him.

This was bad enough, but Masko's next action was much worse. He couldn't send Damek from the house, since he had been appointed there by the king himself, but he had noted my devotion to Lina's welfare in her sickness. He therefore sent me from the house as a gift to the king, to serve as a maid in the palace. Neither my mother's protests nor Lina's pleading – for she lowered herself so far as to beg him to let me stay – made any impression upon his decision; I think rather it hardened him in his determination, for in this way he could at once isolate and hurt her. And so it was, less than three months after the master's death, that I was forced to pack up all my belongings, leave behind everything and everyone I had known, and make the three-day journey to the King's Palace.

Fortunately it was high summer, and the weather remained fine, else my journey might have been more miserable. Masko's thoughtfulness for my comfort extended to an open dray; I was sore from head to foot with its jolting by the time I arrived, but at least I was dry. I was young and frightened and lonely, but I was fortunate enough to meet with kindness; my story after I reached the palace is not so sad.

In the years I spent in the king's employ, I lost touch with the doings of the Red House. I sent letters home every month, but I heard little back: my mother couldn't write, and Lina only sent me one brief missive. This didn't hurt me as much as it might have, since I heard from Damek that Lina was forbidden correspondence.

Damek wrote an occasional letter, until his correspondence broke off entirely. Many years later, I found a short diary that Lina had hidden in her room, in a hole underneath a loose floorboard where we kept our childish treasures. It records some incidents that occurred before she moved to live in the manse. Even if it is sadly disordered, for Lina wrote irregularly and never bothered with dates, and although it sometimes seems to have been written by the Devil himself, it throws a little light on the events that occurred in my absence.

III: LINA

Friday

I have never been more unhappy in my life! For the past hour I have been sitting on my bed holding the red cord on my dressing-gown, but I haven't had the courage to loop it around the beam and hang myself. Finally I threw the cord away – I kept thinking of how it would hurt me, how that red line would cut into my neck, and how my face would turn blue & ugly, and I could feel the awful dread of being unable to breathe even though my body was writhing with the need for air – and I just couldn't do it. I despise myself: I am such a coward in my heart. Yet – perhaps I am not so craven after all: it is not my end that fills me with most fear. I think of Damek – I couldn't endure to so sever myself from him, not for a minute, not for a day, let alone for the empty wasteland of eternity! – For I would go to hell if I killed myself, and he would not, because he is a shining soul who will himself fly to heaven and be with the angels, and we would never ever meet again. – I cannot bear even the thought of that. I would even suffer such despite as I live in now rather than that.

So, I've dragged this old schoolbook out from underneath my bed, as I have to talk to someone, & I am all alone. I don't need the book any more, since Mr Herodias left for the south, so I might as well complain to this paper as to the wall. – It is quieter, anyhow, and no one will threaten me and tell me to be silent. How I wish I could have gone away with Mr Herodias! He never liked me much, but when I threw myself on the floor and begged him to take me & Damek south, he didn't treat me as contemptuously as I expected. He even looked a little sorry. That was the most I was ever going to get from him and his niminy-piminy mouth. I suppose he didn't like me because I didn't like him, but it's strange how much I miss him. I miss everything and everyone. I miss Papa and I miss Anna and I miss how things were, I miss them so badly that it hurts me in every part of my body. If Damek weren't here in the house this minute I think I would die from sorrow.

I am so sad today that I cannot even be angry.

I am banished to my room & the door has been locked, & the key to my own bedroom is now in Masko's fat, sweaty hand, which is humiliation enough! – and Damek is beaten and silent & locked in his own room in turn. That coward doesn't dare beat me! – But today he ordered that Damek be beaten, and that sour old demon Kush thrashed him until the blood came & Damek never made a sound. But he was shamed, he was shamed in his soul, so that he wouldn't meet my eyes even when I rushed to him, and he pushed me away when I sought to comfort him. – & now we are not permitted to speak together. That makes me sadder than anything, to see my dear Damek humiliated – and because he dared to outface Masko, to defend me against his foul, wicked words.

I wish I really were a witch. But I'm not a witch at all. I daren't tell anyone, not even Damek: not being a witch is a worse shame than the mark of magic. I cursed Masko two months ago, and nothing happened: where are the boils & the wasting sickness?– each day I look in hope and I see no mark, not one single sign that the gods heard me and took my part. I think it is I who am cursed.

Masko sits all day in the drawing room, where he has taken down the beautiful paintings that my father set there and instead put up his vulgar daubs in cheap gilt frames, so it is now ugly & graceless. And there he drinks glass after glass of porter and gobbles his messes of pigs' trotters & goose-fat pancakes, and all you can hear is his heavy breathing and slobbering; and then he gets on one of the poor horses, and he goes out to play cards. He is a poison, he makes everything around him vile. I see him looking at me sometimes, his sly eyes rolling in his puffy cheeks: he stares at my front in a way that makes me feel very hot. – Once when my skirts were hitched up to milk the goats – because I am just a servant now! Me, of the royal blood! – I turned around and there he was, not five paces away, and I knew he had been looking at my ankles, and it made me feel filthy, as if I had just rolled in all the dirt in the yard.

I think he is a little afraid, a little, that my words were potent and that he is cursed: and I think that is the only thing that stops him from following his eyes with his fat greasy fingers. I swear if he touched me I would kill him, I would drive even a butter knife through his windpipe, and I would stab out both his eyes with a fork – and it would so please me to see the blood splattering down his ridiculous shirtfront!

There! – I am feeling angry now. And now I am not so sad.

Monday

Damek still lies abed, but I was able to creep in this evening while Masko was out playing cards. He told me to stop crying, and that we should wait until we both grow up, because then we will take our revenge on Masko. He had on his black face when he said that! – He seems then as stubborn as the mountains themselves & as merciless. If I were Masko, I should be very afraid of him! I believe he would follow Masko into the very pits of hellfire itself, to exact his retribution. It comforted me, but all the same, it is such a long time before I grow up! – I might even be dead by then, and I would much rather see Masko at my feet sobbing & wailing for mercy right this minute. I said so to Damek, and he told me not to be foolish.

He knows my curse didn't work, although he loves me too much to say so out loud. – Time will restore all, he said. If it were anyone else speaking, I would believe he was telling me to be a lady and to forget my anger. Damek would never say such a thing to me.

We are still young and we have no money of our own.

Damek says he knows how to get rich. He thinks about money all the time, even when I laugh at him & tell him it's vulgar – he just shakes his head at me and tells me I'm thoughtless & the only way to get back at Masko is to be richer than he is. But even if Masko were in his grave now, the king would not allow me to inherit the estate. Where do you find money? Damek will not tell me. He is very vexing when he chooses to be.

He still cannot lie on his back, but he is so patient & good in his pain! – Truly, he is an angel. Even Anna's ma says so, and she never praises anybody. She's even worse since Anna left, she's all puckered up like a prune, but I can't blame her for that. Everyone in the village says that Anna was only a daughter, and that daughters will always leave their mothers, but that shouldn't mean that a daughter is nothing. In our house it has always been different, at least up to now; but I suppose neither Anna nor I had brothers, and perhaps were more loved – no, I can't think of that! It is too painful.

It is very dull doing chores. I wonder how Anna bore with it all those years. I have to wear such ugly dresses: all my good clothes have been packed away. I wonder that Masko dares to treat me this way! Even Fatima says it is an insult. The people of the village still feel loyalty to the House of Kadar, and do not like to see the family honour smirched – and by such a buffoon! I do not understand why the king hated my father so, that he would send such an heir. What did my father do to merit such ill-treatment? He was a good man, the best of men; and he loved the villagers. I have never seen anyone so upset as when the vendetta came here: his face was white, and he struck his forehead with his hand, & I swear there were tears in his eyes, to think of all the sorrow that would be visited upon his people.

I know why the king hated him, although I do not like to own it. It is because of me & my mother. Anna thought

I didn't know what is said about me: if I mentioned it, she always talked about something else until I stopped asking. But I know. I see the fear & contempt in their faces, as soon as they see my eyes, and I hear the murderous thoughts inside their empty skulls, as clearly as if they spoke them. I know perfectly well that if it weren't for my father, the villagers would drive a stake through me as quick as thinking. If only it weren't the eyes! If witches had strange ears or an extra finger, I could hide those, or chop them off; but I cannot conceal my eyes unless I blindfold myself.

No one dares to say it straight to me, because of the royal blood: at least, until now they did not dare. Masko makes no bones about calling me a witch, and all but calls for my blood, and some cowards follow his lead: Johka of the Low Pastures spat and made the Devil sign when I walked past him today, & I heard the girls giggling in their hands when they saw me in my old clothes, which are covered in darned patches!

The humiliations every day are like burning coals, they scorch me to my very marrow. – But I pretend not to notice, I make sure I walk as proudly as if I were still a princess. Already there are those who forget to call me Miss Lina, who only a short time ago were plucking at my skirts begging to be noticed. I abhor them all – they are small, worm-minded creatures, & they deserve worse than the flames of hell. If I were God, I would lock them in a bathhouse for ever and ever. I can see them already, squashed together in a tiny freezing cold room which stinks of their own rank odours so they cannot escape them! – and I would set them to work sorting pins until their fingers bled and they were mad from tedium, and I would never let them sleep or stop working. That would serve them right.

I was afraid yesterday, when I saw Masko in the square, talking to the Wizard Ezra: my first thought was that they were plotting to kill me, since both would like to see me dead. Masko looked very nervous: he was bobbing up & down with his stupid lace collar flapping up into his face, so that if I had not been so anxious I would have laughed out loud. Then he glanced across the square and saw me there holding my basket, watching the both of them. I swear that he jumped, as if he were guilty, so I am quite certain that he was speaking about me.

Then the most astonishing thing happened: Wizard Ezra, who had his back to me, turned around and stared at me. He had his usual cold sneer on his face, but I refused to look away: and for the first time in my life, he met my eyes and nodded civilly, as if in greeting. Old Yiru saw it too – I saw him standing stock-still with his mouth open in shock! Ezra has never so much as deigned to notice my presence, unless it were to call me a wickedness & a walking blasphemy, or some such vileness. I was never so surprised! – I almost didn't respond, but I remembered in time to make a quick curtsey and then went quickly about my business, as both of those men make my innards boil with contempt & I do not like to be near them.

All the same, I take some hope from what I saw. I believe the Wizard Ezra dislikes Masko even more than he does me. He might refuse to countenance killing me out of spite for Masko. It is almost a good joke. Damek thinks that might be the case, but he tells me to be careful. I no longer have the key to my bedchamber, but now I put a chair under the handle each night.

I am wondering if it is true that I am not a witch. I am almost sure that I am not. – & yet it would be so unfair, to have all the appearance of it, & yet none of the power! If I am to be burned on a stake or stabbed through the heart, then I ought to have some joy of it. – This morning I was serving Masko his breakfast (and trying not to vomit at the sight of that repulsive face, his jowls wobbling like jelly & covered with little beads of sweat as he chewed on his fried kidneys) – I studied him as I always do, and I thought that he seemed *a little haggard, as if he had slept restlessly, and I am certain there is a sore upon his lip. Maybe curses take a while to work. I don't care how long it takes, as long as he dies as horribly as he deserves.*

Wednesday

*L*ife has been so boring that I have had nothing to write about. I've been feeding chickens & chopping vegetables & running stupid errands for ever and ever. Mrs Anna has been kind to me, insofar as she can be kind: at least, she does not chide me for my clumsiness, or not very much.

Something interesting happened this morning. Mrs Anna gave me back my good clothes, and told me that I need not serve in the kitchen any more! Masko told her last evening that my "punishment" is over. He saves face: we all know it wasn't punishment, it was to be my fate in this house. – I think the Wizard Ezra let it be known how little the village people admire his treatment of me. How strange, that my bitterest enemy should speak up for me! I do not trust the wizard any more than I ever did – I'm certain he wishes me no good. But I am so happy to be free from peeling turnips & shelling peas. I have cut my fingers so many times.

It is now two weeks since Damek arose from his bed. Until today, we were not permitted to sit together or even speak –

he could leave the house but I was forced to stay at home – I watched him through the windows as he strode out & away into the plains, all alone – although he would always turn and look to see if I was watching through the window. This morning, I put on my prettiest dress and knocked on his door as if it were the most natural thing in the world. And then, as if he were already grown up, he offered me his arm, and we high-stepped out of the house like a lord & lady – I could barely keep my laughter inside me! No one made to stop us. Masko was still abed, snoring to wake the dead, and the day was yet early and fresh. When we were out of sight of the house, we ran & ran & ran until we were out of breath, all the way to our secret place by the river, and there I stood by the willows and looked over the plains to the mountains and the black clouds lowering over them, and wept from happiness.

It feels years that I have been cooped up in that house! – It was as if I had been blind & deaf & dumb, and all of a sudden God lifted the blindfold from my senses – I could smell the earth itself, and all the rich rot of autumn, and the seeding grasses, and the clean air sweeping down from the mountains with the rain on its wings. The colours burned my eyes, such rich ochres & browns & ambers & endless shades of green – and the sky was every blue there is, from black to the finest most delicate shade, like the shell of a duck egg – and the shadows stretching long and sharp under a lemon storm light –

Everything else has changed, but this place is constant. All my living is here, all my childhood and all my future – here Damek and I are the same as when we first found it all those years ago, pure and whole and free, and nothing mars us. It all belongs to me – and Damek belongs to me – this land and this love are mine, and they can never be taken from me – one might as well steal the blood from my veins! – Not even death will change that! – When I am buried, all these things will still belong to me, and I to them – I will be the sky and the rock and the trees and the wind, and they will be me, and Damek in all, because my heart beats in his breast and his in mine.

Damek says I must not speak of dying. He doesn't believe in God or heaven or even hell, & he claims that death will simply be an endless darkness where there is no thought or light, & that the afterlife the priests speak of is a lie that makes us bear with the hell we know on earth, instead of seeking to change it. I don't know why he thinks these strange things – he sometimes frightens me a little. There is only now! he said – and he took my arm and squeezed it so hard he bruised me. Only now! – and I cried out: Today, I will live for ever! – and I laughed at him and ran away.

Then the wind died down and we knew the rain was coming, so we must needs run home – the clouds burst halfway there. I was wet through at once, and when we arrived home my best dress was all filthy with dirt, but I don't care! – It is too small for me anyway. Mrs Anna told me off roundly. Masko didn't see us – he was still abed, and it almost noon! – He has been out late in Dardan playing cards with his filthy friends, & you could still hear his snores from the drawing room.

Mrs Anna sent me to my room for the whole afternoon. She said I should think about what it means to be a lady, especially if I wish Masko to treat me like one. As if it matters what he thinks of me! That fat slug has now lolloped out of bed – I hear him sliming down the hallway calling for Mrs Anna to make his breakfast. No matter what the king says, this place will never belong to him – never, never, never! He understands less than the smallest worm in the soil, because the worm eats the dirt and is part of it. Masko thinks of nothing except money. I don't care what Damek says. Money doesn't matter. It doesn't matter at all.

Later

Now I am a lady again, I have to eat my dinner with Masko! – It is a sore trial. Damek says I must temper my anger so we might bide our time, so I swallow my pride. It is a good game! – I pretend to be demure & good, and he simpers at me across the table. He has bought a new frock coat, it is made of purple velvet and he wears it with crimson breeches. I never saw anything more ugly & absurd in my life.

April

It is so long since I wrote here, that I had forgot all about it! I was crawling under my bed for a shoe and I found this old book all covered in dust. I am not so unhappy now! – Masko is a fat stupid sot still but we do not need to notice each other, & in any case he spent all winter away in the south. Even though I despise him, I wish he had taken us! – It is so boring here. He came back three weeks ago, but he mostly keeps to his room or is riding off to visit his acquaintances – twice they have come here for dinner & cards, but Mrs Anna makes me stay in my room – she says no good would come of those men seeing me. I hear them laughing & shouting – they drink all night! and last night there was a fight, and I could hear them rolling around and breaking things – but Damek said it was of no account. He says that Mrs Anna is right to keep me hid, and even as bored as I am, I have no longing to see any more of Masko than I do.

Nothing happened all winter. Fatima died of a putrid lung – it was bitter cold this year and she was old. There was no one to take the chickens, for her son was killed in the vendetta last summer and he was yet to marry, and so they were given to us. Her house is empty & sad and already the roof falls in. When the snows came there was no one to shovel the drifts away. She was a silly old gossip but it makes me sad – she never made the Devil's sign behind my back when I was carrying buckets around in my old clothes, and she always spoke well of Papa, and few enough around here have shewn me kindness.

The snows are gone but it has been raining for five days. – It is so heavy that the river flooded and the lower pastures were washed out. – I laughed because Johka's house was waist-deep in water & he was perched on the roof in his undergarments calling for someone to come and get him. It serves him right! – he is a mean-faced weasel and always was & he would have me a corpse if he could. Mrs Anna says the vendetta will likely not touch him, he is last in the list; and it may be that the wizards will find a way to make a truce before then – they often do, she said, before every man in the village is dead. She says that the good are taken & the scum remain.

Saturday

*M*asko says I must give thought to marriage. – So that is what he is plotting! – he will marry me out of the house and so get rid of me. Damek says I am not obliged to marry anyone unless the king says I must, but I fear that Masko will crawl into the king's ear and that will be that. Damek says that Masko will have a hard time finding me a husband, because all my estates have been stolen & I am poor. And also because I am a witch – no one knows that I lack the powers of a witch, not even Damek, because I dare not speak to anyone about this except myself. But maybe it is as well to look like one, even if I cannot curse.

I ran to the kitchen and cried & cried, and Mrs Anna patted my shoulder and said I am a deal too young to think of such things – I will be but sixteen my next birthday. Then Masko came in and Mrs Anna spoke up for me, and he was angry – he said I am full woman & ready to be paired with any man foolish enough to take me, and he pulled me out of the kitchen by my arm. I did not like him to touch me, and I told him so!

He stared at me with his little piggy eyes and I did not like at all how he looked at me. He let go of me at last, but he was still close enough that I could smell his foul breath on my face. – And then he said I was soiled enough, with my bad blood, & it would in any case cost a mort of gold to get any man to even look at me. He kept staring at me – how dare he stare at me like that! – and I slapped his face. He didn't say anything, he just put his hand to his cheek where it was red with the mark of my hand, and he kept staring at me until I ran away. He makes me want to be sick.

I cannot bear the thought of being a wife. To be the drudge of some idiot man, to be at his beck & call, to spend every moment of my day & night as a possession, no better than livestock, a sow to breed squeaking piglets! – I will not give away my name. It is mine and it will always be mine. I hope that Damek is right: maybe Masko will not be able to find anyone to marry me. But what is to stop Masko paying off one of his lickspittle friends to make me an offer, and nosing the king until he sends an order that I marry? I swear if Masko matches me, I will run away! But where can I go? I have nowhere to go.

Midsummer

I'm so angry I would smash every wall in this house! – Yes, & every plate & every bowl & every chair & table – I would break & tear every thing inside & out – & each broken bit I'd break – and when it was all wreckage & splinters grind it under my heels & pound it into the earth – I cannot stop shaking with it, I can barely hold this pen aright –

Later

So *tired now. Damek made me open the door & came in with a broth Mrs Anna cooked for me & so I have eaten although I would much rather not. He is gone now & I would speak to no one else. Everything is quiet & I hear the owl's hoot through my window & the frogs – outside is a tranquil sky with the moon bright as a silver coin throwing shadows over the ground – it is strange how calm the night is, when there is such tempest in my breast! – I have opened the shutters so that the air flows in all peaceful & dries my cheeks.*

Damek told me it is true. He has seen all the accounts. He said everyone in the royal houses knows and I should know too, since I will soon come to womanhood. I can scarce believe – and yet Damek says it is true! – & to have that slug Masko crowing over me is more than I can bear. Him coming into my sewing room & with such arrogance, to tell me that I was to meet with a suitor! & when I said nay & that no ill-bred cur of his low acquaintance would tempt my interest, I, the daughter of Lord Georg Kadar – to have him sneer at me –

I feel such a fool. If everyone knew, why not I?

The noble Kadar, he said, well, there are things you don't know about your noble father. It would make a cat laugh, he said. You sitting there all hoity-toity talking about his fine soul and how he snivelled over the vendetta, like some lily-livered woman. And he said, He was the one who shot that peasant, as the king ordered him, to start the Blood Tax, which had been full-thin from this part of the world because your fine father would not do his duty like a man – & when I said, How dare you speak so of my father when you are not fit to lick his boots! he sniggered & said I should ask the king some time – The revenue needs to come from somewhere, he said, & the Blood Tax is it, and your father was loath to do his share until he was pushed – he was no man! – but he shot his prey in the end, and so be it. & I stood up and called him out like a man, for I swear I would shoot him for my honour and Papa's & why should I not, even if I am a girl? – & he laughed in my face and spat on the floor – That's funny enough, a chit calling for honour! – And in defence of your father, he said, who was famed as the first whoremonger in the land! – & as murderous & greedy & foul as the rest of us. You get off your high horse, young lady, he said, and you will meet your suitor or I'll be damned. – I can't remember any more he said, for I felt that I would faint – I wanted to kill him – I threw myself at him and tried to scratch his eyes out with my nails & he slapped me to the floor & left.

Oh, Papa! And now I know it's true. You took your gun and shot out the eye of that poor man who had done nothing wrong save come to the wrong place at the wrong time. & because of that our house echoes with the wailing of women & the village is pocked with empty houses and ruin! – & it is because of you! You, Papa! – I will never forgive you, never – I curse you in your grave, because I thought you more excellent in your soul than these brutish others! – & you were never so! My heart is torn with it, my life is broken – I hate Masko – but he is just a fat cruel idiot. I hate you more.

Damek said, Where do you think the money comes from? What do you think pays for these fine clothes and the food you eat? What is the wealth of the royal house? – He said, Did you never think of the Blood Tax? Did you never wonder why the vendetta never touches those of royal blood? – Oh, I never did, & I am sick with misery & horror – I would tear off these clothes and go naked, for they are woven of blood! – & every meal I have eaten stinks of death! – I taste it in my breath. I am vile, vile, I will never eat again –

The wizards must know, and partake in it – even Ezra, even as much as I have hated him, I thought that he made his laws according to his knowledge and what he thinks is right, which is not itself wrong. – And yet they are all empty and evil –

If this is what it means to be a grown woman I would have stayed in my mother's curst womb & never been born.

November

How long since last I wrote here? I no longer know or care what the day is. It is wintering now and the winds howl like demons. The snows are coming – I can smell them.

I am so lonely – I want to speak to someone, as if I had a friend. I have no friends now, except this book.

I am shamed to the very pit of my being – broken – soiled as I never thought was possible. My soul has been torn and trampled – if I had thought! – I was foolish and stopped putting the chair against my door since it seemed that Masko would not have me killed. – And the night before last – was it then? or another night? – Masko came home late & drunk and forced his way into my room. Even writing this makes my gorge rise, I have vomited up every meal since –

He broke my rib & I have bruises all over me but none of those wounds hurt as much as the memory of what he did to me. I would cut my own head off to stop that memory. But that is not the worst –

Damek has gone. He tried to murder Masko, after he made

147

me tell what happened. I didn't want to tell but he made me. I wish he had killed him, I wish he had stabbed him right there in the drawing room – but he is still a boy, he is not as strong as Masko, who is tall as well as fat. Masko grabbed his arm & threw the knife away, and he punched him so hard Damek's nose was broke and he was knocked out; and then when he was on the ground Masko kicked him until Kush pulled him off, shouting that he oughtn't to kill the king's bastard, however much he deserved to be beaten to death. – And Mrs Anna & Kush carried Damek into the kitchen and bathed his poor face until he woke up, swearing like the Devil himself. He said that for all the blood, it wasn't so bad, and that Masko couldn't punch to hurt a rabbit, but I don't believe him.

Then he changed his clothes and packed a bag and left. I begged him not to, I fell to my knees & pleaded that he stay – but he said that he couldn't stay now, that Masko would have him killed, and he couldn't protect me here – he said he had a better plan & he would have his revenge. He has gone, I don't know where, and I doubt I will ever see him again. He said he would carry me in his heart, he said if I dared to think of killing myself he would never forgive me. – But what is there for me to live for? – When I told him I would hang myself, he was more angry than I have ever seen him. He told me to have faith, but oh, it is a bitter, tiny thing, and there is nothing to keep it alight. He said he would come back for me. He said he would come back.

Christ Mass

I will not shed a tear on account of Masko ever again. He does not deserve such tribute.

Try how he might, he will never hurt me again, nor demean me, nor cause me to sorrow. Even if he abuse my body, he cannot wound my soul.

I will tend the hatred in my heart as if it is the most precious and delicate seedling, as if it were a nutmeg sent from the palace of the king with the brightest blessings of God. It will sprout into a sapling as graceful as an angel and it will put forth a flower that smells sweeter than ambergris and myrrh and shines like the first sun after winter.

Masko will see it and smile. But when he reaches out his hand to take its beauty, just as he steals everything that is mine, my enmity will strike his heart. He'll wake to a bitter spring! He'll find every green thing withered and every hope blackened. The flower will bear the face of my hatred: its petals will rive open like lips and out from its centre will writhe a serpent that will coil about him and crush the light in his soul. Its fangs will pierce his heart with anguish, and it will devour every moment of all the days of his life.

Even his death will not serve for an escape, for my revenge will gnaw his spirit wherever it goes, for all eternity.

I swear this solemnly, that he has not the honour to warrant being named my enemy.

No, even my hatred is too noble for his kind. No, one day I will pluck his soul from his body as a rat is plucked from its hole and thrown onto the midden, and I will turn away as the gross worms eat out his eyes, for ever and ever and ever. Amen.

IV: ANNA

XIX

Much happened in Elbasa in the years I was away, but I heard only the small scraps rumour fed me, since Damek's letters – the principal mode of my intelligence – ceased after his disappearance. Damek's leaving was generally explained by his attempt on Masko's life, and that in turn was presumed to stem from the cruel treatment he had suffered. Until I discovered Lina's diary, I never knew the real reason for his departure; and I confess that I was never more shocked. I can't imagine that my mother couldn't have known, since she would have had to care for Lina's injuries, but no hint ever passed her lips. Yet it's easy to understand why Masko's shameful crime against Lina would have been kept secret by any who cared for her. If it had become known, Lina likely would have been shot: although she was the innocent victim of his wicked lusts, she would have been held to be as much, or perhaps even more, at fault than the criminal himself. Such is the way of justice in the Plateau.

Like most others, including Lina herself, I presumed that

Damek must have somehow met his death. I missed him, as I missed all those I loved in that luckless household, and mourned his probable fate. At the same time, I was making my own life, and had my own concerns. Most importantly for me, I met Zef, who was then working as a groom in the king's stables, and he indicated an interest in me that I was by no means unwilling to return. When a letter unexpectedly arrived from Lina, petitioning the king to send me back to Elbasa to be her maid at the manse, I was torn: my relationship with Zef was still mere acquaintance, although I already preferred him over any man I had met, and had my wishes been consulted, I would have stayed where I was.

The king decided I should go, and so I had no choice but to leave. My joy in returning home was mingled with regret. Our mutual youth meant neither of us had any power to decide for ourselves where to live and work, and so Zef did not declare himself before my departure. I journeyed home with those feelings usually grouped under the phrase "a broken heart". I can laugh at myself now, since such misunderstandings are long behind us, but it was very painful at the time, as I was sure I should never see him again. In thinking thus, I underestimated Zef's constancy and determination: after he came of age he travelled here speedily and declared himself. And so you see us now, after many years of a good marriage, the only grief of which is our childlessness. They have been unremarkable years to anyone but ourselves, and make no exciting tale, but I thank God each day for my luck, in finding so early in my life a man who honours the qualities of my mind and heart, and who has never disrespected me for my sex. But I digress.

After Damek left, Lina moved out of the Red House and set up her household at the manse. Masko was still officially her guardian, since she was neither married nor of age, but he gave her permission to move; perhaps he was secretly ashamed of what he had done, and was weary of having Lina under his roof, a constant, silent reminder of his crime. Until I arrived, she was assigned a young girl, Fatima's great-niece, Irli, to be her maid, and lived as a recluse, seldom seen in the village except when she attended church. This was so foreign to the Lina I had known that I was astonished, but my mother insisted that womanhood had changed her, and that she had become meek and biddable. I confess that, until I saw her myself, I found this impossible to believe.

The reason for my return also astonished me. Lina was to be married, and I was asked to be the housekeeper for her new household. Her troth had been given to a handsome young man, Tibor Alcahil, whom I knew only by sight, but who was said to be of steady character and minor but established wealth. It was hard to imagine a greater contrast to Damek, and I thought she must be changed indeed to make such an alliance.

It was wise of Lina to distance herself from Masko, by becoming the de facto mistress of the manse; although he continued as her official guardian, her move away from the Red House gained her respect in the eyes of the villagers. In the years that he was Lord of Elbasa, Masko had succeeded in making everyone despise him; not the lowest lackey said his name but to spit. He had no shame in flaunting the women he brought up from the south, in order to scandalize the northerners. He even took his whores to church, thus putting the priests and wizards in a rare unity of outrage.

The wizards and priests grudgingly tolerate each other because the king, for his own reasons, insists that they must; but it is at best a jealous truce. It is proverbial that on any given topic, one side will automatically disagree with the other. On the question of Masko's scandalous behaviour, Father Cantor and the Wizard Ezra actually made a joint representation to the king that he be divested of his property and exiled from the

Plateau. I heard about it while I was still serving in the palace: it attracted much gossip, not only because such a proposition had never before been made, but also because the king refused the submission. It confirmed my belief that the king's detestation of the Lord Kadar was so bitter that he wanted to see his estate entirely dispersed by Masko's extravagance and mismanagement, and had chosen him deliberately, knowing his character, to ensure this design. Masko of course knew of this representation, and when the king refused it, he became more arrogant than ever. But he was even then sowing the seed of his own downfall.

XX

You might imagine with what feelings I packed my trunk and made my way home. Although it was yet early in the year, it was an unpleasant journey: the heat was excessive, and a storm was building. On the final day of my journey bruise-coloured clouds began to pile in the sky, and the air became ever closer and more sultry, so that the sweat trickled down my back underneath my corset. To make matters worse, I was tormented by midges that swarmed in hosts out of the grasses, and which bit any exposed skin. Both the carter and myself were anxious to arrive in Elbasa before the storm broke over our heads. To my inexpressible relief, we reached the Red House just as the first fat raindrops began to fall in the dust.

My mother was glad to see me, although without any demonstration that others might have thought appropriate for close family members who were now reunited after a sundering of seven years. She embraced me briefly, and commented that I had grown tall. She was as shy and awkward as I was: when my mother had last seen me, I had still been a girl scarce out of childhood, and now I was a grown woman. I was shocked by how much she had aged: during my absence she had become old. Her hair was now completely white. Her arms, which had been strong and capable, were grown thin and knotty, and deep, bitter lines ran from her nose to her mouth, writing her unhappiness on her face. We met almost as strangers, and although we both felt moved by our meeting, we were equally unable to express our feelings.

We sat for a time in the kitchen, and she brewed me a tisane as the storm broke over the village and began to hammer the roofs and howl about the trees. It was clearly impossible for me to go up to the manse that night, and gradually, as she answered my questions about what had happened in the village in my absence, the atmosphere between us thawed.

She told me of the major events since I had left, which I have recounted so far as they related to Lina and Damek; but there was much other news as well. She spoke of new marriages, and of births and deaths (there were many more deaths, as the vendetta still burned its slow fatality through Elbasa and Skip). These events, which had once been my first concerns, now seemed to have no relation to my life. This grieved and surprised me; I hadn't realized until then how much my absence had changed me. I attempted to tell her about my years in the palace, and of Zef, who was foremost in my thoughts, but she showed little beyond polite interest and I soon dropped the subject. I went to sleep that night with an oppressed heart, wondering whether I would always feel like a stranger in the place I had thought of as my home.

The following morning the storm had passed and I made my way on foot to the manse. My trunk was to be sent on later, and after the dust and discomfort of the previous day's journey, I was glad of the chance to walk in the cool air, which was cleansed and fresh after the night rains, and to look about the village I had not seen for so many years. It was a melancholy journey: because I was used to the grand halls and fine out-buildings of the palace, Elbasa seemed smaller and meaner than I remembered, and I noticed how many houses, like Fatima's, were deserted and falling into ruin.

Lina was waiting for me at the manse, and embraced me with a far warmer emotion than my mother had. "Oh, Anna!" she said at last, as she stood back and studied my face, blinking tears from her eyes. "How glad I am you're home. I was trem-bling that the king would not permit it. He never would before! And how grown up you are now!"

I was taken aback by her greeting, but couldn't help feeling pleased. "It has been seven years," I said. "It would be strange indeed if I had not changed. But in most respects, I think I am much the same as I was."

I didn't speak my own thoughts, that Lina was changed almost out of recognition. I had been used to thinking of her as strong and robust, the most physically fearless of my childhood friends; and yet here stood before me a slender, pale woman, who seemed almost overwhelmingly fragile. I felt that if I touched her she would bruise, as if she were a lily grown in a glasshouse. It did her beauty no harm; the translucency of her skin made her appear almost luminous. The other strange alteration was that her eyes were no longer the vivid violet I remembered, but rather a dark blue or deep slate grey. It appeared to me that at some stage in the past few years she must have been very ill, and was now in a long convalescence.

She studied me a little more, and then laughed sadly and looked away. "You were always steadfast," she said. "In truth, the major changes are in me. I am grown up now and have put away vanity and illusion. I hope you find me a better friend than I have been, Anna."

This confused me a little; the palace had, after all, strictly taught me to observe my place. "I hope," I said, a little primly, "that I will be a better servant than you remember."

"I could have sought a servant anywhere, Anna," said Lina. "It is as a friend I asked for you. I do not complain of my life – it could be much worse – but I confess it's been lonely these last few years. And who now knows me as well as you do?"

I mumbled something non-committal and I briefly saw a flash of Lina's old impatience, before she turned the subject and said that she would show me the buttery and linen press and other such places that would be in my care.

As she conducted me through the house, we relaxed a little into our old intimacy. As ever when she wanted to charm, Lina was hard to resist, and she was so bound up with my childhood memories that I quickly felt at home. I knew she wasn't lying about her loneliness: I could smell it in her skin. She was absurdly sensitive; although she didn't say so, I could see that my initial withdrawal had hurt her. The more we talked, the more I felt pity for her; sometimes there was almost a feverish edge to her conversation. She was, for example, almost childishly eager to solicit my approval, in a way she would never have cared to before I left, and I particularly noticed that she avoided any mention of Damek. I saw too that she tired quickly, and there were other small signs of damaged health that disturbed me.

My trunk arrived during our tour, so she showed me my chamber and left me to unpack my possessions. It gave me, at last, a little space to myself in which I could think about what I had witnessed that morning. I felt uneasy; I chiefly found myself wondering about Lina's future husband, and my future master. If he were harsh and stern, in the way of most northern men, I feared that she would not long survive marriage. And I then recognized, with a painful adult perception, what I had always known as a child: that for all her faults, I loved Lina as I would have loved a sister.

X X I

It took us a few days to settle into a relationship in which we both felt comfortable, one that at once observed distinction and acknowledged intimacy. It is too easy for a mistress to assume that a servant is at the beck and call of her emotional needs as much as her material requirements; and my sense of dignity demands that such friendship emerge from my own heart, rather than the command of another. But these are trivial niceties which might not interest you, perhaps; I have noticed that not many people concern themselves with the self-respect of those who work for them.

I was pleased, all the same, to be Lina's housekeeper, since it gave me high standing in the village. I was still very young, and I could not but be flattered by my appointment to the position. While the Kadar family had been based in the Red House, the manse had been the working base of the estates, but Masko's low esteem among the villagers had shifted the locus of royal authority to the manse. I'm sure Lina was quite indifferent to this, if she even noticed it. I saw the change in attitude at once, and assumed that her quiet life prompted both curiosity and sympathy; it was also clear that she had become a focus for resentment against Masko's insolence and mismanagement. There was now much nostalgia for the "old days" and the "old master", from those who had been first to slander the Lord Kadar and his scandalous daughter, and the fact that she was supposed a witch seemed quite forgot.

She told me herself that she wasn't a witch. "It was always a mistake," she said. "And so unfair. The terrible things that people said about me... But honestly, Anna, I never felt a single twinge of magic in me, whatever everybody else thought."

I looked at her altered eyes, and bit my lip, and said nothing. I had never doubted that Lina was a witch. I remembered how her powers had flung me against the kitchen wall when we were squabbling as children, and I wondered if she had truly forgotten, or whether in her desire to be like the rest of us she dismissed it as a childish fancy.

She caught my glance, and smiled ruefully. "I knew when I cursed Masko," she said. "Remember that? I never meant anything more in my life. I was sure that he would drop dead at my feet! But it had not the smallest effect. I might as well have saved my breath."

Again, I wondered and doubted. I had yet to see Masko, but I had already heard from my mother that he was much plagued with boils and that he suffered from sleeplessness and continual nightmares, which accounted for at least some of his drinking. Whatever Lina believed, my first thought had been that this was a result of her curse: he had certainly not been so afflicted when he arrived in Elbasa. But perhaps she had since lost her powers; and as she was soon to be married, and clearly wished to live a quiet and respectable life, I judged it best to stay silent. Then, because she perceived my scepticism, Lina told me that she had, two years before, consulted the Wizard Ezra, because he could tell her once and for all whether she possessed the powers of a witch.

"He said I am no witch," she said. "If you don't believe me, surely you would believe him?"

I stared at her, amazed. Lina had changed indeed if she would go to the Wizard Ezra, her bitterest enemy, on such a humbling mission; and yet, alone and untutored in the ways of magic as she was, where else could she have sought advice?

"Did he welcome you in, then?" I asked. "He would not have permitted you over his threshold when I was last here."

"Yes, he let me in. A lot has changed since last you were here. It was strange, Anna, and I was very much afraid: I have always been frightened of him, even if I wouldn't admit it. For a time I thought wizardry was all fraud, but it isn't."

I thought of wizards I had seen at the palace, who could make a man choke although they stood ten paces away and as easily release him, or call lightning down into their fingers and use it to blast a beast or a building, or set a voice in your mind that no one else could hear until it drove you mad. Once in the court, I saw a man punished for some transgression against the Lore. The king's wizard turned him into mist before our eyes. One moment he was a man, standing naked in chains before the king; the next the chains clattered empty to the floor and he was an insubstantial column of smoke that yet held the shape of a man. I remember that he screamed with horror, but his voice was a whisper of a scream, barely audible even in the complete silence of the court. The wizard smiled and passed his hand through his victim's body, and then leant forward and blew softly, so that the screaming head wisped into nothing, leaving his trunk wavering in the air until it, too, dissipated into nothing.

No, it was not fraud. Even the king feared the wizards. I wondered that Lina could have thought so, and then I remembered that she had been forbidden to attend when Ezra burned poor Oti to ashes. That memory still made me shudder, but perhaps Lina had not believed us. It would have been like her, to think herself superior.

I listened to her with a lively curiosity. Lina said that Ezra's mute had opened the door before she knocked, and Ezra was inside, sitting cross-legged on a woven rug laid on the dirt floor. He looked up, unsurprised, and beckoned her indoors, indicating that she should sit on the rug with him. Between them was a large, shallow clay bowl, filled to the brim with water.

"He didn't look in the least surprised to see me," she said. "And I saw why. He blew on the water, and it showed the path outside the house, and I saw on the water's surface an image of myself walking up the path to his door, as I had just done. I was as afraid then as I've ever been in my life. 'I know why you're here,' he said. 'And you have done right. Now, at last, I can help you.' I asked him how, and he told me to close my eyes. He placed his fingers on my eyelids, and they felt cold, Anna, as cold as ice, and it hurt me, but I dared not move a muscle.

"I don't know how to tell you what happened next: a whirlwind was inside me, inside my head, and all of me hurt and shuddered as if I were in the most dreadful fever. But it passed quickly, and then he lifted his fingers off my eyelids and said I could open my eyes. 'You were right to think you are not a witch,' he said then. 'I have touched you to find the magic within you, and there is none. We were mistaken. I will tell the clan Usofertera and the king. You are free to go.' I stood up, but I could barely stand, and he instructed his mute to guide me home; and when I came back here, I slept for more than a day. But oh, I was so relieved, Anna. I am no different from anyone else. It was always a mistake."

I listened to this story with more than a modicum of mistrust; and later questions, which I put in such a way that she would not guess my motive in asking them, confirmed that her ill-health and delicacy had begun around the time she had visited the Wizard Ezra. Yet I couldn't question her desire to be freed of witchery, which all her life had been nothing but a curse and a burden.

XXII

Soon most of my time was spent in preparations for Lina's wedding, which was set for Midsummer Day. Masko offered neither money nor produce towards the festivities. He was annoyed by the betrothal, since it was not of his making: Lina had consistently refused the suitors he had sent her way. He boasted loudly in the local tavern that she should not have a penny towards her wedding, and sealed his oath by spitting on the floor. Lina was therefore coming dishonoured and without family to her bridal day. Feeling in the village ran high against Masko, since our pride was hurt: he made us all look mean-handed.

The task of organizing the wedding fell, by default, on my shoulders. At first I was distracted with worry; it seemed that I had no choice but to make a shameful begging mission to the Alcahil family, to ask for their assistance in ensuring that the wedding guests were fed and watered. Most unexpectedly, and almost at the last minute, the king came to Lina's rescue. I had written to the palace on Lina's behalf, asking for the royal blessing upon the coming nuptials. Strictly speaking, as Tibor Alcahil was a commoner and Lina a woman who would not carry on the Kadar name, royal consent was not necessary. No one else had thought to write, but given Lina's uncertain position, I thought it an important courtesy.

The king's response was swift: a messenger arrived post-haste, bringing with him a gift of fifty gold coins, and a document which awarded Lina the manse and its adjoining fields as a wedding present and dowry. Masko did not take the news well. In his fury, he went so far as to accuse the royal messenger of fraud, which sparked much indignation; but once it was proved that the royal seal was no forgery, he dared make no further protest. The gesture was a clear indication from the king that his favour was wearing thin.

I was much more glad of this news than Lina, who received it with indifference, and not only because I was saved an embarrassing interview with the Alcahil family. The king's ill-favour is a heavy cross to bear in the Plateau. As much as a rebuke to Masko, the dowry showed the world that the king had changed his attitude towards the Kadars; it was an act of patronage beyond duty, and thus doubly welcome.

I still ponder whether it was Lord Kadar's marriage to Lina's mother that had sparked such royal enmity, or whether that decision deepened some earlier quarrel. I suppose I will never know. It seemed to me, as I reflected on Lina's change of fortune, that this recent leniency must be connected to the Wizard Ezra's pronouncement that she was not, after all, a witch, and I marvelled at the irony that it was he, of all people, who had been the means of her deliverance.

I was very curious to see her betrothed, but it was some time before I had the chance. He made a formal visit to the manse with his mother, ostensibly to talk over details of the dowry, but in reality to admire his beloved, and so I was introduced.

I was agreeably surprised: I found before me a slender, rather shy youth, who regarded himself as peculiarly blessed in having won Lina's hand. He had the dark hair and handsome features of the north, and like his mother he had large, sensitive hazel eyes, which reflected his feelings as clearly as if he said them out loud. I liked Mrs Alcahil from the first: she was a sensible farmwife, who concealed the qualms she clearly felt about her son's marriage under a quiet, practical demeanour.

The Alcahil family had no noble relations, but in Lina's case this was an advantage rather than otherwise, since her witch blood made connection with the royal house impossible. They were, nevertheless, well respected: as the principal land-owners of a neighbouring village that had been untouched by the vendetta between Elbasa and Skip, they boasted a comfort-able wealth. Lina's marriage was, as the village women agreed, a much more advantageous match than might have been imagined for a girl so smirched by the scandal of her birth, and with not a coin to her name. However, it was also acknowledged that Lina was the most beautiful girl that had ever been seen in Elbasa, and this, in Tibor Alcahil's eyes, outweighed all her disadvantages. Perhaps Lina's charms also weighed with her future father-in-law, for he made no objection to the match. It seemed that Lina's new-found meekness had erased all the scan-dal associated with her being a witch. No one spoke of it now.

I was relieved to see that Tibor treated Lina with gentleness and respect, and that she genuinely liked him. It was not a pas-sionate match, but I thought that no bad thing. Most marriages in the north between families of wealth or influence are made as alliances between clans, or for one or the other's advantage, and the feelings of the bride or groom are seldom consulted. Even so, they probably have as much of a chance of happiness together as any others, and perhaps more than those who marry in the heat of ardour. I realize this might shock you, since in the south it is fashionable to think differently about love, but in my view, you much underrate friendship as a basis for a marriage. Any woman who finds friendship in a man can think herself fortunate. It runs as deep as passion – nay, deeper – and is a solid ground on which to build a life.

It seemed to me that Lina now had a chance at a life of material and spiritual comfort that had seemed impossible only a few years before and, more importantly, she was no longer an outcast. I rejoiced at this change, and turned with a ready will to the arrangements for the wedding.

XXIII

Lina and Tibor's nuptials were the noteworthy event of that summer, and the celebrations – with the help of the king's largesse – continued for three days, in an orgy of feasting, drinking, dancing and speeches. The villagers, who felt a collective anxiety that Elbasa be shown to its best advantage, were satisfied our honour was upheld, and the Alcahil guests were as generous in their courtesies as the House of Kadar was in its hospitality. Catering for nigh on a hundred people over three days, not to mention dealing with the musicians, dance masters, ecclesiasts, wizards and nobles (in particular, ensuring that each was seated in proper precedence so none was offended) was no easy task. To my relief, Masko decided to leave Elbasa for the ceremony, so that I did not have to deal with the problem of where to seat *him*. I felt all the pride of a difficult task mastered against the odds, and after the final guest departed, I toasted myself with the last of the ratafia cordial and tumbled into bed as exhausted as I have ever been in my life.

My deepest worry had been Lina herself. She was puzzlingly

uninterested in the wedding preparations. If I came to her with one problem or another, she would languidly wave a hand and tell me to deal with it as I thought fit. As the day drew closer, she became withdrawn and ill-tempered: she was clearly anxious, but would not confide in me the source of her unease. She even spoke about cancelling the wedding, and with such low spirits that even my best efforts could not cheer her. She grew thin, which she could ill afford, and bore the signs of sleepless nights. I took advantage of our intimacy to enquire what bothered her, in the hope that confession would ease her spirit, but she refused to answer. At the time I thought it the natural fears of a maiden facing the mystery of marriage. Later, after I read her diary, I understood that she was panicking that her wedding night would reveal that she was not a woman of virtue, as her virginity had been robbed by Masko. Naturally, she could tell no one of her fears; and in the event, fortunately, they proved groundless.

I wondered more than once how she would bear up through the three days of festivities. She did so, and better than I had expected; but she displayed a curious passivity that eschewed both enthusiasm and reluctance. She dutifully appeared at the head of the table with her groom when she was required, and led the dances as tradition demanded; but when her presence wasn't necessary she retired and let others celebrate. Indeed, she looked so delicate in her beauty that no one questioned her need for rest. Tibor treated her as if she were made of glass: when she was at the feasts he fussed about her with a dazed expression, as if he couldn't quite believe this fey, fragile creature was now his own.

The young couple set up their household at the manse, and they settled down to their married life. Lina continued to live as quietly as before, as Tibor had no taste for socializing, and in any case the winter drew in and confined us indoors.

Tibor's days were nevertheless busy: he set his farmer's eye on the management of the property, with plans to redress Masko's neglect, and sketched out the improvements he would make when spring returned. Lina spent her days much as she had before she was married: she concerned herself with household tasks in the morning, and in the afternoon diverted herself by reading or drawing or occasionally playing music. Marriage suited her: the heightened sensitivity that had so troubled me subsided, as a novel content began to suffuse her being. She put on flesh and a healthy colour crept under the pallor of her skin. I looked over these changes with a proprietorial eye, as fussy as a hen with an ailing chick.

Just after the snow melted, Lina came to me and asked how one could tell if one was with child. I think it must have been a rather comic conversation: Lina was embarrassed, which at first inhibited my comprehension of her question, as it was couched in such vague terms. And once I understood what she was asking, I found myself as embarrassed as she was: I was still a maiden, and lacked the frank ease with which married women spoke of these things with each other. I looked dubiously at her slim body, and asked her why she thought she might be pregnant.

"Oh … things," she said. "The blood hasn't come this month. And I am feeling a bit odd. But I'm frightened, Anna, because what will I do with a baby? I don't want to have one."

"You're a wife now, and you're supposed to have babies," I said. Even as I spoke, I felt how useless I was as a confidante.

"Not everybody has babies. I would much rather not. What if I should die, just now, when everything is going right at last?" I knew she was thinking of her mother, who had died in child-bed. "I wish I knew some way to stop it. But if there is already a child inside me, it is too late anyhow. What shall I do?"

"You should tell your husband," I said. "That's what you should do."

"But I don't want to have a baby," she said again, as if the act of telling Tibor would make real what was now mere fantasy.

"Mr Tibor will be pleased," I said. "And perhaps that will make you feel better about it."

She shook her head, and sat for a time in silence, plunged into unutterable gloom. In the end, I advised her to consult the doctor; and after another week of whispered conversations she did so, calling him in on a pretext so that Tibor would not suspect the real reason for his visit. He confirmed that she was, indeed, with child.

XXIV

As spring quickened around us, swelling the river with snowmelt and pushing forth the buds from winter trees, so life quickened in the womb of my mistress. Of course her husband must be told, and he was, as I had predicted, delighted at the thought that he would soon be a father. Lina said no more to me about her reluctance to have a child, and I thought that, as I had hoped, her husband's joy had tempered her fears. She looked to be in the best of health; she suffered from no sickness, and an increase of appetite meant that a bloom attended her beauty that I had not seen in her face since her father had died.

It wasn't until summer, when her pregnancy was well forward, that I found that I was mistaken. I was in the kitchen preparing the midday meal when Tibor entered the back door and sat down at the table. He often did this, as he enjoyed chatting idly with me and the other servants as he cleaned his gun or polished his boots, both tasks he preferred to do himself. Today he had neither boots nor rifle; he just sat down at the table and stared gloomily at its surface, digging into the wood with a knife.

I was busy dressing a hare to make a stew, and so didn't especially note this until I had finished my task; by then he had made a considerable scar in the table.

"For shame, sir!" I cried. "Look what you are doing!"

Startled out of his abstraction, he looked up and laughed mirthlessly. "I'm sorry, Annie," he said (for so he called me). "I didn't mean to make a great hole." He rubbed his hands uselessly over the cut. "I was thinking about something else..." Here he frowned, and almost began to stab the wood again, then saw what he was doing and pushed the knife away. He sighed heavily, and stretched back in his chair, rubbing his hair with his hands until it stood upright.

I saw something was amiss, but didn't like to enquire, and a silence of some minutes fell between us. I felt him watching me as I chopped the vegetables and herbs, and sensed that he might speak at any moment, but it wasn't until I was putting the pot in the oven that he brought himself to say anything.

"Annie," he said. "Do you think it strange that a woman might not like to be a mother?"

My back was turned on him, which gave me time to overcome the immediate sense of misgiving his question set in me.

"It is natural, I think, for a woman to be afraid of childbed," I said. I straightened my back and smoothed down my apron, but I didn't meet his eyes; I was slightly embarrassed, as indeed was he. Although I liked Tibor, and he had been free and friendly with me since first he came to the manse, our conversations had not been intimate. "Do you speak of the mistress?"

Here I did look at him, and his youth then struck me forcibly: he looked then like a lost little boy. He was, in truth, only just a man, as I was only just a woman.

"Aye," he said. "I hope you don't mind me talking of her. But you have known her a long time, and sometimes I don't understand her."

"What don't you understand?"

"She says she would tear the baby from her womb, if she could. She says she doesn't want to be a mother, and she hates feeling the child inside her. It's unnatural for a woman to say such things. Surely every woman is placed on earth to bear children, and should be glad when she fulfils her fate?"

I was shocked by what he reported of Lina's feelings, but attempted to conceal what I felt. I said that perhaps, in her fear, she might speak out and say what she did not mean, and reminded him that her mother had died while giving birth to her, which might make any woman think badly of motherhood.

He nodded dubiously, and sat for a minute more in silence, his brow furrowed. He left the kitchen without speaking further, and I tidied up my peelings, feeling sorry that Lina had so far forgot herself as to communicate feelings to her husband that should have been far better kept to herself. Her anxieties were, as I had told Tibor, not unnatural: what troubled me was the violence, even the hatred, in her expression of them.

After that I kept a warier watch on my mistress, and began to see glimmers of her old, wilful self. She uttered no sentiments to me like those she had shared with her husband, no doubt because she knew I would have disapproved; but as her pregnancy became visible, I saw with concern that her spirits seemed more and more oppressed. Tibor continued in his tender care for her, but the same behaviour that through the winter had given her peace and ease, now seemed to irritate her. She would push away his caresses with impatience, even in front of me, and rejected any care for her bodily safety with a recklessness I had not seen since I had returned from the palace. In particular, she continued to ride horseback, despite the warnings of the doctor, and at last in direct defiance of her husband's orders, until she became too big to clamber into the saddle. It was the sheerest luck that she suffered no mishap.

If her desires were opposed, she didn't lose her temper, as when she was a child; rather she would withdraw to her room, refusing meals and speaking to no one, until she had her own way. I thought this silence was worse than her childhood rages, and it was certainly as difficult to deal with. Although Tibor did not confide in me further, it took no great perception to see that sometimes he was close to despair; he continued to love his wife, and would not abuse her, and yet he had not the force of character to make her yield to his will. Sometimes, indeed, her behaviour towards him was close to contempt.

I still believe that their marriage would likely have survived what were, after all, no more than the early misunderstandings of two very young people but newly wed. In between Lina's bouts of fractiousness, she could be as gentle and sweet as ever; and she joked with me sometimes that she was fortunate to have married such an even-tempered man who would bear with her bad moods. As her belly swelled still bigger and she felt the child kicking in her womb, her resentment seemed to subside; she even began to speak of looking forward to holding her baby. If I could have been sure that her labour would be untroubled, I would have breathed a sigh of relief. It seemed to me then that the worst was passing, and that if only the birth went safely, all would be well. Lina continued in such good health that I suppressed my anxieties on that score, although I lit a candle every Sabbath day, offering prayers to the Virgin, for her sake.

The leaves of the poplars and lindens turned copper and gold and swirled over the sere grasses in gusty winds, early harbingers of the coming winter storms. The shepherds and goatherds came back with their flocks from their summer sojourns in the mountain pastures, the harvests were almost gathered in, and we all began to turn our minds to the long cold. Lina was in her seventh month of pregnancy, and more content than she had been in months. And then Damek returned to Elbasa.

XXV

I was one of the first to know of his arrival. It happened that late one autumn afternoon I left the house to visit my mother. The air was chill with the threat of rain, and I was hurrying so I could get to the Red House before it was dark. Suddenly, a tall man stepped in front of me and called my name. It was as if he had materialized out of thin air, and I started greatly, almost frightened out of my wits.

"Don't you recognize me, Anna?" he said. "Surely I am not so changed?"

He was indeed changed. Since I had last seen Damek, his face had lost the softness of boyhood and he had grown several inches, but in that moment I recognized his voice. I realized then that he must have been standing beneath the pines that shelter the manse from the wind; they cast a deep shadow and had totally concealed him.

"Damek!" I cried. "My dear life, I thought you a demon come to claim my soul! But we all thought you were dead!" I was still not sure that he was not a ghostly apparition, and

I clutched at my cross and made a silent prayer.

"This is a sorry beginning," he said. "I thought at least I would find a friend in you. No, I am not dead, nor am I a demon. I am as alive as you. Look!" And he took my hand in his and pressed it, and my heart stopped pounding so hard, since his skin was as alive and warm as mine. "Come. Are you walking to the village? I will walk with you."

"But where have you been? Why did you not write?"

"That is not your business. I have been away, and I have come back. And I am told that Lina is married. I could not believe my ears! Say it is not so, Anna!"

I confirmed, with some asperity, that Lina was married, and added that she had every right to choose whom she desired.

"I'm also told she is with child," he said, after a short silence. His voice betrayed no particular emotion. I glanced sideways, but it was too dark to see the expression on his face.

"Aye, she is," I said. "We who love her should all be joyful at the news."

Damek was silent at this, but the air between us seemed to thicken, as if some baleful energy were gathering about him. I hesitated, and said, as gently as I could, "She is happy, Damek, and she was very unhappy for many years."

At this he turned to face me, and I saw his eyes gleaming in the shadows of his face. He spoke quietly, but with a force in his expression that made my heart quail.

"I tell you, Anna, no one has been more unhappy than I have been, these past years. Not one day, not one single day, has passed without my thinking of her. Everything I have done, all my struggle, has been for her. And at last I return, and find that I was forgotten the moment I was out of sight."

The injustice of his complaint smote me. "She never forgot you," I said with heat. "And since not one word has been heard from you for years, everybody thought you were killed. What was she to do? You should pity her for what she has suffered."

"What *she* has suffered?" he said, with sudden passion. "Ah, and what of me?" Then he seemed to master himself, and he laughed bitterly. "So I learn a hard lesson!" he said. "It's well said that women are fickle. But I would never have believed it of Lina."

The pain with which he spoke silenced my reproaches; for all the impropriety of what he said, I pitied him. We walked on in silence for some time, each wrapped in our own thoughts. I was chiefly worrying about Lina. I couldn't see how Damek's return would in any way be good for her and, in her delicate state, I feared that he might do her active harm.

As we neared the village, he roused himself. "Anna, I want you to do me a favour," he said.

I cautiously answered that, as long as what he asked was not wrong, I was happy to do him any favour.

"I want you to tell her I am back," he said. "She'll hear soon enough of my return; I'm staying with that pig Masko for the present, and word gets about this village like a plague. But I will come to see her, and soon. I'd rather you told her of my arrival than anyone else. Prepare her for my visit. Tell her that my love is unchanged."

His voice caught, and he paused, which permitted me to interject that I would say no such thing.

"At least give her this letter." He pressed a letter into my hand, but I refused, despite his protestations, to take it. In the end, I said I would inform Lina of his return. I agreed with Damek that it were best to come from me, and I was secretly glad that he had thought to tell me first, rather than bursting in unannounced. I greatly feared how the news would affect Lina's health, and I impressed on him that she had been seriously ill in his absence.

"You will find her changed," I said. "I was shocked by it,

180

when I came back from the palace. She is delicate, and the least thing can throw her. I insist you be gentle, if you care for her at all."

"If I care for her at all! How can you say such a thing?" But at last, on my insistence, he promised to be discreet, and to do nothing that would cause her distress; and with that, my anxieties had to be content.

XXVI

I was to spend the night at the Red House, where Damek too had accommodation. This strange circumstance of an apparent intimacy with his sworn enemy excited my curiosity painfully, but Damek was in no mood to satisfy it. We parted at the gate, he to wander up to the front door and rap on it with a black cane, and me to wind my way through the back garden to the kitchen. My mother was waiting impatiently for me, and ran to the door as I opened it, wringing her hands, to break to me the news that I already knew.

Damek had, she said, arrived only that afternoon, in a richly ornamented closed carriage drawn by a handsome pair of black horses, which caused much speculation as it swept through the village towards the Red House. When Damek had emerged from behind its curtains, and had been greeted at the door by Masko himself, who was clearly expecting him, the amazement of the household was enough for a month of exclamations. The maids were struck by Damek's handsomeness – for he had grown into a striking-looking man – and the manservants by his obvious wealth; and the superior airs of his groom had chastened everyone at the servants' table.

The history of Damek's attempt to stab Masko was, of course, widely known, and so the apparent friendship between them was another mystery. According to Damek's groom, they had met only last month in the city, at one of the gambling houses, and there had reforged their acquaintanceship; and it seemed that Damek had been invited back to Elbasa to stay for the winter, all their differences now quite dissolved. I listened to this story with disbelief: I couldn't credit that Damek had forgiven Masko anything. But I kept my own counsel, and told no one of my private conversation with him.

None of us ever found out where Damek had been, or how he had made his fortune. He never dropped one syllable of information. All that was certain was that he had disappeared for five years, and that he had returned rich. A favourite rumour was that he had made a pact with the Devil, and that his soul was written in blood in the Book of Hell; another was that he had been a privateer in the wars now ongoing in the west, of which we heard distant and belated news; yet another, that he had formed a criminal gang in the city; still another, that he had made his fortune by gambling, and had ruined a great southern family through his audacity and skill at cards. I fancied the privateer theory myself; his swarthy complexion hinted at a life spent much in the weather, and occasionally he would let fall a phrase that bespoke a nautical knowledge. It explained a sudden access of wealth without the taint of criminality, although his steady silence on the question suggested that his story was less than respectable.

Of course, the mystery added to his attraction: and at first, he took great care to be attractive. When I had the chance to observe Damek in company, I saw that he charmed everybody, man or woman; yet a gleam in his eye very like contempt signalled to me that he was playing a role, and that his intentions were far from benign. Also, he never bothered to pretend anything to me. I had known him too long and too well to fall victim to his allure.

I saw no more of him that first evening, in any case. Masko had invited his cronies in for a game of cards, and the festivities were loud and long; the other servants were kept busy ferrying refreshments to the dining room. My mother and I spent our evening quietly in the kitchen, and I retired early since I had to leave before dawn the next day, if I was to attend to my duties at the manse. Despite my early bed, I scarce slept with worry. What was I to tell Lina? How was I to begin to talk about a man whose name had not been mentioned once between us in all the months since I had returned home? And – a worse thought – what if word reached her before I did?

In the event, we were isolated enough at the manse that I was first with the news. I waited until after I had served breakfast and Tibor had gone outside to see to some job, and then sought out Lina. I was so uncomfortable that I fiddled about until she lost patience with me, and at last I blurted it out, without adornment or preparation.

"Damek?" said she, turning white. "You say Damek has come home?"

"I fear so," I said.

"And you've seen him yourself? He is not dead?"

I assured her that I had seen him with my own eyes, and that he was as alive as we were. She turned her face away from me, and I stood uncertainly before her, wondering whether to leave or whether she might need some attention. But in a moment she leapt up and grasped my hands, her eyes shining.

"Anna, I know you would not mislead me. But I can scarce believe my ears! This is beyond everything marvellous! It is a miracle! Damek is come home. Oh, I don't believe it. He is not dead! And he is well? He is happy to be home? Why did he not come to me first? Why is he not here? I must tell Tibor at once! Such news!" Here she began to run from the room, only to halt in the doorway. "Did he say when he would visit me? Did he say when we would see each other again?"

"Soon, he said. Soon. He'll be here soon." I studied with misgiving the hectic flush that had now risen in her cheeks. "Miss Lina, you must not get too excited. Time enough to tell Mr Tibor at luncheon, without running out to look for him. Come, let me pour you some wine."

"Wine? What need have I of wine?" She rushed back into the room and embraced me. "But you're right, I can tell Tibor later. He shall be so happy! I think I have never been happier in my whole life! And what if Damek called and I were out? I couldn't bear it. And he is at the Red House? I should ride there this instant! I can't bear to wait even one minute. I should ride there now. Order my horse, Anna."

She was breathing fast in her excitement, and her eyes were dangerously bright. I begged her to sit down, and poured her a wine which I made her drink. She agreed at last to sit, but it made her no less restless: the words tumbled out of her, expressing her astonishment, her joy, her impatience to see Damek. It took me the best part of an hour to calm her. She only agreed to rest because she became exhausted, and even then she insisted on lying on a sofa in the front room, where she started at every noise in an anguish of expectation. I had not seen her in such elevated delight since my return, and I wished I could feel an equal joy. But I could not like the fever that attended it, nor how her pulse fluttered in her neck, as if a wounded butterfly were trapped there.

XXVII

When Tibor returned to the house, Lina flew to greet him, breathless with her news. At first he responded to his wife's joy – he knew that Damek was a childhood friend long missed – but as the excess of her emotions overflowed, sweeping aside any other topic of conversation, his enthusiasm began to dim. His wife scarce noticed his indifference: she had enough animation for both of them. They were a pretty picture at the luncheon table, one bubbling over with excited chatter, the other becoming more and more morose. At last Tibor's unresponsiveness penetrated even Lina's overwrought perceptions, and she upbraided him for not sharing her delight. He answered curtly, she took further umbrage, and at last he threw his plate across the room and stalked out of the house.

As I cleaned up the mess, I reflected gloomily that this was not a propitious beginning. Irli, who since my arrival had been assigned general duties, helped me to clean the walls, her eyes lively with curiosity, but I refused to tell her what had happened.

Lina, of course, failed to see any good reason for Tibor's actions, and abused him as capricious, ungenerous and cruel.

"I would say he is jealous," I said shortly. I felt little patience with her, as I was behind with my work after the scenes of that morning. "And perhaps that is understandable."

"That is just foolish! He is my husband, and he should love where I do. It is small and mean of him to try to spoil my joy."

I sighed, and took my bucket and cloth into the kitchen without further argument. I knew it was useless. It wasn't long, however, before she followed me. She had already forgotten her quarrel with her husband.

"Anna, do you think Damek will call this afternoon? I think I should visit the Red House, don't you? If he doesn't come here, I mean. Why has he not called already?"

I told her that if she called alone on Damek, it would cause a scandal. I also reminded her that Masko lived in the Red House, and that she would be forced to speak to him as well. Only the latter point gave her pause: she still hated Masko with a passion, and avoided him entirely. I repeated my assurance that Damek would call soon, and bent to my work. After a while, she drifted back to the front room, to hover impatiently by the window. For myself, although I dreaded Damek's visit, I also prayed that he would make it that day. If he did not, I couldn't imagine what state Lina would be in by nightfall; but given his anger about her marriage, it was not impossible he would delay his call. In my anxiety, I found myself wishing that Damek had indeed been killed. Lina's irrationality that morning dismayed me more than I could admit even to myself; when I thought of what Damek had said to me the night before, and of the lunchtime quarrel, I found myself filled with dread. So I didn't think at all: I attended to my tasks, and then I tried to make my mistress take a rest, which she resisted with increasing irritation.

She became more tense with every minute. By mid-afternoon,

Lina was in such a state that the smallest sound – a dog's bark, the shutting of a door – would make her start horribly. I was not much better myself, as her restlessness and anxiety had infected me. Also, I was listening for Tibor as well as for Damek; most of all, I dreaded that they might turn up together, an unlucky chance which would do no good for any of us. When I heard hoofbeats nearing the house, I think I jumped as high as Lina. She rushed to the window, and confirmed it was Damek; she lost her colour, and for a moment I thought she might faint. I rushed to her, holding her arm so she would not fall, and she turned on me eyes piteous with fright.

"I can't see him," she said. "Anna, tell him to go away!"

In my exasperation at her perversity, I could have shaken her. There came a rap on the door, and I swear she went even paler.

"It's him!" she whispered. "Oh, he is here! What shall I do?"

I bit back the sharp words that came to my tongue, and instead asked her to sit down so I could answer the door.

She shook her head, so I made no move; when he knocked again she gripped my hand so tight I felt the bones crunching. She was trembling all over. By now I was half distracted.

"Please sit down, Mistress Lina, I fear that you will fall," I said, and to my relief she did. "I shall tell him you're unwell and can't see him."

"No! No, show him in!"

I looked at her dubiously, but a little colour had returned to her face, and so, lamenting the ill-luck of the day, I left her and hurried to the door.

"Greetings, Anna," said the author of all this discomfort. "How is your mistress?"

After dealing with my mistress all day, his calmness was a severe provocation. "She is not well, Damek," I answered. "Not well at all. I almost curse your coming home, after the morning I've had."

He said nothing in reply, but entered the hallway and gave me his coat. Lina heard his entrance, and called out to me. He stood very still for a moment, his face expressionless, and then turned towards her voice.

"Well then, she is in there?" Without further reference to me, he walked towards the sitting room. I followed, wringing my hands; I felt I ought to stop him, but knew not how.

Lina was seated where I had left her, staring towards the doorway. When she saw Damek, her eyes widened, and her lips parted as if she would speak, but no words came. Damek halted at the threshold of the room, and for a long moment they neither of them moved nor spoke. I think he had not really believed until that moment that she was with child: he stared fixedly, almost with horror, at her swollen belly.

Lina couldn't but notice this, and she blushed and put her hand protectively on her stomach. Then she seemed to recollect herself, and she stood up, stretching out her hand in formal greeting.

"Damek!" she said. "How – how wonderful to see you!"

He strode towards her and, taking her hand, stared earnestly into her face. "And to see you!" he answered.

A long silence fell between them, but their eyes remained fixed on each other's face. He kept hold of her hand, and she did not withdraw it. At this point I thought it politic to interrupt, since they seemed to have forgotten altogether that I was present.

"Mistress, shall I bring some refreshments?"

Lina turned to me, startled. Her face was radiant, as if a light inside her had been suddenly unveiled. "Refreshments? What for?"

"For you and your guest," I said.

"I think we will not need anything, Anna," said Damek, with a meaning glance. "Except, perhaps, a little privacy."

"I think the master would not like his wife to be alone with a man..."

Here Damek interrupted with a profanity and, to my distress, Lina laughed. Now that Damek at last was present, her anxiety seemed to have vanished all at once; indeed, the mocking glance she turned on me was more like the old Lina than I had seen since my return to Elbasa. She pressed Damek's hand to her breast as she spoke.

"Anna, don't be so ridiculous. Damek is no stranger. He might as well be my brother, and there is nothing improper about my being alone with him. Now, you go and do all those jobs you were complaining about before. We have much to say to each other, and we don't need a chaperone."

"Off you go, Anna," prompted Damek. "You heard your mistress."

I had no choice but to leave the room, if with many misgivings at their folly, and Damek took care to shut the door behind me.

XXVIII

The pair remained closeted up for nigh on three hours, and all that time I was in a constant alarm, lest Tibor would come home and discover them. I confess too that I was burning with curiosity: I wondered what they were saying, and what they were doing. Lina did little to satisfy this last vulgar hunger; after Damek had left she simply said that they had been exchanging news, while giving me an ironic look that showed she was perfectly aware of my interest. If Damek revealed to Lina where he had been for the past few years, she never told me.

It seemed that Tibor was still angry with Lina, as he stayed out late that evening and didn't come home until well after dark. Damek left carrying a lamp, for Masko was hosting a card party that he wished to attend. And so the meeting I dreaded between Damek and Tibor did not take place, on that day at least. Their encounter was inevitable, but as St Matthew says, "Sufficient unto the day is the evils thereof", and I was happy to take his advice.

After Damek's departure Lina was strangely calm; she seemed abstracted, but biddably ate her dinner and took the foul-tasting tonic the doctor had prescribed her without protest. She retained that radiance, which gave an almost supernatural edge to her beauty; as she sat in her sitting room, a book open but unread on her lap, her chin resting on her hand, she seemed like a figure carved of alabaster, lit from within by a soft but intense flame. When Tibor at last returned, she greeted him languidly, but without hostility; and he, no doubt expecting a petulant greeting, was unexpectedly disarmed. He ordered a late supper and they sat quietly, speaking together without rancour. Anyone who saw them would not have imagined them to be anything but the most content of couples.

As I prepared myself for bed that night, I wondered if my fears were unfounded. Whenever I thought of Damek's conversation with me, I felt uneasy: I did not see that he would accept Lina's marriage with any complacency, and I knew he had little respect for the conventions that ruled the rest of us. On the other hand, I thought, if he truly loved Lina, he would see what was in her best interests, and put his own desires aside. After all, he had even forgiven Masko, with whom he seemed now on the most cordial terms, and that suggested anything was possible.

That I entertained such thoughts shows the foolishness of wishful thinking. Damek could be patient, more patient than anyone I knew, in pursuit of his desires, putting aside immediate gratification if he needed to; but the thought of relinquishing the passions that drove him never entered his head. I think he was the most single-minded person I ever met. And I had forgotten Lina's wilfulness; I had thought it controlled, when in fact it had simply had no object. Well, I was soon to be disabused of my hopeful fancies.

Damek arrived at the manse after breakfast the following

day, not long after Tibor had left the house; he was then supervising the building of some outsheds which, now the burden of the harvest was over, he hoped to have finished by winter. I was surprised to see Damek, but Lina was not; they spent an hour or so talking alone in her bedchamber, which scandalized me, and then Lina called for her cloak and boots and they left the house, striking out towards the river, even though the air smelt of rain. When Tibor returned for his lunch, they were still out. He asked me where Lina was, and I answered with some confusion that she was out walking with Mr Damek. He flushed with humiliation and anger, but said nothing in response, and finished his meal in silence. I felt sorry for him, and annoyed with the pair whose thoughtlessness was causing such pain.

An hour after lunch, the wind changed and it began to rain. At first it was a light shower, and I thought it would pass, but after a half-hour I saw the bad weather had set in. I watched the veils of rain sweeping over the back courtyard as I worked in the kitchen, and fretted uselessly over Lina's foolishness. She was exposing herself to a bad chill, at best; at worst, in her delicate condition, she was putting not only her life, but her baby's, at risk. A little later, Tibor came in the back door, nodded towards me as he divested himself of his wet outer clothes, and went upstairs.

It seemed an age before I saw any sign of the others, although I think it was perhaps less than an hour, and only my impatience made it feel so long. There was no let-up in the weather, and I began to be seriously worried, and wondered whether I ought to send out someone to look for them. At last I heard a disturbance at the front of the house, and hurried out, wiping my hands, to see Damek and Lina, soaked through from head to foot, standing in a puddle of water in the hallway. Lina was clutching Damek's arm and laughing; she was panting, as if she had been running – and in her condition!

"Oh Anna!" she cried when she saw me. "Look at us! The rain came down in buckets when we were by the river. We tried to shelter under the old willow, but it did not pass, and we were going to be as wet there as here, and so we have run home!"

I hurried forward, scolding the both of them. Lina's eyes glittered with a dangerous elation, and when I touched her arms as I stripped off her dripping cloak, the skin felt as cold as a corpse. Aside from a flush high on her cheeks, she was deathly pale, and her teeth were chattering.

"Mr Damek, you ought to be ashamed! You must have known better than to make her run in the rain!" I said. "She is not a child any more, and she has been sick! If she falls ill and dies, then it's your fault and no one else's."

I saw his eyes flicker towards her face when I said that, and knew that what I said had hit home.

"Don't be silly, Anna," cried Lina. "I have never felt so well! How could I die now? Now, when I am more happy than I have ever been?"

Her voice rang out over the hallway, and carried to the ears of Tibor, whom I now saw was standing at the head of the stairs, just about to come down. He halted like a man who had been slapped, and then all but ran down the stairs. Ignoring Damek, he grabbed his wife's arm and swung her round to face him, demanding to know where she had been.

Lina tore her arm out of his grasp. "How dare you touch me like that!" she said, with all the hauteur of a princess of the blood. Tibor had not seen this mood before, and he stepped back a pace, surprised and abashed, as she continued, "You do not speak to me like that. You should address me with respect."

"I'm your husband," said Tibor, who was shaking with anger. "Or have you forgotten that?"

"Of course I haven't," she said.

"You're acting like a whore," he said. "Not like any wife of mine."

Lina gasped, and Damek's face went black with anger. I think he would have punched Tibor there and then if I had not shouted at both the men to come to their senses, and to stop behaving like children. I was out of patience with all of them, but mostly I was concerned that Lina change into some dry clothes; and so, before anything else could be said, I hurried her upstairs to her bedchamber, stripped off her damp dress, and scrubbed her hard with a towel before a warm fire until the colour came back into her face. As I did so, the baby began to kick, and she put her hand on her belly to feel its limbs writhing beneath her skin.

"You'll kill your baby, and yourself, running about wild like that!" I told her. "And you'll drive Mr Tibor to distraction."

"Nay, Anna!" She had been standing passively as a small child, not helping me one bit, except to lift an arm or a leg if I asked. "The baby is joyful too! It loves freedom as much as I do!"

I shook my head at her wilfulness. When she was warmly dressed, I studied her closely. She didn't appear to be feverish, but I didn't trust the sparkle in her eyes. I told her to stay in front of the fire until her hair was dry, and went downstairs to check what had happened to the men. Neither was anywhere to be found. I asked Irli if she had heard anything, and she said that they had both left the house directly after I had taken Mistress Lina upstairs. I wondered briefly if they had gone out to knife each other, but at the time I was too cross to care. Good riddance, I thought, to the both of them.

XXIX

To my astonishment and relief, Lina didn't catch cold. It was as if something had ignited inside her which drove off the possibility of chills. The fragility that so concerned me was still evident, and she was more easily exhausted than I liked, but at the same time she was consumed with a fierce energy that made her seem stronger than she was. She breakfasted sulkily with Tibor the following day, refusing to speak to him at all until he humbly apologized for his insult the previous day; but once he did apologize, she smiled radiantly and reached across the table to stroke his face.

"Why are you so cross about Damek?" she said. "He is as close to me as my brother, and I'm so happy that he has come home! Don't spoil it, Tibor, please. Surely you should love him as I do? I have told Damek that he has to love you, and it's not fair if it is only one way…"

Looking cornered, Tibor swallowed and spread out his hands in mute protest. I watched as Lina exploited all her charm, hoping in my heart that he would find it in himself to resist, but he could not; a mouse might as well hope to bewitch a snake. As soon as Tibor had been persuaded that his happiness depended upon Lina's (which, to a certain extent, it did) all was lost. She sat back in her chair and, smiling brilliantly at him, told him that Damek would call in later that morning.

"He said nothing of any visit to me," said the poor man, in some confusion. I suspected that the previous night he might have told Damek never to darken his doorstep again.

"But he did say so to me," said Lina. "And he never breaks his promises. You mustn't go out this morning; you must stay and say you're sorry and make friends, or I shall be so unhappy!"

I did almost laugh when I showed Damek into the sitting room later that morning, for him to discover Lina and his rival bent over the table, talking over plans for the farm. His brows contracted in a frown, and he looked sharply at me, as if this situation were my fault. I would not be bullied by him, and met his gaze sternly. For his part, Tibor looked uncertain and embarrassed. Lina, unconcerned by the moods of both men, smiled in welcome and invited Damek to sit down, and so the three of them sat together making stilted conversation for the next quarter-hour, until Tibor suddenly remembered an urgent task and hurried out of the house. I saw his face as he left, and felt sorry for him; he wore the expression of a trapped animal.

After that, Damek came every day, always leaving at nightfall to play cards with Masko. Sometimes he and Lina went for long walks, although they heeded my pleas about not repeating their adventure in the rain: Damek had at least that much concern for Lina's health. A strained civility continued between Damek and Tibor, but Damek's constant presence at the manse began to spark gossip in the village, and I judged it only a matter of time before it reached Tibor's ears. In short, although there was a truce, I thought that it would not continue long.

I told my fears to Lina, but she laughed at them; she said she didn't care about the opinions of some silly old women and that everyone concerned was perfectly happy, an observation which did not coincide with mine.

I began also to hear rumours that Masko was losing hugely to Damek; it was said that Damek had a luck with cards that was diabolical. It was about then, I think, that the stories began about his pact with Satan: he had sold his soul, it was said, in return for the riches of the world. After that, his friendship with Masko was no mystery to me: I didn't doubt that part of his revenge was to strip from Masko the riches that should have been Lina's. I'm sure Lina knew of his plan, as she never protested his leaving the house, and always waved him off with a smile which held an edge of malice. Unlike Damek, who was as rapacious for wealth as any man I've met, Lina never cared a straw for money, but she was as invested in revenge against Masko as he was.

Things continued in this unease for a fortnight or so. Then it happened that Old Kiron, the latest victim in the vendetta, was shot on the hill above the manse. Tibor found his corpse early in the morning, and brought the body home on his horse. It was laid out in the front parlour, where no one sat except on formal occasions, until the family could come to claim it. Kiron's son arrived a little later, pale and speechless, with his wailing sisters. They were escorted by Damek, who had met them on the pathway. Lina refused to leave her room until the body was gone, as it is bad luck for a pregnant woman to see a corpse, and so Damek stood with the family as they wept over the dead man, and helped Tibor to place him on a rough bier, to be pulled home by the family donkey.

Tibor accompanied the family to their house, as a mark of respect, and Damek and I watched them down the path.

"Damn it, I'd forgotten this barbarity," said Damek. "Is this still the same vendetta as when I left? You'd think enough blood had been spilt. And enough coffers filled. It's enough to make you spit!"

I mumbled something indifferent in return; in truth, I was a little shocked at his voicing so directly sentiments which, even if I felt them, I did not dare to say.

"I hate this place, Anna," he said then. "I hate it with all my heart. Look at it! Those mountains there, ugly as sin, and these barren plains, and a climate straight from hell – I swear that if it were not for Lina, I would never have returned. I don't understand what binds her here. Why will she not leave?"

"But Damek, she is married!" I said, shocked again. "And she is with child! You cannot ask—"

"Marriage to that witless fool is no marriage. Even Lina knows that. So what if she is with child? I'll wait, Anna, until she's had the babe, but after that she has to reckon with her desires. I'll not be cheated by anyone, not even Lina."

I couldn't think of any response, though felt that his statements required strong objection; and before I could shape a rebuke, Damek had leapt up the stairs to tell Lina that the corpse was gone, and that she could now come out of her chamber.

X X X

After that conversation, I watched Lina and Damek with a lively suspicion. While Damek's intentions were clear, Lina's were much less so: she pursued her intimacy with Damek as if it were the most natural thing in the world, and expressed surprise or anger at any objection to it. Tibor made no comment one way or the other, but only the most determinedly self-deceiving could take his silence for consent. As the days went past, he left earlier and earlier in the morning, and came home later and later at night. Often when he came home he stank of raki, and Lina – who was keen enough for his company when Damek was not there – was often resentful of his absence, accusing him of neglecting her and mocking him for drinking with the peasants. This would generally escalate into a row, which sometimes continued into the following day. Usually they had made it up by breakfast time, and everyone was briefly content, only for the same pattern to repeat a day or so later.

What I could not work out was Lina and Damek's present

relationship. While Damek had made his position unambiguous to me, I could not be sure that he had been as frank with Lina. When she said Damek was just like her brother, and scoffed at the vulgar minds of anyone who claimed otherwise, I swung between thinking her disingenuous, and believing that she said only what she thought was the truth. For all the conflict between Tibor and Lina caused by Damek's presence, they seemed – when they were not bickering – as fond of each other as ever; Damek's scornful estimation of his rival never seemed to infect Lina's view of him. In short, I was as painfully puzzled as I was full of trepidation. I began to look forward impatiently to the birth of the babe, as Damek's absence would then be enforced, and there would be some peace.

The impending birth clearly was weighing on Damek's mind as well. In her final month, Lina's body swelled: before then, her belly had been obvious, but had never impeded her movement. I think that Damek had, after his first shock, been able to wipe it from his mind. Now she complained of a sore back, and had trouble rising unassisted from a chair, and was afflicted by severe tiredness, which caused me much concern. It seemed to me that all the extra exertion that she had indulged since Damek's return was now presenting its payment, and with interest. On the positive side, her exhaustion forced Damek to leave the manse earlier than he planned several days in a row.

"When will she have this brat?" he asked me one afternoon as I showed him out, after Lina had dismissed him with especial petulance. "The Devil curse it! The damned thing is a parasite, and it steals her away from me."

I bit my tongue, knowing it was of no use to rebuke him for his sentiments, and said she had a few weeks to go yet, all being well. He snorted, and took his cane and strode home in a black mood.

I returned to Lina's room, where she was lying on a chaise

longue, her eyes shut. When she heard me come in, she sat up and asked me to pour her some water. The energy that had driven her over the past weeks was now all dissipated, and without its force, she seemed more frail than ever.

"They tire me so, Anna," she said. I nodded, but said nothing. "Always pulling me, this way and that! If I as much as mention one, the other throws a tantrum! It drives me to distraction!"

I ventured that this was the logical result of the situation she had herself set up, and that perhaps it would help if she saw a little less of Damek.

She struggled to sit up straighter and then, to my surprise, seemed to think this over. "See less of Damek! Oh, Anna, how little you understand! What good would that do? He would be fretting and pawing the ground, like a bull in a stall, and I would feel it in my bones. I cannot be calm if he is so vexed. Why can't he be satisfied, like he should be? We are together, after all, and that is everything that either of us have ever wanted."

I regarded her with some astonishment, and after a short time of reflection, decided that now might be as good a time as any for some plain speaking.

"Mistress Lina, you must know that Damek wants you for his own. He will not be content until you belong only to him. He will never regard Mr Tibor as anything else but a rival; and in my view, Mr Tibor has some grounds for feeling alarmed and jealous."

"Tibor is being a child," said Lina. "I don't listen when Damek speaks like that. It is foolish and selfish of him, Anna, do you not think?"

"It is," I said. "But it is also foolish and selfish to so disrespect your own husband. It is no wonder that Damek thinks as he does, with the encouragement you offer him."

Lina was roused out of her lethargy. "Encouragement? Disrespect? Anna, why do you speak to me as if you were one of those village crones nodding over their knitting? You're as bad as Tibor and Damek. Both of them are like the farmers that squabble over three almond trees, or a goat. I am not a creature to be owned, or a piece of land to be arbitrated by some upland wizard. I don't expect Tibor to understand anything else... I love him dearly, but he is what he is. Damek knows better! If he has my heart, what need has he of anything else?"

"Your heart belongs to your husband alone," said I. "Did you not listen to the vows you made in church?"

"And all this time I thought you had some understanding... Listen to me: Damek and I are but one being – to speak of our separation is nonsense! I might as well tear the heart from my own breast! I cannot wake, but he is in my thoughts; I cannot sleep, but he is in my dreams. When I thought he was dead, I died: now he is back, I can taste my life at last."

"If you feel such things, you should never have married Mr Tibor," I said hotly. "That is more selfish than anything I have ever heard in my life!"

"Selfish? But I love Tibor." She stared at me as if it were astonishing that I should think otherwise. "He is tender, and he cares for me so. He is like a calm lake. Remember in the south, when we used to go swimming in that shady pool near the house, with the willows dropping their branches in the water? It was always so peaceful, with the doves cooing in the trees, and the ducks splashing, and everything so green and soft and the water so clear. Tibor is like that. And maybe when winter comes, the pool will freeze and the trees will be all naked, and I'll not love him any more; but now he is a haven, Anna, and I need him. But Damek – Damek is like the rock beneath my feet – I cannot escape him, any more than I could escape my own soul. I know he is selfish and I know he has no God. He doesn't care for me, any more than the mountain cares for the storm, or the storm for the mountain. He is myself, Anna, the bedrock of myself – there is no tenderness there, no pleasure, only necessity…"

"Then you did wrong when you married Mr Tibor. And you do wrong by your child, and by everyone around you."

Tears shone in her eyes, and for a long moment she was silent. "If I am wrong," she said at last in a low voice, "there is no right, either."

"You *are* wrong, Lina, and you know you are wrong," I repeated, feeling no pity for her tears. "You have made your bed, and now you must lie in it."

"Don't you preach to me, Anna." Her eyes flashed with a sudden, deadly rage. "Or patronize me with your threadbare proverbs."

I protested that I was speaking sense, and that she knew it; but this only made her so angry that she was white to her lips. She screamed at me to get out of her sight. I saw there was no benefit in staying, and cursing my over-eagerness, which had done more harm than good, I turned tail and fled.

XXXI

The following morning as I rose from my bed, I looked out of my bedchamber window and saw the Wizard Ezra in the distance, walking towards the manse. I stared for a long time, to be certain, but his figure and gait, and the stunted body of his mute, were unmistakable. It was still first light: the sun was a pale phantom through the early haze, and mist lay in shallow pools on the ground, so that the wizard was wading knee-deep through a white sea. It looked uncanny, as if he were floating footless above the ground.

I dressed hurriedly and ran downstairs, my heart beating fast. I had not spoken to the wizard since my return; in truth, I had barely seen him, aside from glimpses on my errands to the village. As I hovered in the kitchen stoking up the fire in the stove and waiting nervously for his knock on the door, it occurred to me that perhaps he was on some mission to the hills behind the manse, perhaps to investigate the death-site of Old Kiron. This seemed more likely than his coming all the way on purpose to the manse, since vendetta is true wizard-business.

I told myself to calm down, and began to fill the kettle for a tisane to steady my nerves. But no: there was a loud rap on the front door that made me jump so badly I spilt the kettle. I threw down a cloth over the water on the floor and hurried to answer his summons.

He stood on the front doorstep clutching his blackthorn staff, looking no different than he had looked when I had first gazed on him, when we returned to Elbasa all those years ago. I had the strangest sensation, as if history were being repeated: it was as if I were my mother, standing terrified to her marrow by the front door of her home, gathering herself to defy him. I wiped my hands on my apron to gain time, greeted him respectfully and asked him his business.

"I will not come in," he said, as if I had invited him. "I want to speak to you."

"To me, sir?" Involuntarily I met his eye, but he was not looking at me unkindly.

"I hear you are a woman of virtue and good sense," he said.

If I had not been so frightened, I might have laughed at this description. Not that it was entirely inaccurate, mind, but it was so much a man's description of a woman he barely recognizes in the street. Instead, I mumbled something inane, feeling my face burn, and waited. He surely had not stridden all this way to tell me that.

"I also know that you have known Mistress Alcahil since you were milk sisters." For a brief moment I wondered why he spoke so of Tibor's mother, before I recollected that it was Lina's married name.

"Aye, sir, we have known each other since we were children," I said cautiously.

"She will trust you as a messenger, then. I wish you to tell her something. Tell her the peace she sought from me will be withdrawn, if she continues as she does."

I understood him, but I asked him what he meant all the same, ready to bristle in defence of Lina's honour.

"You tell her. I'll not tell her myself. She barely deserves the warning." He turned his face and spat, and then, without any further speech, gathered his cloak around him and walked back the way he had come.

I watched him and his mute until they vanished in the mist and trees, and then I realized that my knees were trembling. I went back to the kitchen and mopped up the water I had spilt. Then I made myself a tisane, and sat coddling it until the rest of the household began to descend and I had to attend to the business of the day. I wondered about Ezra's claim that Lina had no witch powers, and if it were really true, and what the wizard wanted from her, and whether Ezra had also spoken to Damek. The wizard's words seemed to be freighted with an ominous weight beyond their immediate meaning, a shadow which I sensed, even if I failed to understand it. I felt that I stood shelterless and alone on a wide plain, watching as giant thunderheads rolled down from the Black Mountains, their looming darkness veined with giant lightnings, to bring a storm beyond my imagining.

I told Lina of the wizard's visit after breakfast, just after Tibor had left the house. Things were still a little stiff between us after the scene of the night before, and after that and my fright that morning I was in no mood to humour her. A momentary scepticism crossed her face, making me suspect that she thought I was making it up to drive home my argument, but she thought better of voicing her disbelief. Instead, she thanked me with a distant politeness and walked heavily across the room to rest on her divan, drawing her shawl around her shoulders, and picked up a book. I saw that she was only pretending to read, and took it as a sign that she was more disturbed by what I had told her than she allowed. But it could have been simply tiredness and distraction: her face looked puffy and pale, and her movements were sluggish and awkward.

Once I had seen she was comfortable, I went back to my chores. From her appearance that morning I thought, without knowing anything about it, that she must be very close to her time, and wondered whether we ought to call the midwife up from the village, and whether to alert the doctor as well. As so often with Lina, I found myself torn between concern and irritation, fear and love. I was, after all, no older than she was, but lately my responsibilities felt as heavy as those of a mother for a small child. It might have been bearable if I had the experience and wisdom of another twenty years under my apron, but I didn't. I knew myself unequal to the task in every way.

Damek arrived as usual after breakfast. Before showing him to Lina's room, I took him aside and told him of Ezra's visit that morning. He looked at me narrowly, and then showed me a silver ring, very like the one you wear, which he bore on his middle finger.

"I care that for a petty village wizard," he said. "Don't think I didn't come here without protection."

"It's not you I fear for," I answered tartly. "It's Lina. She's close to her time, and what with you and Mr Tibor squabbling over her like a couple of dogs she's beside herself. The last thing she needs is the Wizard Ezra sticking his nose in."

This made him thoughtful. He studied my face, as if he were seeing me for the first time.

"A dog? Is that what you think I am, Anna?"

"You might as well be," I said. "It's not like you ever think about the position Lina is in. She's a married woman, and you are bringing scandal to her name when even she says she's finally happy! If you knew what was good for her, you'd just go back where you came from."

"I'll wager if you said as much to her, she would tell you to go to hell," he said.

I couldn't deny that, after what Lina had said the night before, but I had had enough. "All the more reason for you to leave, if she can't make the right decision on her own. You might take some pity on her, Damek."

Damek laughed. "Pity Lina? You should know her better than that! You should tell her to pity *me*."

If I had dared, I would have slapped him for his selfishness. He must have seen it in my face, for his expression changed, and he took my arm, holding it so tightly that I cried out.

"If you knew what I suffer! I live under a curse, and she is the witch that has cursed me – my heart is in a red-hot vice, and every day it is jabbed and rent by demons, every day the wounds bite deeper. And they will not heal – no, not as long as I draw breath. I know that you despise me because I do not believe in God, Anna. But believe me, I know that hell exists. I know, because I live there. And Lina knows it, she knows it in her bones. She sent me there when she betrayed her own heart. No, I won't pity her. She doesn't deserve it."

All this was said in a low, urgent voice, with such rapidity and passion that I scarce understood what he said. I pulled my arm away, and at last he let me go, and I stepped back from him.

He laughed again at my white face, although there was no mirth in it. "I know you think me a monster. Maybe you always have," he said. "But I tell you, I am not so inhuman. I wish I were. With all my soul, I wish I were." And he brushed past me and went upstairs, where Lina awaited him in her bedchamber.

XXXII

I returned to the kitchen and tried to gather my scattered wits
together by chopping vegetables and gutting a chicken and
other sundry tasks, but my hands were shaking so badly I
could hardly hold a knife. Finally I poured myself a nip of plum
brandy, and that helped with the shakiness. I had poked up the
fire and set myself to stuffing the chicken when a scream echoed
through the house. I knew at once it was Lina, even before she
called my name. Then I heard Damek running down the stairs
and shouting for me.

I have no recollection of moving from the kitchen to Lina's
room: it just seemed that suddenly I was there. Lina was curled
up on the bed, panting like a wild animal at bay; her hair was
disordered and her bodice was ripped. I thought that they must
have been making love and my heart plummeted at the scandal
that must surely follow, but I didn't have time to reflect on this.
Lina groaned and lifted herself on her hands and knees, and
I saw that blood was seeping through her skirts.

I turned, wondering whether to run for the doctor or to stay with her, and saw that Damek was just behind me. He looked panic-stricken, the only time I have ever seen the like in him: all the blood had drained from his face, and his knuckles were white. In my distraction, I grabbed his shoulders and shook him.

"What have you done? What have you done to her?"

He didn't deign to answer me; instead he asked in a shaken voice what was wrong with her.

"It's her time, you fool!" I was beyond caring what I said. I didn't know anything about childbirth, but it looked wrong to me, and I didn't know what to do. "What do you think is wrong?"

Lina heard me, and twisted on the bed, calling my name, so that I ran to her and took her hand. She grasped it blindly; her eyelids were shut tight, although tears escaped from beneath them and coursed down her face. "Anna, it hurts! It hurts so! Ah, I've never felt anything like that..." Her heart was pounding so fast I could see its pulse in her breast, and her hand was cold as ice and slick with sweat. I murmured some words of comfort and wiped her forehead, and she grimaced, and then sighed.

"It's gone now," she said. She opened her eyes and looked up at me, and I cried out and almost snatched back my hand in my shock: for the eyes that blazed out of her white face were the violet eyes of a witch. In that moment I thought that she wasn't Lina at all, but some hellish apparition sent to torment me. Then I recollected myself, and tried to think what to do.

"You're bleeding, Lina," I said, as firmly as I was able. "I am going to get the doctor."

She gripped my hand even tighter. "Don't leave me!" she said. "Don't go away!"

I stroked her hair and told her to be calm, but she wouldn't let go of my hand until I promised that I would stay with her.

I gave my promise, and then persuaded her that I had to organize some help.

Damek was standing still as stone by the door, watching us. I went up and talked to him in an undertone, because I did not wish Lina to overhear.

"God rot that man in hell," he said. "He's killing her with his brat."

"No, it's you killing her," I said. "I told you she was near her time! I told you to take care! What have you done? Her eyes…"

"She is Lina again, Anna." He grasped my shoulders and stared intently into my face. "She is herself at last. Do you not see? I could burst with the joy of it! But now…"

"But now she will die, if you do not help. Get out of here – this is no place for you. If you value Lina's life, you will ride for the doctor this instant."

He stared at me a moment longer, then thrust me aside and rushed to Lina's bedside, and snatched her violently in his arms, kissing her wildly all over her face. She wound her arms around his neck, and I saw that she was sobbing.

"It has stopped hurting, my dear," she said. "My dear, dear Damek."

Damek did not answer; he gathered her greedily in his arms, and I saw that his shoulders were shaking. Then he mastered himself, and raised himself up so he could see her face.

"By God, Lina, how could you do this to us?" he said in a low voice. "How could you? What if you die? What would I do without you?"

Lina laughed shakily, but it was a poor imitation of her usual mockery. "Dying? Who's talking about dying? I told you I would live for ever… I'm only having a baby. Life, not death…"

"But you're so pale," he whispered. "And why all this blood, Lina?"

"There's always blood," she said.

"So much?" he said, lifting her sodden gown. "Surely not so much?" He kissed the cloth, and then kissed her face, so that her mouth and cheeks were smudged with the bloody prints of his lips.

I stood irresolute – I felt I should stop them, but didn't know how. Then there was a timid knock on the door. It was Irli, who was come to see what the fuss was about. She craned her neck to see into the room, but I would not let her look, and shut the door behind me; then I hurriedly gave her instructions, telling her to send for the doctor and the midwife, as quickly as she was able, if she valued the life of her mistress.

I paused on the landing a short time, to catch my breath, and then returned to the chamber. Lina and Damek were no longer embracing; Lina lay on her side, her hair scattered over her pillow. Her belly seemed enormous, almost as if it were not part of her body. Damek was seated next to her on the bed, stroking her face. Even as I neared them, Lina's belly rippled, like the earth during a quake, and she groaned, and her back arched violently, so that Damek was pushed off the bed. I saw that she was still clutching his hand, but by then she was in such a state she knew not what she was doing.

I wrenched their hands apart, and she clutched at mine instead, as if she were drowning. Damek stood like a man stunned, until I screamed at him that he had done harm enough, and that he should go. I was then too busy dealing with Lina to see what he did: but when I next was able to look, he was gone.

XXXIII

That was the first childbed I attended. If it had been my last, I would say that childbirth was the worst thing that could ever happen to a woman, and bless my childless state. Since then I have seen many women in travail and learned that, while birth is a great labour for every woman and never without pain, for most it is not the ordeal that it was for Lina. I have sometimes marvelled at the strength of women, whom men so lightly claim are the weaker sex: they only can claim so, who have never seen how stoically women endure the toil and anguish of their bodies, and with what gladness, when at last they hold in their arms the child they have given to the world.

Lina was not one of those women. It seemed that her body was at war with itself: she thrashed about in her pain and panic, crying out that she had never suffered such agony, that she was being ripped by a monster, that claws and teeth were rending her in two. I thought she must be right, for I could not stop the blood: I had soaked a blanket before the doctor arrived, and he arrived quickly, for by luck he was in the village. He assessed her condition swiftly, and immediately administered a tincture, which took the edge off her suffering and stemmed the bleeding. I lost all sense of time, and in truth do not remember the following hours very well; I just did what I was told, and prayed. The child was born just as the sun set. As the doctor took the tiny scrap in his arms and cut the cord, a ray of the westering sun shafted through the window and gilded the scene with an unreal brilliance. I remember being surprised: if anyone had asked me, I would have said it was deepest night. All that day seemed like a dark tunnel.

In no time at all, or so it seemed, the midwife had bathed the baby, and Lina was washed, and the bloodied sheets tidied away for the laundry and new linen brought, so the room no longer looked like a slaughterhouse. Lina, dressed in a fresh nightgown, lay back on her pillow. She was white to her lips, like a corpse: the only part of her that seemed alive was her eyes, and they blazed unnaturally, like giant violet orbs in her haggard face.

I showed her the swaddled babe, and she smiled faintly. "Is that mine?" she whispered.

"It's a little girl," I said.

"Lina," she said. "A little Lina. Damek should be pleased."

Even in my exhaustion, I was disturbed by what she said. "What has this to do with Mr Damek?" I said. "He's not the babe's father. I should think that Mr Tibor is the one most nearly concerned."

"Tibor?" she said, as if she didn't know whom I meant. She shut her eyes, and turned her face to the wall. When I offered her the child and told her it needed to be fed, she shook her head irritably and waved me away.

The doctor drew me aside, and said that we would need a wet nurse, since he didn't believe that my mistress would be able to suckle the babe. I stared at him, and asked him straight out if

Lina was going to die. Now she had had the baby, I had thought in my innocence that the worst was over. He looked grave, and told me that she was weakened by the birth and had lost a lot of blood, and that much depended on the next few days.

Tibor was finally permitted to see his wife and child. I was conscience-stricken that he was the last person I had thought of alerting, but perhaps it had been as well that no one had remembered to get him until Damek was out of the house. He timidly entered the chamber, as if he were not sure that he was allowed in. His face was almost as white as Lina's; I realized that he must have been sitting downstairs for hours, listening to Lina's screams and the bustle of people running up and down with bowls of water and cloths. God alone knows what he had been imagining.

I handed him his daughter, and he looked down at her wrinkled, red face with speechless astonishment, as if a babe were the last thing he expected. He smiled crookedly, and then looked anxiously towards his wife.

"Mistress Lina is very tired," I said.

"It was a hard birth," said the doctor, who was wiping his hands. "I suggest you ask in the village for a wet nurse."

Tibor nodded – though I'm not sure he had heard a word either of us said – and went to Lina. She stirred when he perched on the edge of her bed, and rolled over towards him. He flinched when he saw how her eyes had changed, but he said nothing. Lina frowned slightly, as if attempting to remember who he was, and then she smiled.

"It's all over," she said. "I'm so glad."

She spoke so softly that he had to lean close to hear what she said.

"Do you like her?" asked Lina.

"Like her?" Tibor glanced down at the baby. "I – I suppose I do."

"She's a little Lina. Look, she has black hair, like me."

Tibor nodded, and sat in silence until Lina whispered that she wished to sleep. He kissed her brow and, handing the baby back to me, left the room. I didn't know what to say to him: he looked dazed and ill. I think that somehow he already knew that, whatever happened, he had lost Lina.

Twilight had now turned to deep night. Lina fell fast asleep, which eased my heart, and I told Irli to watch her while I had something to eat in the kitchen. I was ravenously hungry, although I was so tired that it was an effort to chew. The doctor had a private conference with Tibor, and then told me that he knew of a village woman who had lately given birth and who could be trusted to wet-nurse the baby. He took me down to the village in his carriage with the child. Once the proper arrangements had been made, we went to the Red House and asked my mother to come up to the manse to help with Lina's care. Masko gave her reluctant permission; the doctor made it difficult for him to refuse. While my mother was packing some essentials, the doctor offered to drive me home. I declined, despite my exhaustion; it was a clear, moonlit night, and I knew the path well. I was longing, with all my soul, for some time to myself, away from the endless demands of other people.

I don't think I had a single thought as I walked home. I could hear the night birds crying in the distance and the occasional hoot of an owl, and the plains lay serene and still under the moonlight. I soaked the silence in through my very pores, wondering at this peace without when there had been such terrible struggle within. When I reached the pines near the manse, Damek stepped out of their shadows and accosted me. I was too tired to be startled, but I was annoyed that my precious solitude was broken, and by Damek, of all people.

"Anna, tell me, is she dead?" he said.

"No, and no thanks to you," I said, snatching back my arm

from his grasp. "She had a little girl."

Damek said nothing, but I heard his breath catch in a sob. Then he stepped into the moonlight and I saw his expression. Despite myself, I was moved to pity. I am not sure that I have ever pitied another human being more than I did Damek in that moment. He had told me that morning – was it really that morning? – that he lived in hell. I had thought that he was exaggerating, out of self-pity; but when I saw his face that night, I believed him.

"Thank God," he said. "I have been standing here these hours, since I can't be with her, and when everything went quiet, and I saw you leaving in the carriage with the baby, I was sure she must have died. I could hear her screaming from here."

"It wasn't an easy time," I said, more gently. "She's sleeping now. Damek, you should go home and sleep yourself. You look wretched."

"Nay, what if she died in her sleep, and I was not here?"

"The doctor says she will be fine," I said.

He studied my face. "I know you're lying. What did the doctor really say?"

I hesitated, and then told him what the doctor had told me. He was silent, and then took my hand.

"You're a good friend," he said, with unexpected warmth. "You reassure me. God's truth, I have been standing here since sundown, sure that she was dead, and not daring to ask a soul if it were true. You don't know the demons in my head – I was making sure to hang myself. That would be a rebuke to her murderer, a corpse grinning from his tree, a gift from my broken life! But what would be the point? There would be no point even in that. Such blackness in my heart, Anna! Not one glimmer of light to guide me! Do you know, I prayed. I prayed to God. Me! And my prayer went out in the empty universe among all those dead stars, and nothing came back, nothing.

There was nothing there. I've always known it, but I've never felt before how big that nothing is, and I alone in the darkness with nothing to comfort me…"

I drew my hand away from his. His words frightened me, but his face frightened me more. His teeth flashed white in the moonlight as he spoke, and his eyes glared out of his harrowed face. I was sure that he was mad.

"She is sleeping now," I repeated. "And so should you."

He laughed shortly. "Sleep? If only I could. I cannot sleep. I thank you for caring, you alone of all creatures in this godforsaken world. No, I'll stay here and watch over her. You needn't fear, no one will see me. You go back to Lina."

I wished him God's blessing, though I'm sure I didn't know how it would do him any good, and walked slowly back to the house. When I reached the doorway, I looked back; if I searched, I could just see his dim figure standing straight against the trunk of the pine, holding his senseless vigil in the shadows.

XXXIV

Clouds gathered during the night, and by the time the sun rose it was raining steadily. Before I began my morning tasks I checked on Lina, who was still sleeping. My mother had sat with her, and she told me that Lina had suffered some bouts of restlessness. I noticed there was a flush in her cheeks, and returned to the kitchen feeling troubled. I looked outside to see if Damek was still there. He had gone, but underneath the tree where he had stood the grass was flattened and churned from his pacing about. It looked as if cattle had stood there.

The events of the previous day had left me with a heavy weariness in my body and a melancholy in my soul. The rain, which continued all day, grey and unremitting, matched my mood: I felt dull and slow, and wished I was back at the palace, where my duties were clear and undemanding. I missed Zef, and out of sheer loneliness considered writing him a letter. I thought better of it; he had not spoken, and it would have been a forward act. I was not Lina, after all.

With all this in my mind, I was glad of my mother's quiet,

practical help. It lifted a weight of responsibility off my shoulders. After a brief visit to his wife, Tibor spent most of the day in the kitchen cleaning his guns. He got under our feet, but no one complained, since he so clearly needed the comfort of womanly bustle. Not one of us said a word about the sudden transformation in Lina's eyes, but we all knew about it, in the way that knowledge is mysteriously transmitted without any visible conversation. I was sure that it must have reached the village by now, and lived in hourly dread of a visit from the Wizard Ezra.

The doctor arrived as he had promised, checked her temperature and looked serious. By then Lina was awake, demanding something to drink and refusing, against all our persuasion, to eat any food, although she had scarcely eaten the day before. We forbore to press her when she became agitated. She complained that her breasts were hot and painful. It was because she was not suckling the baby, and the doctor showed me how to ease her, which was difficult because she flinched at my touch. It was the worst of several unpleasant tasks I now had beyond my usual duties. The doctor said her milk should dry in a few days, and that we had to watch for milk fever.

Lina slept most of the day, and deigned to take some broth for supper. That evening she seemed merely tired, and her skin remained cool, but there were moments of irrationality that disturbed me. I had to change her sheets again, and sat her carefully on the chair by the bed. She made no protest, and at first seemed quite herself, but then she turned to me, her eyes shining.

"Anna, how beautiful the birds are!"

I answered that birds were indeed beautiful, and she smiled radiantly and reached out her arms. "See, they even perch on my hand! Oh, I never knew their feathers were so bright!"

I stared at her in alarm, but in the next moment her eyes had clouded, and she seemed to have forgotten that she had seen any birds at all. She then asked irritably where Damek was. Grateful that Tibor wasn't present, I said that Damek could not come, and tears welled in her eyes, just as they do in a small child denied a sweetmeat.

"He cannot come! But he promised! And he never breaks his promises. He said he'd come to me even if I were at the ends of the earth, even to hell!"

I made soothing noises, and helped her back into her bed, saying that I was sure that Damek would be along presently. She lay down obediently, and then started up, as if an ugly thought had struck her.

"Anna, is it that I am in heaven and the angels won't let him in? He is too black-hearted, Anna; he has too many mortal sins on his head and he says that God has cursed him – but surely he could come to get me, if I was in heaven? I'm sure it's a mistake—"

I told her that she was not in heaven, but in her own bedroom at the manse, and at last that seemed to calm her, and after a while she was speaking rationally again. I gave her a dose of laudanum, and at last she drifted off to sleep. I watched her eyelashes fluttering on her cheek and reflected that not once during the whole day had she asked after her baby, or Tibor.

The following day she seemed much improved, and even managed to be pleasant to her husband. We judged that she was well enough for my mother to return to the Red House; but by evening her wits began to splinter again. For a short time she thought she was in her childhood bedroom at the Red House, waiting for Damek to come and play with her. I dealt with each incident as it arose, pressing down my fears. I suspect that I was protected by my ignorance; Lina's mental disorder was not so different, after all, from some of her ravings when she was a young girl, and I treated her as I had then. Their difference in quality I put aside from my thoughts, just as I did not permit myself to believe that her illness might be fatal.

You can guess the pattern of the following days. Our hopes rose and fell with each hour: at one moment, she would seem to be recovering, while the next would bring a relapse. Most of the care fell on me, in part from my own inclination, but also because I was the best at soothing her deliriums. We set up a bed in her chamber so I could sleep there, in case of any emergency during the night hours. Although she asked for Damek every day, she didn't insist: it was enough for me to say that he would come later. I think even Lina knew she was too ill for such a meeting. Sometimes I glimpsed Damek outside when dark fell, keeping his vigil in the freezing wind, although no one else saw him. I didn't attempt to speak to him, and he never accosted me. I assumed he had his own means of obtaining news.

After that first day, Tibor scarcely spoke about his wife at all. He would make a brief formal visit in the morning, and then leave the house to supervise the building of his outsheds, which he was anxious to finish before the snows came. Certainly, Lina gave him little incentive to stay with her; once, she had made so plain her disappointment that he was not Damek that he turned pale with anger and stalked out of the bedchamber. It seemed to me that, aside from the disturbances caused by Damek, he was repulsed that she appeared to be, after all, the witch that rumour had claimed. I confess a small part of me despised him for it, and thought less meanly of Damek as a result.

Tibor's mother arrived two days after the birth, and my mother then returned to the Red House, although out of her anxiety for Lina she visited almost every day. The presence of Mistress Alcahil meant an extra pair of hands in the household and cheered Tibor, which gave me one less person to worry about. Understandably, she was curt with Lina, even though her actions were always benign; I think word had reached her of Lina's indiscretions. Once, after she heard Lina speaking of

Damek, she went so far as to observe to me that it would be no bad thing if Lina died. She crossed herself as she said it, and apologized after; but she was angry on behalf of her son, and I could not blame her for that. I was sorry, because I liked her, and knew her to be a generous soul. It was neither her fault nor Tibor's that they found themselves in their present distress.

A week passed in this way, seeing neither an improvement nor decline in Lina's health. Most of the time she was lucid, although she regarded her physical incapacity with impatience. Sometimes she would struggle out of bed, claiming she was well enough to go for a walk, only to find that she could barely reach the door without her knees buckling. Her lucidity was punctuated by periods of delirium during which she lost the sense of her surroundings, but these always passed swiftly. The doctor was concerned by her lack of improvement, but counselled patience. I think he was puzzled, as against all expectations she had developed no fever and he could find little explanation for her mental distraction.

As the days passed, my thoughts kept turning to the Wizard Ezra's words to me on the morning of the birth. I couldn't but wonder whether he had placed a curse on her. I said my thoughts to no one, but clearly my mother feared likewise. Without saying anything to me, she had placed fresh sprigs of rowan above all the windows as soon as she arrived in the house and sprinkled the thresholds with salt, and I saw her checking the cold iron that was routinely set over all Plateau doors, to ensure that a wizard could not enter without invitation. She also placed a silver teaspoon beneath Lina's pillow, as silver is commonly supposed to be a means of warding off the evil eye. From my time at the palace, I knew that silver is in fact useless unless smelted by a wizard; but I felt strangely moved when I saw this humble piece of cutlery and left it there, as a talisman to hope.

XXXV

O n Sunday, after a few days of clear skies, the snows
started. When I opened the shutters, the house filled
with a diffuse golden light, so dull it scarce illuminated
anything, and I saw heavy yellowish clouds lowering over the
plains. At noon the first flakes spiralled down, and by evening
a cover of snow had turned the world white. It was a light
fall, but the first of many to come. Mistress Alcahil had now
to decide whether to return home to her village, a distance of
some ten miles; if she did not leave soon, she would be forced to
stay with us for the winter. I didn't know whether I would pre-
fer her to leave or stay. On the one hand, my duties in caring for
Lina took up much of my time, and more help in the house was
very welcome; on the other, since her arrival I could not but
notice that Tibor's attitude to Lina had changed from confusion
to hostility, a transformation I attributed as much to his mother
as to Lina's own behaviour. Mistress Alcahil now regarded her
son's marriage as an unambiguous disaster.

I still, perhaps foolishly, held out hope for the couple. I was troubled that neither Lina nor Tibor had shown the smallest interest in their daughter. Lina's condition argued some excuse, but I urged Tibor to go down to the village to see Young Lina. I had made two visits myself and saw that she was a bonny babe, with a shock of black hair and dark, surprised eyes. I think I was the only one of that household to feel any motherly inclinations towards the poor little mite. I thought she was beautiful and hoped that the sight of his child would reignite Tibor's affection for his wife. Perhaps fearing the same thing, Mistress Alcahil always found an excuse not to go.

However, the coming snows forced the question. The following day dawned clear, and Mistress Alcahil decided to return home while she still could. I assessed the household staff, and decided that if we employed a cook there would be sufficient help for winter: all the autumn bottling and preserving and smoking had been completed, and our cellars and storehouses were well provisioned for the coming cold. Thus it was that Mistress Alcahil, myself and Tibor found ourselves in her carriage to the village, to forward our various ambitions: we would look in on the babe (whom I was careful always to refer to as Tibor's daughter); I would engage a cook, since I knew of a widow who would be glad of the work; and Mistress Alcahil would continue her journey home.

Even Tibor's mother was not proof against the charms of a newborn, and despite herself dandled the babe and exclaimed over its likeness to its father. As I said, she was a generous woman, if soured by circumstance. To my disappointment, however, Tibor remained stolidly indifferent: he regarded the child almost with dislike, and barely concealed his impatience to get away. We left the wet nurse's house and walked along a small alley back to the carriage, which was waiting in the square. By bad chance, as we exited the alley Damek and Tibor almost collided. Neither said a word to the other, merely stepping back in surprise, but the glance of hatred between the two fairly crackled the air. I don't think Mistress Alcahil even noticed the encounter: she didn't know Damek from Adam, and was in any case already hurrying towards her carriage, exclaiming against the cold. Once the farewells had been made, and the carriage rumbled off, Tibor sighed heavily.

"Well, Annie," he said to me, with unaccustomed directness, "my life is a bad joke. My mother says that if I had any honour, I should kill my wife." He stood in black abstraction, twisting his hands. "I am not sure I have that much honour," he said at last. "How could I kill Lina, even knowing what she is? I pray every morning that she will be dead, and save me the trouble. If she does not die, what then? Do I let that black-hearted thief take her away? Will that wizard curse me, for being married to a witch? What shall I do?"

I was so taken aback that at first I had no idea how to answer him; yet he demanded an answer, as he spoke from the fullness of his heart.

"Mr Tibor, I don't know how to advise you," I said. "But surely there has been enough death in this village already, without you adding to it."

"I know you are on Lina's side," he said. "But even you must acknowledge that she is a faithless whore. She has deceived me in every way, and I cannot forgive her. And yet I still think of her with a soft heart, and wish that she might love me. My mother says she has bewitched me."

He looked so forlorn that I forgot myself and took his hand. "God save you, sir," I said. "You have a good heart. Let's have no more talk of killing! I'm sure things will work out for the best."

"God moves in mysterious ways, eh, Annie?" He squinted up into the sky. "I wonder what I've done, that I should be so punished."

Again I had no answer, and there was a short silence. "Well, there's one comfort," he said, and laughed bleakly. "And I can find that at the bottom of a glass."

He went off towards the tavern, and I followed him with my eyes, feeling sorry for the whole mess. In truth, I could see no way out either, although I could not hope as he did for Lina's death. I began to wonder if it would not be best, after all, if Lina went away south with Damek. If Tibor would not kill her to save the honour of the Alcahils, his father might. And even should the Alcahils decide to spare her, there was the threat of the Wizard Ezra, whose ill intentions I didn't doubt and didn't dare to guess. Yet Lina could not travel south in her present condition, even if she agreed to leave (which was doubtful), and in any case soon the roads would be impassable. Winter was on our heels, and I did not know how we would survive it.

I made my errand, engaged the cook, and walked back to the manse with a heavy heart. When I arrived, I found that Lina was out of bed, and with Irli's help had bathed and dressed. She was seated on her window seat, looking down over the snow-clad path that led to the house. She looked up as I entered her room and smiled cheerfully.

"So, has that bitch gone at last?" she said.

I demurred at her expression, and she laughed at me. "You know whom I mean, Anna. Don't get all prim with me. I thought I should burst if that woman were here any longer. If looks could kill, I'd be dead a thousand times! I swear she has been all but pulling the iron down from the doors."

I didn't answer, except to confirm that Mistress Alcahil had, indeed, left for her own house. "On her way, she and Mr Tibor went to see your daughter," I said pointedly. After my gloomy thoughts that morning, her mood was grating. "I wonder that you haven't asked after the poor child."

"You'd tell me if she fared poorly," said Lina. "How strange, to think I am a mother now! If it weren't for how bad I've been feeling, I'd swear it was a dream."

"It's not a dream, Lina, and it were well you woke up," I said. "If you are feeling as well as you look today, you might give some thought to what you should do now. Your husband tells me he ought to kill you, since you and Damek have so smirched his family honour, and the Wizard Ezra is out for your blood, and Damek is stalking about Elbasa looking like murder. I swear, I do not know which way to turn."

"Kill me?" Lina stared at me with the purest astonishment. I could have slapped her. "How could Tibor think to kill me?"

"If you don't know, Mistress Lina, then I do not know how to tell you."

"You *are* in a bad mood, Anna!" She contemplated me for a moment, and then turned back to watching the pathway. "Are you jealous?"

"Jealous?" said I. "Jealous of what?"

"I suppose you wish you had men fighting over you?"

The pure cattiness of this remark took my breath away. I addressed the back of her head – I knew she could feel my gaze, although she would not turn to face me – and let her know that envy was the least of my complaints. I was weary to the bone. Not only did I have to attend to the running of the house; I had spent nearly all my waking hours nursing her, worried sick about her health, and on top of that had been dealing with Tibor and his mother and with Damek, not to mention the wizard. And this, I said, is the thanks I get for my trouble.

I would have gone on, but Lina silenced me. Her voice was cool: she seemed not in the least agitated, and there was something in her posture that made the hairs rise on the back of my neck.

"Listen to me, Anna," she said. "I am well. I am tired, but

I think I am recovering. The birth was nothing to what I have suffered before. I feel clearer in my head today than I have for, oh, for months and months. Maybe for years. Since that first moment the pains started, I understood that my body has always been at war with itself, that I have always been at war with *myself*; but at last this morning I am at peace. And all these days I have been thinking. I am not a fool, whatever you think; I know perfectly well that bitch wants me dead. Tibor couldn't kill me, even if that woman poisons him against me; but now she is gone, perhaps he will think of me gently again."

"He says that you have betrayed him in every way, and that he cannot forgive you!" I said.

She made an impatient gesture, continuing her contemplation of the view outside her window. "Oh, that," she said. "Of course he will forgive me."

I feared, rather than wished, that she was right: the complacency with which she spoke of her husband angered me. "But what about Damek?"

"Damek will learn to respect me," she said. "I have not had the strength to deal with him these past days, and I am glad he did not come, no matter how I long to see him! He speaks so easily of betrayal, he who abandoned me and left me alone for so many years! And he knows I am married in the sight of God; and he also knows that nothing I can do can betray the friendship between us."

I sighed for her folly and blindness. "I doubt that Damek will see it that way," I said.

"He will," she said. There was a steel in her voice I had not heard before, not even when she was a young girl. "He will learn that I am not a pile of gold, to be won and held and used – for that is how he thinks of me, Anna. He has always wanted to own things! No one loves money more than Damek – Tibor's just as bad, in his own way. I swear I am tired of men. Why can neither of them love me unless they can jingle me in their pockets? The way they both behave, they're no better than that pig Masko."

I listened to her in mounting astonishment. "That is the way men are," I stammered.

"That is the way men are!" As she mocked me, I pictured her scowl. "And I suppose that is the way women are, too, and they become petty tyrants in their turn, like Mistress Alcahil, bullying their husbands and sons! And so we all chip each other to pieces, until there is nothing left save a pathetic pile of rubble, and that's where the king puts his throne and lords it over all of us! Anna, sometimes you are so stupid. Who makes these laws that bend us out of our proper shapes? Why should men be like that? Why should I? I won't be beholden to those laws any more. I swear before God that from now on I will be myself, and myself only."

She turned to face me, and I felt an unreasoning fear thrill through me, like a flood of icy water through my veins. Her eyes were blazing, and I thought that her skin was shining, so that the shadows fled the room. She laughed when she saw the expression on my face.

"Yes, Anna, I *am* a witch. At last I understand! All these years I have been so afraid of myself, and why? Because everyone wants me to be afraid, because they cannot face the pettiness in their own hearts. They have crippled me, and forced me into a vice, so I am all bent over like a blasted thornbush. But there is nothing to be afraid of. I will stand up straight. I will fear no longer!"

I stared at her, not knowing what I thought, and yet despite my own fright, I cannot deny that part of me delighted to hear her say such things. It was like standing in a keen breeze that blew away cobwebs from all the secret corners of my mind. "But you can't stay on the Plateau then," I said at last. "What of the Wizard Ezra?"

"He cannot hurt me," she said. "He fears me. And rightly too. He always knew I was more powerful than him. That's why he took away my powers, and why he doesn't want me to have them back."

"I hope you're right," I said dubiously. I reflected that if she lived openly as a witch, it wouldn't be just Ezra out for her blood: the entire wizarding tribe would declare war on her, and the king himself would draw up her death warrant. "It would be well to be cautious, all the same."

"Of course I'm right." She laughed and the light inside her faded, so that she seemed shrunken, an ordinary woman sitting in the afternoon dimness. "And never fear, I will be cautious. I just wish I were not so tired. But that will pass, as everything does. And then I will live *my* life, as *I* choose."

In that moment, such was her certainty, I almost believed her.

XXXVI

While these events were occupying my mind to the exclusion of almost everything else, the villagers were turning their attention to the Red House. Perhaps they felt that the dramas at the manse were, at least temporarily, at a pause, and could be safely left to be gossiped about another day. Also, I was careful not to feed the rumours, protecting my mistress as best I could from calumny, and the main actors had no incentive to talk freely about their private business. Beyond malicious speculation – of which, admittedly, there was no shortage – there was not much profit to be had from the tangled affairs of Lina, Tibor and Damek. Such was not the case with Masko, whose bullying of his servants meant that he inspired no loyalty, and who was, to say the least, indiscreet in his words and acts. As a result his most private affairs were discussed over every kitchen hearth in the village.

His chronic ill-health was common knowledge, and I was not the first to connect it with Lina's youthful curse (which was also widely known, and had been given new currency by her recent change). Much hilarity was had at Masko's expense when one of his visiting women let slip that he was impotent, and the intimate nature of his boils was a standard joke. I had more reason to dislike Masko than most, but I could not hear these obscene speculations without discomfort and sometimes found myself feeling almost sorry for him. Even before winter came, he was almost completely alone: his gaming friends deserted him in his illness, and my mother and Kush were, in the end, the only servants who remained in his employ.

The day Young Lina was born, Masko's health took a sudden and dramatic turn for the worse: he suffered some kind of fit at the card table. He was carried as a dead man to his bed and the doctor was roused from his sleep to attend to him. The following day he was recovered enough to leave his bed, and he dismissed the doctor with impatience and returned to his drinking, which he claimed did him more good than any quack's potions. I guess that alcohol served to numb his physical pain; he had always been a heavy drinker, even by the standards of his peers, but now he called for raki from the moment he awoke, and drank steadily until he fell down in a stupor in the evening.

His decline from that day was alarmingly rapid. His only interest was gambling, and since Damek was now available all day, he played cards with him for as long as Damek would sit. My mother told me he would scream for Damek like a madman every morning until they sat down at the table and dealt the pack. Damek would play on until Masko fell face-down on the table, unconscious from exhaustion and raki. After each game, Damek would insist that my mother fill a basin with warm water, and he would wash his hands thoroughly with soap, as if he had been doing something filthy.

Certainly Masko was no pleasure to be around. He stank as if his body was rotting from inside and, unless he was gambling, he was in a constant rage. My mother often visited the manse simply to escape: the Red House had become a purgatory. Once I took Irli down to help with the cleaning, which was too much work for my mother alone, and as I left the house I saw Masko for myself. I was shocked at the change in him. He had lost weight, and his skin seemed to be hanging off him in great folds, and was pocked with suppurating boils.

One morning, about ten days after his fit, Masko was in the breakfast room, shouting as usual for Damek to come and play cards. My mother told me how no one could find Damek, and how Masko had worked himself into a blind fury by the time he finally appeared. Damek was dressed in black from head to foot, and such was his expression that Masko was silenced by the sight of him. It was, my mother said, as if the Devil had entered the room. Masko had in truth thought Damek was his friend: he had spent drunken nights lamenting the perfidy of others and sentimentally toasting Damek's loyalty. Damek had played his part, never once revealing his real feelings. In that moment, Damek removed his mask, and I think that Masko recognized his fate before Damek said a single word.

Damek told Masko that he would not play with him, as he did not game with paupers. He threw down a sheaf of papers onto the table. Masko picked up the document with hands that trembled so much he could scarce hold it, and he read it and read it again, as if he didn't understand what it said.

"You own nothing. I have won everything, even the clothes on your back, you filthy thieving slug," Damek told him. "You own less than the poorest beggar in this village and all that you stole is now restored. Now, get out of my house before I kick you out."

My mother told me that Masko turned a sickly greyish-green, and was too shocked to say a word; and then he just burst into tears. She said that she didn't know what to do: she loathed the man, but she couldn't leave him like that – he was still the master, after all...

She tried to get him to lie on a sofa, as he sobbed and shook. Damek told her to throw him out of the house, as he would not have such vermin on his carpet. When my mother ignored him, Damek irritably repeated his orders. She objected that it was not his house, and so he showed her the deed, made out to Damek; and when she protested that he could not throw a sick man out into the snow, he said that Masko should be treated with the mercy that he had shown others.

Masko heard it all, but had nothing to say on his behalf: he just sat and wept. My mother swears she has never seen a man so broken. At last, at my mother's insistence, Damek agreed to wait until the doctor arrived, and a place was found for Masko in a village house, more from the respect felt for my mother than from any compassion. That household's hospitality was not of long duration, as Masko died that night; and everyone in the village said he had his just deserts. So he met his death, unpitied and unlamented, unless you count that impulse to common decency felt by my mother and myself. So Lina's curse was fulfilled, and she and Damek had their revenge.

My mother – and I honour her for it – was horrified by Damek's behaviour that day, and never regarded him with the same eye afterwards. To pretend friendship where there was none for so long – for even she had believed Damek's professions – and to throw a mortally sick man out into the snow, revealed a ruthlessness that transgressed her deepest principles. Masko may have deserved such a mean death, she said, but that was for God to determine, not Damek. Ever after, she believed Damek was a demon, and crossed herself whenever she saw him.

Even so, it must be said that Damek's ownership of the Red House improved my mother's lot considerably. For all his capacity for cruelty and vengefulness, he was a fair master.

The servants who had left the Red House were reinstated and others hired, and she found herself all at once the head of a substantial household. My mother's first task was to burn all Masko's clothes and linens, which cleansed the air considerably, and Damek's next order was to empty the house of Masko's belongings, which were either sold or given away. The former master's old furniture was taken out of storage and his pictures replaced on the walls, and when next I visited, the Red House was restored to its original comfort. With the many willing hands, this took less than a week.

Once the house had been fumigated of Masko's presence, Damek took over as master of the house and, it turned out, lord of the village. Many years later, he told me that he had taken the precaution of seeing the king before he came to Elbasa and had made sure that Masko had worn out his royal usefulness, and that Damek would not be frowned upon as a replacement. This did not surprise me: by then I had learned how cold-blooded and meticulous Damek could be in pursuit of his revenge.

XXXVII

News of Masko's fate spread quickly, but it took a day or so to reach us: the first winter storm meant there wasn't much congress between the manse and the village, and when the skies cleared again the ground was six inches deep in snow. My mother tramped through the drifts to see me: she was much shaken by what had transpired, and made the walk despite the icy wind, which belied the mild blue sky. She sought tea and a comforting ear, and I willingly gave her both.

Lina was upstairs resting, and Tibor had gone out to help the village men in clearing the roads. Keeping the village pathways navigable is the major labour through winter, and a necessary one. Although it is inevitable that the outlying houses will be cut off during the worst storms, we attempt to keep the pathways clear for as long as possible. I confess that year I thought it would be no bad thing if we were isolated, since Damek would not be able to visit. I had just said as much to my mother when Damek himself walked in the back door, stamping his feet on the floor to rid his boots of dirt and ice.

My mother and I stared at him in amazement.

"Don't gawp at me like a pair of old crows," he said impatiently. "I came in the back door so I wouldn't have a stupid time-wasting argument with Tibor, and I'm in no mood to put up with you two."

"Tibor's out clearing the roads," snapped my mother. "And you should be too. They need all hands."

"I don't remember the Lord Kadar ever digging snow," said Damek. "You should remember who I am. I need to see Lina, and at once. Is she in her room?"

"I don't think she needs to see you," said I.

He didn't deign to respond, and casting his great coat on the settle, leapt up the back stairs. My mother and I exchanged glances, and I followed him, attempting to persuade him that he should not disturb Lina, as she was sleeping. He took absolutely no notice of me, and didn't even knock on the door of the room before he entered.

Lina was awake and dressed, and was lying on her couch, staring out of the window. When she saw Damek she started up and flung her arms about him.

"I knew it was you!" she said, her eyes sparkling. "Tell me, Masko is dead, isn't he? I dreamt and I saw him drowning, and then I dreamt again and he was lying in the snow like a fat blue pudding, all naked. I've never seen anything more disgusting, awake or asleep. I'm sure he's dead."

"Yes, he's dead," said Damek shortly. "But—"

"I'm so happy, Damek! At last – I have so longed for this. Did you make him suffer? Oh, I hope you ground that worm into the dirt…"

I felt almost ill with shame and disgust. After my mother's distress, I was in no mood for such unholy glee. Lina had much reason to hate Masko – more than I knew at the time – but even so, justice is one thing, and joy in another's suffering quite another.

"Yes, he's dead," I said. "And if you were a good Christian, you'd be praying for his soul, instead of gloating over the poor man's suffering. You were cruel, Damek, and you know it."

"No crueller than he was," said Damek, turning on me a look of contempt. "Save your pity for a better target. That man deserved every pang he suffered, and more. Anyway, that's not why I'm here." He grasped Lina's shoulders and looked seriously into her eyes. "Lina, you have to leave with me, and now. Ezra means to kill you."

Lina pushed away his hands. "Don't be ridiculous, Damek. The Wizard Ezra can't harm me."

"He has already cursed you."

"I feel nothing. He cannot hurt me, Damek. I am stronger than he is, and he knows it. And you can't come in here telling me what to do—"

"I'm serious, Lina. Come away with me – we can make it south before the hard snows, if we leave now. Come to the city with me – remember how often we talked of the things we would do? We can do it. But we have to leave now."

For a moment, I saw raw longing in Lina's eyes, and she wavered; but then she laughed, and the moment passed. "Damek, I will do what I choose, not what you choose. I am married! I have a daughter! I'm not leaving them, just to please you."

"You must leave now, or die here," said Damek. "There was a gathering of the clan yesterday, and you have been declared a witch. They have said that you are to be killed, and your body burned. Ezra has already begun the purification rite, and I judge that he will be here within the hour. It was only the barest chance that I found out at all…"

"So?" Lina looked scornful. "I'll make them pay for even daring to think of harming me."

Damek stared at her in disbelief. "Did you hear what I said?"

"I heard. But I'll not run from those peasant wizards. I'm no coward."

Damek opened his mouth to argue, and then thought better of it. He turned to me. "Anna, start packing a trunk. We can go by the back route – I have a horse and sleigh with me for the luggage, and my carriage is ready to go when we reach the Red House. Haste!"

Such was the urgency of Damek's command, I found myself running to Lina's wardrobe and pulling out some warm clothes. I was by no means as sanguine about the Wizard Ezra as Lina was, and his news put me into a near panic. Lina turned on me like a furious dog.

"Put those back! Don't be such a hen, Anna! Damek, you get out of here. This is my house, and I'll thank you to remember it!"

"I'll not have you dead, Lina!" said Damek. "Did you not hear what I said? Do you really think you could outface all the Usoferteras? It's not just Ezra; it's the whole clan. And do you think the king is a friend to you, when he thought your very birth was an insult? He tolerates you at best. The slightest trouble, and he would order your death. Do you think you'll see next spring if you stay here?"

"I'll be as alive as you." Lina's lips were set in a stubborn line, and her eyes flashed dangerously. "I'm not your damned goat, to be hauled off where you want, when you say. I fear no wizard and no king. Now get out of my house."

Damek knew that expression as well as I did: in this mood, Lina could not be moved, even if the house were on fire.

"You can't mean that, Lina," he said, and he stretched out his hand to hers. She turned her back on him.

"Get out, I said."

Damek stood irresolute. I think it had been a long time since anyone had resisted his will, and he did not know what to do.

"Listen, Lina. I came here for two reasons: to kill that louse Masko, and to get you—"

"I'm glad you destroyed Masko," said Lina. "But I'm not something you *get*."

She turned to face him, the light in her body again, and my skin prickled into goosebumps. I swear I saw sparks in Lina's hair, and that it floated about her head as if she were underwater.

"I said, get out. Both of you."

She didn't speak loudly, but it was impossible to resist her order. Both Damek and I found ourselves on the other side of the threshold, looking in at Lina, who seemed now the only luminous object in a room that was suddenly full of shadows. And then, without any human agency, the door slammed shut in our faces.

For a few moments we were both silent, from astonishment. Then Damek turned to me, trembling with rage and fear.

"I could shake her to pieces," he said. "Her pride will kill her. Why will she not listen?"

He began hammering on the door and calling Lina's name, as I vainly tugged at his arm to stop him. When she didn't answer he rammed it with his shoulder, and at last the bolts gave and he fell into the room.

Lina didn't seem to have moved: she still stood in the centre of the room. Damek threw himself towards her, intending perhaps to pick her up and carry her out by main force, and she simply lifted her hands in a gesture of prohibition. It was as if he'd run into a wall. He fell stunned to the ground.

"I said, go away." Lina's voice was hard and expressionless.

Damek looked up, and to my surprise I saw tears in his eyes. "Why won't you listen?" he said.

"I'm not the one who is deaf," said Lina.

"I couldn't bear it if you died," he said. "Without you, the sun is dark in my eyes. Without you, the world is a desert of thirst, with no spring anywhere. Without you, I have no soul, no life. Don't you understand?"

For a moment Lina faltered, and I saw doubt fleet over her expression. Then she smiled, and it was such a smile as I picture on Satan's face as he looks over his cohorts in hell: sweet and beautiful almost beyond imagining, and yet expressive of a diabolical will.

"I'll not die," she said. "And even if I did, do you think you would be rid of me? Do you think I would not beat in your heart, Damek, and look out through your eyes? Why do you keep demanding what is already yours? Are you so greedy?"

Damek slowly scrambled to his feet. "Come with me, Lina," he whispered. "I beg of you."

"No." She turned away, dismissing both of us. "I'm tired. Come back tomorrow, and we'll talk."

Damek glared at her with sudden hatred. "Damn you then," he said. "Damn your stupidity and damn your petty arrogance. Damn you to hell."

He turned on his heel and walked out of the room. I heard his footsteps receding down the stairs, and the slam of the door as he left the house.

Lina stood still as stone, listening to his departure. And then she swayed and fell to the floor in a faint, even as I ran to catch her.

XXXVIII

y mother had come upstairs when Damek left, and she helped me carry Lina to her couch. We set about chafing her cheeks and waved hartshorn under her nose, but she did not revive. After a half-hour of no response, we became anxious: her breathing was faint and her face was bloodless. I ran downstairs and told the groom to ride for the doctor, instructing Irli to mind the door, and then ran up to her room again. I poked up the fire and we undid her stays gently and dressed her in warm nightclothes and laid her in her bed. At last this roused her: she blinked and opened her eyes.

"Anna!" she said. "How strange! I thought I had fallen into the well."

"You should take care of yourself," said I. "You are still sick."

"Nay," she said, and struggled to sit up. She could not, and lay back on her pillow. "Why am I so weak? Where did Damek go?"

"You sent him away," said my mother. "And quite right."

She seemed stricken by this news. "I sent Damek away?"

"Yes," I said. "Don't try to sit up, Lina; you should rest."

As we spoke, I heard with relief a hammering on the front door. "That'll be the doctor," I said. "He must have been close!"

"I don't want to see the doctor," Lina said petulantly. "There's nothing wrong with me…"

I ran onto the landing so I could speak to the doctor before he saw Lina, and I heard voices rising from the hallway. My heart stopped. It wasn't the doctor: it was the Wizard Ezra. Irli must have let him in. I cursed myself: in my anxiety over Lina I had completely forgotten Damek's warning. How could I have been so thoughtless? Irli was only a child, and she couldn't be expected to defy a wizard demanding entrance. I stood frozen on the landing, gripped by total panic. Then I ran back into the chamber. There was no way of bolting the door, as Damek had broken it earlier, and my first confused thought was to move Lina into another room.

"It's the Wizard Ezra!" I hissed at my mother, as I hauled off the bedclothes and attempted to pick Lina up.

My mother went pale and crossed herself. Lina pulled herself up, supporting herself on the bedstead, and stared at me.

"Ezra?" she said. "In my house?"

"Hurry," I said, desperately trying to push her out of the room. I could hear heavy footsteps on the stairs already.

Lina swore obscenely and shook me off. "I don't care about Ezra," she said. "Stop behaving like an old woman, Anna."

"Lina, he wants to *kill* you!"

She laughed shakily. "As if he can!" she said. I stared at her: she was holding herself upright by force of will, and looked as if she were on the verge of collapse. I judged that she would have trouble defending herself against a moth.

I opened my mouth to argue, but at that moment Ezra strode through the door. He came in wrath, his staff held out before him like a weapon; his white hair flew about his head and his eyes were bottomless black pits in his face that seemed to suck all light out of the room. Despite my terror, part of me watched in wonder: he was such an incongruous figure in this feminine chamber. I realized that I had never in my life seen Ezra indoors: I had only ever seen him at the door or striding over the fields or through the streets of the village. It was as if a wolf had invaded the bedroom.

He stood framed in the doorway, and my mother and I cowered against the wall. He didn't even glance at us: his whole attention was on Lina, who stood before him in her nightgown, her knees shaking with weakness, white-faced and vulnerable and small. He didn't shout: he spoke quietly, with a dreadful deliberation that made the hairs stand up on my neck.

"Serpent of Satan!" he said. "I bring the judgement upon you. I bring fire to burn you and water to drown you. I bring iron to pierce you and salt to cleanse you. I bring the tooth of the wolf to cut out your tongue and the wing of the owl to blind your eyes, and I bring the curse of my heart against the filth and evil of your soul."

He raised his staff, and Lina staggered backwards as if he had struck her. Until then I had been frozen to the spot, but when I saw Lina fall back, a blind fury rose within me. She looked so fragile and ill, and the injustice of it smote my heart, so I scarcely knew what I was doing. I threw myself at Ezra and grasped his jerkin and shook him, crying at him to leave my mistress be.

He stepped back in surprise. For an awful moment his eyes met mine, and there was such malignance in his gaze that I thought I was stabbed to the heart. I fell back against the wall as if I had been thrown, although he hadn't lifted a hand against me, and slid to the floor.

Lina scrambled upright. She no longer looked small and ill: now she loomed in that tiny room, and a viciously bright light seemed to emanate from her form, banishing all shadows. Her hair was coiling about her face like a nest of snakes, and her eyes were violet fire. On her face was an expression of such demonic hatred that I recoiled.

She merely lifted her right hand, and the wizard stood transfixed, unnaturally still: some seizure had afflicted him and he could not move a muscle. His mouth and eyes were wide open, and his hands were arrested mid-gesture, so that he seemed caught out of time: only his eyes, rolling in his head, showed that he was conscious. His attitude was one of complete terror, and that in itself was frightening. In that moment, I remember, the room went completely silent, as if all sound were sucked away; I couldn't even hear the beating of my own heart.

As I watched, every loose object in that room – the water jug and basin, the oil lamp, the chamber pot, the bedclothes, Lina's undergarments, the fire irons, even the nursing chair – became airborne, spiralling around Lina's head, so that she seemed the centre of a nightmarish domestic whirlpool. The Wizard Ezra's eyes were now rolled up in his head, so I could only see the whites. Then Lina flung her arms out in a violent gesture, and the objects flew at the wizard with terrible force. Those that were brittle, smashed; I heard a loud crack as the chamber pot broke against his skull, and the wizard fell over, tangled in the linens and blankets as in a diabolical net. Then everything went still, except for my mother, who cringed against the wall, sobbing and shaking, and I realized I could hear my heart again, hammering in my chest.

I stared at the carnage dully, too dazed to react; but then I saw that the broken lamp had spilt its oil and set fire to the fabrics. Within moments it was blazing merrily. I realized that if I did not act we would all be burnt to a crisp, and somehow I tore the brocade curtains off the bed and with them stamped out the flames. When I had finished I stood for a short time, regaining my breath. Lina had collapsed, so I picked her up, and dragged her onto the stripped bed. She was so still and white that at first I thought she must have died, but if I laid my ear to her mouth I caught the faintest breath, and her heart was fluttering lightly in her breast, fast as the heart of a bird. Then, unwillingly, I checked the wizard. I saw at once that he was dead: the poker had been driven through one eye with such force that it had pierced his skull, pinning his head to the floorboards. There was a deep depression on the side of his head, and blood was seeping out of his mouth and ears. Despite the evidence of my eyes, I felt for his heartbeat, trembling the while that he might wake and grasp my hand.

"He's dead," said my mother, who had crept up beside me. Her face was ashen, and I'm sure mine was the same.

"What shall we do?"

She stared at me, shaking her head, but had no answer. I drew the charred bed-curtain over his face, so I did not have to look at that terrible sight, and we crawled away from his body. My mother caught my hand, and we sat together on the floor of the destroyed bedroom, unable to move. I don't know how long we sat there. Everyone else had run out of the house when Ezra arrived, in fear of their lives; no one came to disturb us until the doctor arrived. He walked through the wide-open front door and came straight up to the bedroom. He stared at the destruction and his lips tightened, but he made no comment. He checked Lina's pulse and sighed. Then he whipped the cloth back from the wizard's body, and as quickly covered him again. There was clearly no need for his ministrations there.

He went downstairs, returning quickly with a bottle of plum brandy and some glasses. He poured a large glass for my mother and myself, and insisted we drink it all. Then he poured one for himself, and that's when I noticed that his hands were shaking.

XXXIX

Perhaps you are wondering why, when I saw her terrifying capacity for violence, I did not leave Lina's employ at once. The truth is that I was never personally afraid of her; the wizard's death appalled me more than anything I had seen in my life, yet afterwards I felt, if anything, more loyal to my mistress. Lina could exasperate me beyond measure, and she often alarmed me, but I never thought her a monster. It is easy too to forget how young we were! All of us, Lina, Tibor, Damek, myself, were scarcely out of childhood. What hope did we have, even the most self-willed of us, of ruling our own destinies? When I look back, I wonder what we might have been, had we been born into another world. But that is almost the same as wondering how our lives might have turned out had we been completely different people.

In the end, I was the most fortunate of us all, and that because I was the least important: there is a luck in being born ordinary. As I had no fortune and no status, I had the more freedom to be myself: it mattered little to anyone beyond my intimates what

I did. Lina, on the other hand, was scrutinized by all eyes from the moment of her birth; all her life she had been the object of attention, and there was not one person she knew, including myself, who had not attempted to shape her wild being into a more biddable form. She was like a thorn tree which to its misfortune is bent into an espalier against a wall, and which cannot but betray its spiky and unruly nature, no matter how sternly its growth is pruned and directed.

That day I understood that Lina's extreme behaviour was forced by circumstance, as much as by her wild nature. Left to herself, she might have found her level, but tormented as she was by others, tugged now this way, now that, she could never attain the balance within herself that she so sorely needed. From her birth, she was thought to be unnatural, a demon, a monstrous creature who must be destroyed. If she had not killed Ezra, he would have murdered her: was she then to offer her throat to his knife, like a lamb to a butcher? If Ezra had succeeded in his aim of killing Lina, no one would have lifted a hand against him, for he had the weight of the Lore in his hand. If a man had defended himself as Lina had, no one would have said a word, because that man would have been a wizard. The affair would have been considered "wizard-business", and thus none of our own.

Lina's only real crime was to be born a woman, with powers and instincts that were thought proper to belong only to a man. She was not the first, and certainly not the last, in her situation. Yet I knew her well, and for all her faults, which I understood better than anyone, I could not think her unnatural. Why should any of us be deemed monstrous for heeding the simple bidding of our hearts? Why do we bow before the chains that bind us, spilling our blood into the coffers of the king and strangling the longings in our breasts? Is that the real reason why someone like Lina must not be suffered to live, because her mere existence reveals our private, unadmitted shame, our poverty of spirit?

These questions burst on me that day with the force of a revelation. It was as if a veil was removed from my sight: I perceived everything afresh, like one newly born. I had always felt for Lina the compassion and love of a sister; now I felt too the loyalty and indignation of our common sex. She ignited an anger within me which has never been quenched, at the rank injustices of this world.

The wizard's body was taken away that afternoon – with some difficulty, I remember, as the poker that affixed his corpse to the floorboards was driven right through the wood – and Lina herself was removed to a spare room, out of the wreckage of the bedroom. She seemed dead herself; she did not wake or move all that long day. I was in a daze, attending to my ill mistress while also attempting to cope with the distress and shock of my mother and the servants. It took all my powers of persuasion to stop the servants leaving at once.

Tibor arrived home in a panic, having heard that the Wizard Ezra was intending to kill his wife; when he was told what had happened, and saw Lina lying white and still on her bed, he withdrew to his room and would not come out. I think he simply did not know what to do. I didn't know what to do either, and would have been glad to shut myself up and demand to be left alone, but since everyone turned to me, and there was no one else, I had no choice but to take charge.

Damek arrived not long after Tibor, in a state of some dishevelment and distress. He insisted on seeing Lina, but I would not permit him into her room. I was in no mood for his bullying. I told him she was deathly ill, and his presence at such a delicate time would do more harm than good, and then I angrily asked why he did not take up his responsibilities as Lord of Elbasa and calm the villagers, otherwise the entire population would be at the manse with pitchforks and brands. At this he stared at me hard, and to my surprise left without further argument. I think he did as I demanded; certainly, no mob turned up at our doorstep, as I had half expected might happen over the next few days. I wondered too when we would hear from the wizards. Ezra had been the only wizard in Elbasa, and it would take at least a day for news to reach the other clans. Again fortune was with us: the day after the wizard's death came the first heavy snowfall, and I judged that since communications would be delayed, I need not fear a response for a few days, at the very earliest, and perhaps not at all that winter. There was little enough to be thankful for, to be sure, but I was grateful for that small mercy.

Lina herself lay insensible to everything, as the wind whirled the snow about the chimneys. She showed no outward sign of harm, aside from a bruise on her temple; but her breathing was barely perceptible, and she hardly stirred. After two days of this, I was beside myself with worry. The doctor showed me how to give her nourishment, soaking a rag with broth so she would not choke. This was a time-consuming and difficult task, and I was grateful when Tibor came out of his room and offered to help nurse her. In the sickroom he proved gentle and surprisingly skilful, which I put down to his mother's teachings, and I sighed again for what might have been. Strain and grief had made him gaunt, and his eyes were red-rimmed. He looked a man in the grip of terrible sorrow, although our conversation was limited to practicalities and he said nothing of his feelings to me. Sometimes, from the hallway, I overheard him talking to Lina, as if she could hear him, but I could never make out what he said.

Lina regained consciousness on the third day, but that was scarcely an improvement: with consciousness came the high fever that I had been dreading since she was brought to bed with the child. The first I knew of it was in the small hours: she screamed and threw off her blankets, waking me up, then scrambled off her bed. I leapt up to attend to her, and she flinched away from me in horror.

"I'll not come now!" she cried. Her voice was hoarse and cracked. "Back! Away from me, foul ghoul! Take your net elsewhere!"

"It's me – Anna! Come, Lina, back into bed – you'll catch a chill!"

She blinked and, to my relief, recognized me. "Oh, Anna, I thought you were Death come to claim my soul! I saw him there with his net and scythe, just where you're standing – his eyes were burning, Anna, burning cold—"

"Now Lina, it's just a bad dream. Look, there's only me!" I put my arm about her shoulders. Her skin was clammy and cold, and her entire body was shaken by violent tremors. Her nightdress was drenched and in the candlelight her face glistened with mingled sweat and tears.

"I don't want to die. What will happen to me when I die? Why must I die?"

"You won't die, my dear, but you must get back into bed. Come now … come, I'll sing you to sleep."

She took my hand like a child, and the trust in that small gesture wrung my heart with fear and pity. I wiped her face, wrapped a shawl around her, and poked up the fire that was slumbering in its embers. She permitted me to change her clammy nightdress and to tuck her back into bed, and at last she drifted into slumber. I dared not sleep after that, and sat up and watched her. She did not wake again, but she stirred often and muttered, and sometimes she cried out. Mostly I couldn't understand what she said, but she twice called for Damek, and once she seemed to be speaking to Tibor.

When dawn came, dim and blue, she slept more peacefully, so I woke Irli and bade her sit with Lina, and went down to the kitchen. There I splashed my face with cold water and made a tisane with liquorice and honey, to wake myself up: I was exhausted, but I could not see myself resting that day. The storm's violence had abated but it was still snowing. I realized with dismay that the doctor was unlikely to make his morning visit, and I was far from confident of my ability to nurse a delirious fever. I knocked on Tibor's door, to tell him his wife had woken from her stupor. He was dressed when he came to the door, but he was unshaved and smelt unwashed. I thought he must have slept in his clothes, and his manner was vague and distracted.

"I thought I heard something in the night," he said. "But then I was sure it was voices in the wind. I heard a voice, Annie, calling my name, and someone rattling my shutters ... but who could be outside my window? I swear, it's thirty feet up if it's an inch."

"No one, Mr Tibor, for sure," said I, my heart sinking to hear his incoherence. I wondered what I should do if my master became as mad as my mistress. "It is only the wind. It was high last night – it made the whole house shake."

"Yes, that's what I thought. But it called my name."

"I'm sure it was a dream," I said.

"It couldn't have been. I haven't slept a wink these past three nights," he said. "Will she forgive me, do you think? What if she dies and leaves me unforgiven?"

"I'm sure that Mistress Lina knows there is nothing to forgive," I said. "Now, don't you worry yourself, sir. You need some sleep and you need a good hot meal. I'll get the cook to make a nice broth for now and I'll send Irli up with some hot water, and once you're washed and fed you'll feel much better. Then you can see Mistress Lina, although I fear she has the fever."

Poor soul, he wrung my hand and thanked me, although whether it was for the broth or for my news, I wasn't sure.

X L

Tibor spent the whole morning sitting with Lina. I was sent away, and took the opportunity to snatch a little rest in my own chamber, which was chill and musty from disuse. I was too tired to light a fire, and simply piled all my coats on the bed and lay down fully clothed. When I woke up, it was early afternoon. The clouds were gathering again outside, and it was so dark that I thought I must have overslept. I neatened myself up hurriedly and went to Lina's room. She was sleeping, and Irli was on duty. She told me that Tibor had only that minute gone to bed himself, but she had no opinion on the condition of either Tibor or Lina. I derived a little hope, nevertheless, from Irli's report: it seemed a good sign that Tibor was sleeping, and Lina's fever seemed less severe, although she still slept restlessly.

Lina woke not long after I sat down. She seemed rational, but spoke with a disturbing rapidity, halting often to catch her breath. She never mentioned the wizard once, for which I was grateful; it seemed, in fact, that she had forgotten the terrible scene of three days before altogether. Instead she talked incessantly of Tibor and Damek, attempting to parse the virtues of both men.

"You're right, Anna," she said to me. "I should never have married Tibor. He is too gentle and good, and I fear I've broken him. He asked me to forgive him – me! Oh, it breaks my heart!" She paused, as the tears rolled unnoticed down her cheeks. "It's no use feeling sorry, I know that. But I'm sorry I'm going to die, and that it's too late for anything…"

Her words disturbed me: they had too much of the air of a confession for my taste, and I did not like her talk of dying. She was certainly ill and weak, but to my eyes was not beyond recovery. I said so, with more certainty in my voice than I felt. She shook her head impatiently, but didn't argue, and returned to her train of thought.

"Damek is hard as a tree root. Not like Tibor, who thinks I am something else, despite everything … he is wrong, wrong! But both of them betray me, although they do not know it, both of them destroy me… Do you think either of them ever really cared for me? Or did they just love a phantom, whatever they saw when they looked at me, and forgot to love me? I wonder that, Anna, and it makes me feel so lonely…"

I was at a loss to answer her, as I had wondered the same thing myself, so I just stroked her hand and said nothing. She soon continued her anguished meditation. "Nothing would destroy Damek … not even me. But could I live with that? I am not that strong – I hunger for gentleness… It is like being loved by a wolf, who only knows love as a devouring … and yet, what am I without him? I need him. It isn't love – it's worse than that. What could I do? What could I do…?"

She trailed off and was silent for so long that I thought she had fallen asleep. Then she struggled against her pillows, and sat up. "Where is Damek?" she demanded, in a voice that was suddenly preternaturally clear. "Is he dead too? Why have I not seen him for so long? If he's dead you must tell me, you mustn't lie, I must know at once!"

I assured her that he was as alive as I was, and was only kept away by the snowfalls, but nothing I could say would calm her fears. She became more and more agitated over the next half-hour, and I saw the hectic flush heightening in her cheeks and became afraid. She clutched my hand and wept, and called out for Damek, and swore that if she did not die she would kill herself so that she might join him in hell. I tried to make her lie down, but in her delirium she was too strong for me and succeeded in hauling herself out of bed and stumbling to the window. Little enough was visible outside, but she pointed and cried out that she saw Damek's ghost walking through the snow, and then she fell to the floor. She was so weak that she could not pull herself up. I called for help, and Irli and I had just succeeded in placing her back in her bed when the cook came running into the room, out of breath, to tell me that Damek was downstairs in the kitchen and wished to speak to me.

I was astonished by the news – it was still snowing too heavily to walk safely anywhere. But I had no time to answer, for Lina overheard the whispered communication. She turned on me like a wild thing. "Damek? Here? Bring him here, at once!"

"Hush now, Lina. You are too ill to see anyone!" I said.

Her nostrils whitened with rage. Fury brought back her strength, and she had swept off the bedclothes and was making for the door before I could stop her. She refused point-blank to lie down again until I had promised to fetch Damek, and such was the extremity of her agitation that I was thrown into a panic. A visit from Damek could only worsen her condition, but denying his presence was equally dangerous. And if I did admit Damek, what should I say to Tibor?

I was still hesitating when Damek himself entered the room,

closely followed by the cook, who was wringing her hands helplessly, having failed to stop him coming upstairs. He had thrown off his coat, but his hair was starred with snow, which was melting in the heat of the house, and his trousers were wet to his thighs. When he saw Lina, all the colour fled from his face; then he attempted a smile, but it was more a grotesque grimace than any expression of joy. He was clearly struck forcibly by her condition. It was as if his perception wakened my own and I observed her afresh through his eyes; I saw, with a clutch of the heart, that she was a shadow of the shining termagant who had thrown Damek out of the house only a few days before. She stood holding onto the bedpost, a frail, tiny figure, her hair sadly tangled, her nightdress disordered. Her face was absolutely white except for her lips, which had a bluish tinge. When she saw Damek she froze, and her eyes grew luminous and blurred with unshed tears.

"Lina," he whispered, and he grasped her hand and kissed it. "What have you done to yourself? What have you done?"

Lina leant her head on his shoulder and clasped his neck, and her shoulders shook with sobbing. I turned and hissed for the others to leave – I did not want strangers in the room, even if Damek and Lina were oblivious to their presence. I did not dare to leave myself, and yet I felt all the discomfort of staying.

"I was sure you were dead," said Lina at last. "Did I dream it? It was too cruel, for you to die a second time! Surely I have grieved for you enough?"

"Not enough, Lina! I swear, I would wish you a lifetime of grieving, if it meant you were alive."

"You know that I am dying." Lina said it with indifference. "I think I do not care any more. What good was I to anyone? But I am still afraid…"

Damek groaned and buried his face in her hair. "You are so cruel, Lina. You can't die and leave me all alone. I swear, I do not pity you. You chose this, and you have killed me as surely as you killed yourself. I will never forgive you, not as long as I draw breath in this world..."

Lina gasped as if she were in pain, and I sprang up with a cry. Damek turned and gave me a look that set me straight back in my chair.

"You're strong, Damek. You don't understand what it is not to be strong enough," said Lina. "How could you understand? And now I will die, it is too late anyway. Death came for me this morning and Anna chased him away, but I can see him waiting in the corner..."

She began to cough violently, and Damek patted her back until she recovered and then lifted her up in his arms and wildly kissed her face. He was now weeping openly, and he held her so roughly that I saw his fingers imprinting bruises on her white arms, but she made no protest, and simply tightened her arms about his neck.

"Death hurts so much less than birth," she said. "Why is that so, Damek? Why does living hurt so much? Come, you must not cry like a little boy. Come, Damek, I do not think it is sad. Remember how I said I would be part of the sky and the earth, and every flower will be my face?"

"I don't want any flowers," said Damek brokenly. "I only want you, Lina. Only you."

I saw with alarm that she was drooping as if she had fallen into a faint, but Damek grasped her to his breast and snarled at me when I dared to come close. I thought in truth he was a wild beast then; he was bereft of human speech, and his eyes rolled in his head as if he were in a death agony himself. Then he sat on the bed, still holding her close to him, and I feared at that moment she was dead. Damek wouldn't listen to anything I said, or permit me near her, and so violent were his responses that I became frightened and left the room.

I sat downstairs for some minutes, trying to gather my wits, but I was so worried I soon went upstairs again. Damek sat on the bed with Lina in his arms as before, but the fit of fury had passed. He looked deathly tired.

"She has fainted," he said. It seemed a struggle even for him to speak. "Look, she still breathes…"

"Aye," said I, attempting to hold in my anger. "And no thanks to you, Mr Damek. She needs sleep and care and none of this fuss and talk of dying, if she is to see another day. I think you must go now."

He sighed heavily, and then placed Lina in her bed, and tucked the blankets around her as tenderly as if she were a child. I rushed to her and checked her forehead: the skin was dry and burning, and her body was limp.

"What have you done?" I so forgot myself that I shouted. "You have killed her, you selfish fool!"

At this Damek flinched with such an expression of anguish that I was taken aback and wished I had not said those words.

"Selfish, Anna?" he said, and was silent for a time, watching me lave her brow. "She was dying already," he said at last. "I saw it the moment I walked in this room… I've seen many people die. I know the signs."

I shut my ears to him, although the blue shadows gathering on Lina's face made me fear that he was right. I took her hand and felt for her pulse, which was barely perceptible, and the tears started in my eyes.

Damek touched my arm, with a shyness that made me turn around in astonishment, and I looked up straight into his face. For a moment I saw there the stoic boy I once had known, who concealed beneath his impassivity unknown sufferings, and part of me relented. He was neither a beast nor a demon, only a man whose entire being was a wound. A wound may be monstrous, but that doesn't make him who bears it inhuman.

"I'm sorry, Damek," I said softly, and his hand tightened convulsively.

"*You* are not selfish," he said. "You have the right to judge me, which I give no one else. You have a heart, and you have eyes to see. They are precious rare in this world, Anna, and you mind what I say, because I know. Most people might be made of stone, for all they see and feel. If I am selfish, I am not alone."

There was a raw justice in what Damek said, that I couldn't but acknowledge, even after everything he had done. He leant forward and stroked Lina's hair, and then he kissed her forehead.

"I told her I was nothing without her," he said. "She never believed me, but I only told her the truth. I was not strong; she was all my strength. If I have killed her, you can be sure I'll be punished for it, every day that I walk on the face of the earth. I am a dead man now, Anna."

I couldn't speak, so I merely nodded. He lightly kissed the top of my head, and quietly left the room. I didn't see him again for a very long time.

Tibor never knew of Damek's visit; for better or worse, we were all of us too afraid to tell him something that would only add to his distress. Lina never recovered consciousness and she died at midnight, with Tibor weeping at her side.

Afterwards I threw open the shutters to let in the fresh air, as the room was stifling and full of sour vapours. The night sky was still and clear: the snow had stopped falling at last, and the whitened Plateau swept away before me to the mountains, a long, glimmering slope under the dark sky. The moonlight shafted in through the casement and silvered Lina's face with an unearthly beauty. For a wild moment I was sure that she was only sleeping, that the past few days had been but a nightmare from which I had now woken, and that the next day I would be scolding her as

261

usual and making her breakfast. But it passed, as every moment does, and I saw how still she was, how her eyelashes no longer fluttered on her cheek nor her breath lifted the tendrils of her loose hair. It was only then that I understood she was dead.

XLI

That was a bleak winter, with the household in mourning and Lina's body kept frozen in the preserving shed, for the ground was hard as iron and she could not be buried until the spring thaw. I washed her and arrayed her in her favourite dress, and crossed her arms on her breast, and placed her father's crucifix around her neck so she might be buried with it. Despite the bitter cold, which preserved her body in the icy air, Tibor spent many hours in the shed. I also suspect that Damek made his own visits; although none of us saw him come or go, the snow betrayed that someone from the village visited the shed.

The events of the previous months left me exhausted and sad and without hope for myself or anyone else. I went through that winter like one of those automata you can see in the southern cities. I performed my duties as required, but I thought I would never smile again; I could only see a black spring before me, with no expectation of renewal.

I missed Lina more than I can say. The house seemed strangely pregnant with her absence; it was as if she had merely stepped out for a walk and might return at any moment. I couldn't rid myself of the expectation that I would hear her voice summoning me the next minute, or that I might see her rounding a corner on some mundane errand. Sometimes I even saw her, a slight form standing under the cypress outside, or vanishing from a room that I had entered. In this I wasn't alone: Irli claimed that she saw her in the bedroom where she died, as clear as day, and Tibor came downstairs one morning white with shock and said that he had woken to find Lina leaning over him, her hair brushing his face.

I was not surprised that Lina, so unquiet in life, should be a restless spirit. Unlike the others in the manse I didn't fear these hauntings – perhaps by then I was beyond fear – but they made me sadder than ever. It seemed to me a further injustice that even death could not bring Lina peace.

The thaw came with all its attendant inconveniences and I found myself busier than ever, which in its own way was a comfort. The first task was Lina's burial. The priest initially refused to accept her into the church cemetery, saying that she was a damned soul and ought to be buried at a crossroads like a suicide, but Tibor railed against him with such uncharacteristic fury that he was forced to relent. Her grave may still be found in the Kadar family plot, next to her father's. Her married name has been obliterated from the headstone, which merely proclaims the name LINA and the dates of her birth and death. Surely only Damek could be so offended by that name as to take the trouble to chip it out, but the true source of the desecration remains a mystery, as the gravestone was defaced when Damek was far away in the south. Master Tibor replaced the headstone a few times, but at last this silent battle over a name seemed pointless to him, and he left it as it was.

Damek himself left Elbasa for the south as soon as travel was possible. After his departure we saw no more apparitions in the manse, and life began to settle into a domestic routine. Although Damek was in regular contact with the employees on his estate, as until recently he was always strict about the care of his properties, he continued as an absentee lord for many years.

We heard nothing at all from either the wizards or the king. Lina's death contented their desire for revenge, I supposed, and they preferred to forget about her altogether. With the death of the Wizard Ezra there also came the end of the vendetta. Perhaps the wizards judged that Elbasa had suffered enough, or perhaps they were alarmed by their colleague's death, or perhaps the cycle of revenge had run its length; in any case, once a new wizard was appointed the proper restorations were made, and representatives from Skip and Elbasa met at the border and formally declared peace. With this shadow removed, it was as if the village was reborn: a new life seemed possible.

So the days widened and the early flowers bloomed, and slowly I began to feel less desolate. On one of the first warm days I decided to beat the carpets, which had become musty and close over the winter months, and with Irli's help I had carried them out and hung them on the washing lines. I remember that I was stretching my back after the labour of carrying the heavy rolls when I saw Zef standing by the gate. He bore in his arms an enormous bunch of spring flowers that he had gathered for me.

I couldn't believe my eyes. I blinked and looked again, but there he was, as real as the gatepost next to him. He was a handsome man in those days: his hair was as brown as coffee and his eyes as blue and mild as the skies of high summer. As he stood strong and sturdy in the pale sunlight and laughed at my astonishment, I am sure no angel could have looked more beautiful to my eyes. I stood still as a stone, unable to speak: I had been all ice, and that minute my soul broke open, as if my feelings were a river in flood. I found I was not so numb after all, and that I could do more than smile: I laughed for sheer joy, even through my tears.

Our courtship was brief: we had already spent too much time apart, and were each impatient, as all young people are, to reach our bliss. He spoke and I consented; the rest was a matter of practical decision. I was reluctant to leave the manse, and I approached Tibor and asked him to employ Zef as a groom, to which he gladly assented. We were married in the autumn, once the time of mourning was over.

I can't pretend that my happiness was unalloyed; the events of the previous year had left their mark, and I still mourned Lina's death. I felt older than my years, as if I had lost for ever an innocence that until then I hadn't known I possessed. Sometimes I wished fiercely that Lina could have had the peace that I had found, although at other times I wondered whether her restlessness meant that, even should she have lived, she would never have found content. How do we measure such things? My love for Zef was neither star-crossed nor tragic, and our marriage concerned no one but ourselves. Perhaps I never suffered the ecstasies that possessed Lina; but I believe that, in my own way, I felt no less deeply; and I have certainly been happier in my life.

It seems wrong that there is so little of interest to say about happiness. The next fifteen years were the most content of my life, and yet are soon told. There were sorrows: my mother died a few years after Young Lina's birth, which caused me much grief. At around the same time, Zef and I accepted that we were fated to be childless. After an initial sadness, I found that I was very content as I was: I liked my work, and I was loved by a good man, and that seemed to me to be very sufficient. If I had married another man things would have been very different: I knew of women who had been sent from their husbands for not bearing a son. As with all things, Zef followed his own mind.

He said that if God had decided not to send us children, who was he to argue? In any case, he said, it meant that he had me all to himself.

This wasn't entirely true, as the chief care of Young Lina fell to us and in truth we loved her as if she were our own. By winter the baby was old enough to be weaned and she was brought to the manse. Of course we wondered – not without anxiety – if she would inherit her mother's violet eyes, but in a few months we could lay our fears aside: her eyes were like her father's, brown and soft as a milch cow's. I supervised her growth through her childish maladies and mishaps with all a mother's pride and anxiety, and watched her grow into a sweet, biddable girl. She had none of her mother's wilfulness and almost all of her beauty: it was as if she united the best features of both her parents.

Tibor was never the same after Lina's death. Ever after there was a delicacy in his constitution which expressed itself in periods of melancholy. After an initial period of indifference, Young Lina became the darling and consolation of her father's heart, and her innocent play could rouse him out of all but the worst of his dejections. He ran the manse with a farmer's sense and, barring the ups and downs of normal life, we all prospered. Young Lina's sunny nature seemed to make up for the evils that had afflicted her mother, and we all believed that the curse of the Kadars had at last burned itself out.

XLII

I was, of course, reckoning without Damek. When Lina was fifteen, Damek returned to live in the Red House. As ever, he told no one of what he had been doing for the past fifteen years, although from scraps of gossip that came my way over the years I understood that he had worked himself into the highest affairs of the country.

I couldn't regard his return without trepidation and was relieved when it seemed that he was, if anything, disposed to avoid the manse. His presence stirred old scandals that had long lain dormant, and some reached Lina's ears. I was forced to tell her some of her mother's story, which up to then I had kept secret. I carefully culled what I told her, but she listened wide-eyed, excited that she had such a romantic history. I'm sure that she supplemented the little I related with accounts from her friends in the village, which were no doubt exaggerated and highly coloured. She was of an age to fill her mind with penny novels that her indulgent father purchased for her from the south, and her imagination was set afire to think that she was the daughter of a witch who had been cursed by the king himself. I couldn't approve her nonsense, but at the time it seemed harmless enough.

It wasn't long before I met Damek in the village. He greeted me with neither enthusiasm nor dislike, seeming rather indifferent to my salutation, and showed none of the intimacy that had marked our relationship many years before. I studied him curiously: somehow he was changed, although outwardly he seemed little different from the last time we met. His eyes were hard and calculating, and there was that in his manner – a coldness that seemed like the obverse of the fierce passion I had once seen in him – which made me keen to go no further in our relations than common civility. I was puzzled why a man of affairs as he had reportedly become should consider living in an isolated village and, prompted by curiosity, I asked him why he had moved here. His reply was at first no more than I expected.

"What business is it of yours?" he said. "Surely a man can live in a house he owns without exciting impertinent speculation?"

"Of course he may," I said, feeling the rebuke. "But you must own that there is little here to interest a man of your tastes."

"What would you know of my tastes?" said he, and I thought that was that, and prepared to take my leave. But he had not finished: he gave me a narrow look which made me feel very uncomfortable, and then asked me why I had remained in this place, when I was so clearly not cut of the same cloth as my neighbours. I was taken aback by his question and answered confusedly, saying that I had ties of blood and habit that made it dear to me.

"I too have ties of blood," he said then, with sudden intensity. "If not habit, blood. Every thing that ever happened to me, happened to me here. There are ties that call, whether a man likes it or not…"

I shuddered: for a moment I saw beneath his mask of indifference, as if I had glimpsed a monstrous creature at the bottom of a dark pond. I remembered with a vivid clarity our last meetings, when I had been sure he was out of his mind. But Damek swiftly recollected himself, and the mask was resumed; he gave me a mocking look, nodded and passed on.

I was discomforted enough by this conversation to be grateful that our paths seldom crossed. He never attended church, and at most we would pass each other in the street, where neither of us did more than acknowledge the other.

So events rumbled along unexceptionally for a year, and my charge turned sixteen and became of marriageable age. Her beauty and her father's property made her the object of several courtships, which caused the usual flutterings and excitement. I did not for a moment fear that she deceived me, and so allowed her more laxity in her movements than was wise, a circumstance I now rue bitterly. To be short, Damek covertly presented himself as one of her suitors, flattering and charming her as only he knew how. Citing the ancient enmity between her father and himself, Damek swore Lina to secrecy, and her mind was so full of romantic nonsense that she fell in gladly with his schemes, believing everything he said about his role in the matter. Don't get me wrong: she loved her father dearly, and had no desire to hurt him. But in her innocence, she thought what had transpired between her father and Damek was no more than a tragic misunderstanding, which time and love would eventually heal.

I have no doubt that Damek had been nourishing this plan for many years, perhaps ever since he left Elbasa, and had been waiting patiently for the time to ripen. From his point of view, marrying Lina was the perfect revenge. He knew it would destroy Tibor and, since he also blamed Lina unequivocally for her mother's death, he could punish the child as well. Since she was her father's heir she would inherit the manse and its properties on his death, which appealed also to his grasping nature, since all the property would pass to him.

Suspicion was so far from any of our minds that Lina was able to keep the affair to herself right up to the moment that she ran away with him. She left a letter full of foolishness and prattle: she was in love, and she was away to be married, and would return after her honeymoon as mistress of the Red House. She begged our forgiveness for her secrecy, but had feared her marriage would be forbidden since her father had such an unjust dislike for Damek, but she was the happiest woman on the face of the earth.

My whole world fell apart. My master collapsed with the shock, and was bedridden for a week. When he rose from his bed, he was a different man; he oscillated between towering rage at his daughter's betrayal and a dangerous lassitude brought on by large amounts of laudanum. It was a medication he used to combat his melancholy, but after Lina's flight he resorted to taking it every day. Not anything I could say would make him think of his daughter with compassion, and if he had not been so ill he would have disinherited her at once. He certainly claimed the intention. For myself, I could not imagine that Damek felt any real love for my nurseling; yet I nourished some hope that he could not be too cruel to a young girl who was, after all, the flesh and blood of the woman he had loved so passionately. That hope was dashed in less than a month, when I received a desperate letter saying that her marriage had been a terrible mistake and begging to be allowed home. This, despite all my representations, was refused by her father.

Damek and Lina returned in three months, no doubt so Damek could flaunt his revenge in Tibor's face. As soon as I heard, I hurried to the Red House to see her. You might imagine how my heart broke when I saw what had happened to my innocent girl. All the happy light in her had been quenched: she was cowed and frightened, and I saw evidence of her husband's cruel treatment in the bruises she showed me on her arms. She told me she had tried to run away to escape his constant abuses, but Damek had always followed her and brought her back. Such was my anger that I later confronted Damek, and ordered him to treat his wife with respect and consideration. He laughed in my face.

"What, and lose the sweet revenge I have planned for so long? There is little enough pleasure in my life, but knowing how Tibor squirms and suffers in the vice has given me a reason to live. How can you deny me that? What do you take me for?"

"A human being," I said. "I once thought you were at least that. But I see that I was wrong, and those who say you are the Devil must surely be right. How could you treat such an innocent so, and she Lina's own flesh and blood? Do you not know that you are breaking my heart also? And I'm sure her mother would weep, if she could know what you are doing..."

"Don't you speak of her mother to me!" he said. "What she said was all too right: she is with me every day. She has cursed me. I was cursed from the moment we first met. And yet I never see her! A glimpse in the corner of my eye, a snatch of laughter in another room – oh, she is clever enough to give me enough hope to keep me in constant torment, but never to satisfy me. Don't mention her in the same breath as that puling brat! She doesn't deserve to bear her mother's name; she is all her father."

I had no reply to this, because it was clear to me that Damek was no longer a rational human being and, in truth, I feared that he might strike me. I shuddered and asked then, without any hope that it might be granted, that he permit Lina to come and live with me, even if we went to the south. He laughed again, saying she was his property to do with as he wished, and dismissed me.

Damek had all the joy he desired, for Tibor sickened and

272

died before the year was out. Tibor had never found the spirit to change his will, and all his property passed into Damek's hands. He called for his daughter on his deathbed, but Damek refused to let her attend; indeed, he seemed to take a diabolical pleasure in forbidding Lina to attend the funeral or even to wear mourning, although Damek himself was seen at the edge of the cemetery, no doubt gloating over his vanquished foe. He moved his household to the manse, where my poor girl had spent her happiest years, appointing Zef and myself to look after the Red House, as you find us, since he is now our master. If it were not for Young Lina, I would have long left his employ. I visit the manse when I can, and bring such comfort as is possible. There is this at least, that Damek does not forbid my visits. And so it has been these past two years.

I can find it within me to forgive, if not excuse, Damek's previous actions, despite the terrible harm he caused; but even a saint could not forgive the injury he has done to Young Lina, who did nothing to excite his hatred except to be born. I pray that some justice will be dealt him, but I cannot see how, as he has the king's favour; and even should he decide to blow out his unhappy brains with a rifle tomorrow, the damage he has inflicted will never be undone. If I can be said to hate another human being, I hate him. After Lina's death, he was nothing, as he had told me, and he built a fortress on that emptiness that even now stares blackly over us all, forbidding all joy and gentleness. I had not known a human being was capable of such barren savagery.

Since he removed to the manse, Damek has lost even his former regard for his property. He remains as miserly as ever, but what was once carefully maintained is now left to decay. That is partly because villagers refuse to work there because they say the house is haunted: the only servant who remains is Kush. The main reason is Damek himself. He doesn't care any more to conceal his nature, and he is widely feared. Myself, I think that each month Damek's insanity grips him more deeply.

There are many stories circulating in the village – some say they have seen Damek speaking with the Devil, and others claim that he is the Devil himself. I do not credit all of them, since gossip gives wings to flights of fancy, but I think even the wildest rumours contain a seed of truth. A few weeks ago, for instance, Father Cantor found Lina's grave disturbed, with all the earth dug up. Poor man, he crossed himself in panic, believing that Lina must have clawed her way out of her coffin and was now stalking the cemetery. I think it more likely that Damek, in one of his fits, sought to look on the face of his dead love, even in her bodily decay. I confess, the thought of such perverse passion fills me with greater horror than the thought of Lina walking abroad.

And again, early this spring a young herder who was out past sunset searching for a stray goat stumbled across Damek by the river. Damek, he said, was scrabbling in the mud, begging and pleading like one in torment. The boy thought he was ill and, overcoming his fear, sought to help him, and Damek turned on him like a wild animal, snarling and cursing. The boy swore his eyes were rimmed with demonic flames. Whether it's true about the flames or not, it is certain that the boy ran all the way home in terror for his mortal soul, and ever since won't leave the house after nightfall.

Rumours of demons aside, the manse is a wretched household! Nothing can mitigate the atmosphere of misery, although I do what I can to lighten it. Young Lina, who is trapped in this noisome hell, is becoming as disturbed as the rest of them. Although she says she has never seen any ghost, she believes that her mother is punishing Damek for his ill-treatment of her. So deep is her hatred of Damek now that I think that this faith in her mother's infernal love and her joy in the thought of

Damek's agony are the only things that are keeping her alive. He has in truth driven her half mad.

Even so, I still see inside this unhappy woman the young girl I love, however wounded and tormented, and my only hope is that I can tend her until such time as healing is possible. In short, the only way out I can see is Damek's early death. Yet, for all the stories of his mad behaviour, he continues as strong as an ox, and mostly appears to be as rational as you or I. Sometimes I believe the real answer to our distress would be if I picked up a gun and shot him myself. I quail at the thought of committing a mortal sin: yet is it not true that we shoot rabid dogs for their own sake as much as for our own, as no creature deserves to suffer so?

For all that, I can't but feel it is for God to make such judgements, not mortals such as ourselves. I cannot rid myself of the thought that redemption may be possible even for a soul as ruined as his, although I find it nigh impossible to imagine. Like the rest of us, I cannot know the truth of another's heart.

I confess that recently, in my disquiet, I have begun to visit Lina's grave and speak to her. Perhaps this only confirms that these events have finally disordered my wits, although I can report in my defence that she has never answered me. I went there yesterday: it comforts me to sit alone, disturbed by nothing more than the distant cries of rooks and the sleepy buzz of bees at work in the wild crocuses that star the grass. In such peace I can believe that my love for Lina, my sister, my other soul, is not wholly without meaning, and that one day at last her unquiet spirit will find healing in this quiet earth.

EPILOGUE:
HAMMEL

It's some weeks since I last wrote in this journal, and now I find my return to civilization is imminent. To be sure, until yesterday there was little enough to record: the dramatic beginning of my visit to this unremarkable village by no means signalled the tenor of its life. Existence here is almost unrelievedly dull. I can't say that I am entirely sorry for the lack of excitement: I still flinch at the memory of that hellish night spent at the manse, and I will bear the marks of that filthy cur's teeth to the end of my days.

Aside from my mad landlord, I have few grounds for complaint about my treatment here: I have been most comfortably lodged! I swear that during my convalescence I put on quite two inches about the waist, and Anna was forced to let out the waistband of my breeches. She whiled away the time by telling me the history of Damek, which is indeed a wild and strange tale. I thought at first it might make material for a novel, but on reflection discarded the idea. The story is too rough and grotesque for civilized taste; there is a coarseness about its narrative which would not appeal to the manly literary palate, and a moral taint about these disagreeable characters which might outrage a polite readership. It would at best make a penny romance that could only appeal to maidservants, and I would not sully my reputation with such vulgar stuff.

But now to yesterday's events, which I record because it seems that I have unwittingly played a small part in this melodrama. After I recovered from my fevers, I had to suppress – discreetly and politely, as is my wont – the familiarity with the housekeeper my enforced idleness had encouraged, and so I was unaware of the recent developments. It seems that since my unfortunate visit to the manse, my landlord, whose rationality has long been uncertain, has lost the final remnants of his sanity. He spends days on end striding about the countryside like a madman, and often sleeps under the stars. This is no great hardship in the midst of summer, as the nights are balmy and short, but it is certainly conspicuously strange behaviour.

Naturally I have avoided Damek since the dreadful night I spent in his company. On rare occasions while out walking, I have seen him approaching in the distance, and took good care to alter my direction to escape any awkward encounter. Until yesterday, this strategy seemed to work very well, since he clearly had as little desire for my company as I did for his.

I was out for my usual constitutional when, on an impulse, I decided to strike out towards the river, an area I had not yet explored. Although the sky was clear it was a hazy day, with the sultriness of an approaching storm, and by the time I reached my destination I was uncomfortably hot. I paused for refreshment in a likely place, and was splashing my face with water when a hand gripped me roughly and pulled me with such violence that I was thrown onto my back.

The source of this outrage was, of course, Damek. He was standing above me, glaring and breathing heavily, but not saying a word. I scrambled to my feet and asked him the meaning of his behaviour. I confess that I was alarmed, but I felt all the unseemliness of my position.

His lip curled with contempt. "You!" he said. "I might have known."

"You have no right to treat me thus, sir!" I said.

"And you have no right to be here!"

"To my knowledge, I have not trespassed," I said, with as much dignity as I could muster. "And I would have you remember that I am paying you a significant rent to partake of these amenities…"

He gestured impatiently. "This is no *amenity*," he said mockingly, imitating my manner of speech. "And it is forbidden to come here. Do you hear?"

"Forbidden?" I said. "On whose authority, sir? I believe my lease permits me the easeful enjoyment of this estate…"

"On my authority. *Mine*. That should be enough for you, as it is for everybody else."

I was now as eager to leave as he was to have me gone, and I bent down to gather my pack, proffering an apology for unintentionally offending him, when he grasped my elbow and pulled me up to him, so close that I could feel his breath on my face. His eyes searched mine with an unholy passion, and his grip was so brutal that I afterwards found bruises on my arm.

"Why did she show herself to *you*?" he muttered. "It's driving me mad. What cruelty, that a poor specimen like you should see her, when I have longed for years… Not one sign, not one sighting! And yet you stumble into the house…"

He took my chin and turned my face, inspecting me closely as I unavailingly attempted to loosen his hold. I felt as helpless as a rabbit in the jaws of a wolf. He let me go so suddenly that I stumbled, and we stood facing each other. He was still glaring at me, his face so distorted that he was scarcely recognizable as human. I was too frightened even to move.

Then it was as if a spell broke, and the moment passed. Damek laughed at me. "Look at you! All but pissing your pants with terror. How she would have despised you. And yet – if you knew how I envy you! I would be you, even if it meant having your sorry, insipid soul, for one glimpse... Just one glimpse... And there you stand, blind to your good fortune. My God, I could kill you for it..."

By now my only thought was to get away, and I confess I forgot my pride and ran. I am still shaken, a day later. The man is clearly out of his senses, and a danger to everyone about him. I am deeply glad that my removal a fortnight hence makes any further meeting unlikely. I briefly told my adventure to Anna, who said that I had mistakenly stumbled on his meeting place with his lover, and so roused his wrath, and that if I avoided the place I should be safe enough. However, given his manifest jealousy that I seem to have seen this ghost, I feel some trepidation that he might seek me out further.

I have followed Aron Lamaga's instructions, and each night drop a little of the green liquid from the glass phial he gave me on my pillow and at my bedroom door. I felt foolish anointing every threshold in the house as if I were an anxious old woman, and so, until last night, my vigilance somewhat slackened on that count; but these measures seem to have protected me from malignant powers, even if they haven't quite prevented the recurrence of nightmares. My fear now is that this lunatic might assail me here, but Anna shows so little alarm at this prospect that I feel reassured. I suggested we should employ some sturdy fellows to guard the house, but Anna thinks it unnecessary. Surely she would know her own master well enough to judge the risk?

But now to happier thoughts. Confined indoors, I have spent the chief of my time on my manuscript of poems, which has confronted me with technical challenges enough to while away the hours pleasantly. I believe that at last my native talent, which I have long felt stirring within me, has burst forth in full flower! At times I have almost felt a divine power coursing through me, as if I were the vessel of a god. It is not I who speaks, but the Muse of Poetry, who bends to my ear and whispers a language of such transcendence and power that I am sometimes awed. I am impatient to return to the city and show my achievements to S—; I am certain he will be as taken as I am. It must be enough to establish myself as more than a minor poet in the undistinguished annals of an ignored country. So much for those myopic critics, who took such exception to my original expression and mocked my rhymes: will they dare to sneer at this force of inspiration? I will have to stop myself from shaking the book in their faces. Surely even their benighted sensibilities will be stirred out of their foetid darkness? Surely my genius can no longer be denied?

My dear Grosz,

I have now seen my second month in this godforsaken hamlet, and I am as anxious to return home as ever I was to come here. There is, I've found, precious little to be gained from an exile from the city, save a keener appreciation of civilized life. Unvarying and limited company, a sullen landscape, and the grim visages of the populace conspire to induce in me the most poignant melancholy. As you know from my previous letters, I have an anecdote or two that will give me some currency in those fashionable watering holes I think of now with the most acute nostalgia, but I have discovered that one can have too much peace. I was never more bored in my life!

I can see you laugh, given my trepidations in travelling here. My residence has not been all bad, however. The nervous condition which plagued me through winter has vanished entirely; I have never felt better in my life. It is, I fear, the influence of clean country air and healthful walks; I have little else to do except walk and breathe. I have seen more of this countryside than anyone could wish; it is, after its initial romance, bereft of all interest, since all it offers is undistinguished hamlets and dull plains and endless rain. The local wizard, whom I have seen plodding about the fields and streets, is sadly disappointing, and has done nothing more dramatic during my stay than to rebuke a peasant for stealing a goat. Sadly, my infected leg and the bad cold that went with it meant I was never able to make that visit to the Black Mountains, which might have given me at least a little picturesque splendour to justify my visit.

I have completed my manuscript of poetry, of which I have high hopes. I am excited, Grosz; it is my best work yet, and surely will establish my reputation in the city. Maybe, I dare to think, even further, if only I could find a reputable translator. I have settled on calling it *Black Spring*, and after much thought have decided to dedicate it to L——; the dedication gives the book a certain romantic mystery, and surely it is ambiguous enough to cause no impertinent comment? Tell me what you think of this.

I must relate the events of the past week, which have livened the tedium considerably, if not enough to make me sorry to leave, and have kept the peasants in an uproar. They concern my mysterious landlord, Damek, who has finally taken leave of his senses. Amusingly enough, the locals believe he is the Devil himself and cross themselves when they mention his name. I think him to be no more than an unusually unpleasant man – he is, for example, a notorious miser – but his countenance is such, saturnine and brooding withal, that you can see why such superstitions have arisen.

I'm sure you remember that vision I saw in the bedroom mirror in his house; I am not ashamed to confess even to you, Grosz, that this witch still appears in my nightmares, and no amount of scepticism will induce me to remove the wizard's ring from my finger! It seems that Damek was convinced (as, too, was my housekeeper) that I saw a vision of an unfortunate woman called Lina, a local witch who was in fact the mother of my landlord's present wife. I had a most unsettling encounter last week, in which Damek threatened to kill me out of jealousy that I, not he, had sighted this phantom. Have you ever heard anything more curious and primitive in your life?

My housekeeper saw him shortly after I did, and told me that he was fairly quivering in some strange ecstasy of delight, claiming he had seen Lina for himself, and that he soon would join her beyond death. It seems that he refused all meat and drink, and stayed out in all weathers, scaring half to death any peasant who encountered him. Anna, good soul, was convinced he was possessed, and was full of anxiety for his wife, a poor beaten slattern who had once been in Anna's care and who, she assured me, was, for all her disagreeable manner, of gentle upbringing.

Two days ago, Mr Damek locked himself in a bedroom – I assume it was the same bedroom in which I stayed, which my housekeeper tells me must be the room where this witch died – and would not answer any summons. In the depths of the night the household was awoken by a shot, and Mr Damek's manservant became alarmed and shouldered down the door. He found his master's form stretched across the floor, lifeless from a bullet to the head. I am sure it is the man's excited imagination, or perhaps shame at the disgrace of his master's suicide, but, according to Anna, this manservant claims that he saw the witch standing over the body holding the gun, and that she turned and smiled diabolically before she vanished into thin air, leaving the weapon to clatter to the ground. Moreover, he maintains that the placing of the head wound means it is impossible that the man had shot himself.

Since he was locked in a room all by himself, this seems a difficult tale to credit; but the simple peasants around here all claim that he was shot by the ghost of his erstwhile lover, in revenge for his cruel treatment of her daughter. Anna takes issue with this verdict, arguing rather that the man has been released from his torment at last, and his curse expiated. Pious woman that she is, she has been praying for the redemption of the two unhappy souls.

These events have tediously impacted upon my domestic well-being, since Anna has been away at the manse looking after my landlord's widow, leaving me to the mercies of the undercook. That good woman has kept me from starving, to be sure, but with small delight.

It is an outlandish tale, no? For all its air of ignorant superstition, it almost makes me think of picking up the idea of the novel again: but even should I evade the perils of entering such a narrative, I fear such stories are going out of fashion. Those Naturalists are now making the pace, and I should be better off writing about accountants or miners or suchlike. I'll stick with poetry; I might indeed get a creditable poem out of the story's uncanniness. One never knows.

In any case, I will see you next week, thoroughly cured of any desire for solitude. How I shall appreciate the luxuries of cultured companionship and post offices and hansom-cabs and electric light! I shall never complain of the tedium of the city again.

I remain
Your obedient servant,
Oskar Hammel, Esq.

THE BOOKS OF
PELLINOR

THE FIRST BOOK OF
PELLINOR
The Gift
ALISON CROGGON

THE SECOND BOOK OF
PELLINOR
The Riddle

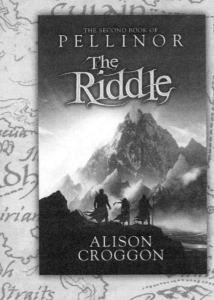

ALISON CROGGON

THE THIRD BOOK OF
PELLINOR
The Crow
ALISON CROGGON

THE FOURTH BOOK OF
PELLINOR
The Singing
ALISON CROGGON